PENGUIN BOOKS

THE MALCONTENTS

C. P. Snow was born in Leicester in 1905 and educated at a secondary school. He started his career as a professional scientist, though writing was always his ultimate aim. He won a research scholarship to Cambridge, worked on molecular physics, and became a Fellow of his college in 1930. He continued his academic life in Cambridge until the beginning of the war, by which time he had already begun the 'Lewis Eliot' sequence of novels, the general title of which is *Strangers and Brothers*. The eleven books in the sequence are, in their correct order, which is not that of publication: *Time of Hope* (1949), *George Passant* (1940) – once known by the series title, *The Conscience of the Rich* (1958), *The Light and the Dark* (1947), *The Masters* (1951), *The New Men* (1954), *Homecomings* (1958), *The Affair* (1960), *Corridors of Power* (1964), *The Sleep of Reason* (1968), and *Last Things* (1970).

In the war C. P. Snow became a civil servant, and because of his human and scientific knowledge was engaged in selecting scientific personnel. He has had further experience of these problems since the war, both in industry and as a Civil Service commissioner, for which he received a knighthood in 1957. His Rede Lecture on *The Two Cultures and the Scientific Revolution* (1950), his Godkin Lectures on *Science and Government* (1960), his address to the A.A.A.S., *The Moral Un-Neutrality of Science*, and his Fulton Lecture, *The State of Siege* (1968), have been widely discussed. He received a barony in 1964, and was made Parliamentary Secretary to the Ministry of Technology.

In 1950 he married Pamela Hansford Johnson.

C. P. SNOW

The Malcontents

PENGUIN BOOKS

Penguin Books Ltd, Harmondsworth, Middlesex, England
Penguin Books Australia Ltd, Ringwood, Victoria, Australia
Penguin Books Canada Ltd, 41 Steelcase Road West, Markham, Ontario, Canada
Penguin Books (N.Z.) Ltd, 182–190 Wairau Road, Auckland 10, New Zealand

—

First published by Macmillan London Ltd 1972
Published in Penguin Books 1975

—

Copyright © C. P. Snow, 1975

—

Made and printed in Great Britain
by Richard Clay (The Chaucer Press) Ltd,
Bungay, Suffolk
Set in Linotype Granjon

I

In the mild January night, a young man was waiting outside his father's house. A single bell rang, and kept on ringing, from the cathedral tower. The young man, whose name was Stephen Freer, was used to bells, having lived since he was a child in that house close by. Six fifteen on a Saturday evening: the spoken evensong without a choir: not paying attention, concentrated on his own thoughts, he watched a couple of figures, and then another, move towards the radiant porch.

Stephen moved down the lane and stopped at the bollards at the end. The lane, cut off from traffic, Georgian houses on the further side, was as near a precinct as the cathedral could provide: but in fact the cathedral had until recently been only a parish church, promoted when the town itself was promoted, and the lane was a relic, piously preserved by local antiquarians, Stephen's father among them, of the old eighteenth-century town.

Stephen rested against one of the bollards and gazed up at the sky. It had been a warm and gusty day, but now the wind had dropped. The spire, elegant and high, a piece of Victorian reconstruction, stood out against some early stars. Stephen knew something about the cathedral, and a good deal about the stars: but he paid no attention to either, no more than he had to the sprinkling of old people going in to the evening service. He was not given to thinking of two things at once. He was waiting for a friend and ally. He was in a state, almost pleasurable to him, though he might

5

not have recognized it as such, not so much anxious as keyed tight; a state in which he wanted to decide and act.

The cathedral clock had struck the half-hour. Minutes of absorption. The street outside empty in the evening. No noise from this part of the town. Then quick, familiar steps.

'Hallo,' called Stephen.

'Hallo,' said Mark Robinson.

An Englishman would have guessed at once, listening to their tone, that they came from privileged homes.

'I wanted to catch you,' said Stephen.

'What's on?'

'Something's come a bit unstuck.'

'Oh hell.' In the dim light, Mark's expression wasn't any more anxious than his companion's, but eager, enthusiastic, pure. 'What is it?'

'There's been a leak.'

'Hell. Now that we didn't want. Serious?'

'Difficult to say.'

The two young men walked back up the lane together. As they came under the first of the eighteenth-century iron lanterns (gift of Thomas Freer), they made a physiognomic contrast. Both were tall, both looked active and intelligent. They were dressed alike, in polo-neck sweaters and corduroy trousers, and their hair, Mark's shiningly fair, Stephen's darker, was thick at the nape of their necks. But Mark, six months younger than his friend, who was nearly twenty-two, had a face without much written on it – with the kind of handsomeness, luminous-eyed, which is also innocent. Stephen had none of that. He was long-headed, with features clear and aquiline, already set and unlikely to alter until he was old. His glance was very sharp. Often, as now, he appeared brooding, except when he broke into a sarcastic

6

smile which, surprisingly, gave his face warmth and made it younger.

It was that smile which Mark expected, didn't need to look for, when he heard Stephen's answer about his father. The young men had known each other since they were children: they had been at school together: they talked with most of the explanations left out. How they felt about the 'leak' didn't require saying: the action to be taken, they argued about without fuss. Mark, however, was curious as to when and how Stephen had heard. That afternoon, after tea, said Stephen, actually only an hour or so ago – and from his father.

'Who it came from I don't know, one of his lawyer friends, I fancy.'

'How much have they got?'

'Anything they've got, it would be better if they hadn't.'

Thomas Freer hadn't said much, there wasn't enough to go on. Mark asked how had he taken it, what had his attitude been?

'Semi-detached,' said Stephen.

As for immediate action, they couldn't do it all that Saturday night. They would have to stay at the Freers' dinner party until ten o'clock, for decency's sake or rather to seem unaffected: afterwards, they could talk to Neil in the pub.

Mark would go off at once and ring him up: he wouldn't have time to collect the 'core' that night, he had better be told to arrange a full meeting for tomorrow.

'Don't explain why over the telephone,' said Stephen.

Mark smiled. That wasn't necessary. In spite of all his openness, he had learned discretion, or at least the rules of secrecy. Saying that he would be back in time for dinner, he was leaving Stephen, when he suddenly thought to ask whether they could get everything in order by Monday. He had planned to return to Cambridge then.

'Your guess is as good as mine,' said Stephen. 'It might be rather a long weekend.'

They were at the top end of the lane, where it was crossed by another silent and empty street. Mark gave a wave of the hand as he plunged off, leaning forward in his eager walk.

2

THE drawing room in Thomas Freer's house was entirely in his taste. That wasn't because his wife was negligible; there she was, sitting among her guests, all present except Mark Robinson, who, she remarked equably, was not often late. She was a big strong-muscled woman, whose forehead, deeply lined, seemed out of harmony with the heavy body: it was easy to believe, if one looked only at the fine and delicate features, that she had once been beautiful. Now, despite the harassed skin, she seemed content, able to absent herself from trouble, amused by what had happened to her.

Her husband was the same age within a year and they had had Stephen, their only child, when they were in their thirties. But Thomas Freer looked younger than she did, and did not absent himself at all. In this company he was in command. It was a bourgeois gathering, and he liked it: the Bishop and his wife and daughter, his own wife and son and his son's cultivated friend, just arrived, with polite apologies. That was all, and as it should be. Thomas Freer was himself a bourgeois, but of an unusual kind: to himself he might have smothered the word patrician. His grandfather had been a prosperous solicitor in this town, and his father, and now himself. He could afford to let his partners do most of the firm's practice, and indulge himself as Registrar, the layman responsible for the cathedral's legal business. Like others of the few remaining old families in the town, his had started as Unitarians, but his father had moved into the Anglican church. That suited Thomas very well. He enjoyed a small society, he would have detested being taken out of it, he liked his own position. He liked being able to devote himself to causes already lost, such as Union Now and the local Liberal Party.

He had a good deal of taste, and all of it was good. He would have thought it vulgar, and certainly unhistorical, to envisage this fine Georgian drawing room of his furnished only in its own period: that wasn't how things had gone, or how they ought to look. So, round the walls, there were a couple of Cotmans, a small Boudin, his prize possession, and then, in the same latitudinarian spirit, a William Scott.

It was his own taste to live in the house, in the deserted centre of the old town, which might be picturesque but was also inconvenient. The Provost (who would have been called the Dean if the cathedral had not been a modern creation) lived next door, but then he had to. Otherwise no middle-class family, let alone one as well-off as the Freers, slept at night within the same square mile. That seemed to Thomas Freer appropriate, and gave him a devious, or perhaps an aesthetic, pleasure.

He was a slender man, as tall as his son, though there wasn't much family resemblance between them. The father was also personable, but in a neat-skulled, small-headed fashion, with the first sign of nutcracker jaw and nose. His manners were easy but sometimes seemed as though he were parodying himself. When he went round the circle and asked, 'Bishop, may I give you another glass of sherry?' he might have been a diffident parson addressing a prince of the Church, or alternatively a connoisseur thrusting priceless liquor down an uncomprehending crop. Certainly the Bishop was puzzled, the more so as Thomas Freer often called him Bert.

The Bishop was only just getting used to his Registrar's

dinner parties. In fact, the Bishop, scolded into them by his wife, a woman as large as Kate Freer and many times more dominant, was only just getting used to dinner parties of any kind. He was a small square man with a roseate complexion and a comfortable north-country accent. He had come from a humble family in Lancashire, made his way by scholarships through grammar school and Oxford, and had no social pretensions or pretensions of any kind at all. Despite his rise up the ecclesiastic hierarchy, he was, of the people in that drawing room, still much the poorest.

The Freers had both inherited money: Mark's father was a hosiery manufacturer and well-to-do: whereas the Bishop was paid on about the same scale as a university lecturer. He could manage to send his daughter, a short sturdy pretty girl who had been whispering to Stephen, to the local university, and lived not very differently from his own old headmaster in his native town. But it was the Bishop who, during dinner, took it upon himself to change the conversation. The party had moved downstairs, for the dining room was on the ground floor, smallish after the big room above, another example of Thomas Freer's carefully anachronistic taste, with Queen Anne chairs older than the house, candles on the rosewood table. The food was fine, though not in large quantities: the wine was good, but didn't circulate often. What Thomas Freer did circulate was a set of reflections which didn't seem – except to hypersensitive ears – to be coming to a point.

He was sitting with Mrs Boltwood, the Bishop's wife, on his right and on his left her daughter Tess. At the other end of the table, the Bishop and Mark were flanking Kate Freer, with Stephen interposed between the Bishop and Tess. Thomas Freer, in his easy modulated tones, appeared to be addressing no one in particular when, after the soup, he set about asking the air at large some questions, as though engaged in a labyrinthine exercise in introspection.

'I sometimes wonder, don't you know, what one would do if one could get the faintest glimpse of the consequences. Do you think I'm wrong? Of course, I'm not very clever at foreseeing consequences. But I wonder how many people are? Doesn't one get into a situation, I'm sure I have, of trying to do good and finding that evil comes of it?'

The three young people were silent. From the other end of the table, Kate Freer gave a sound which tinkled like a distant chuckle, or even a giggle.

'Thinking of doctors, don't you know.' Thomas was weaving away. 'I've often thought that being a doctor would be a decent way to live. Does that make sense? And they've kept children alive, that was a nice thing to do, they've kept them alive all over the world. With the consequence that there are going to be more people than the world can cope with, so they tell one. I only wonder, but mightn't that be a classical case of doing good so that evil might come? One can't see one's way –'

'Of course they're doing good,' said Mrs Boltwood, nose protruded in indignation.

'Maybe. Who is one to judge?' Thomas was weaving again. 'Or take the October Revolution. I suppose that, if we'd been Russians in 1917, everyone round this table would have been for it, we should have thought we were doing good, don't you think we should? But looking back, of course I'm very ignorant about history, should we have been? If the Russians had muddled on without it – one might have saved millions of lives. Looking back, if there hadn't been the revolution, there wouldn't have been much chance for Hitler – we could have escaped another war, one might have thought. One hopes so much, don't you know, but I wonder if we could see the consequences of what we hoped for –'

That was the point when the Bishop broke in. It was not so much that he was out of sympathy with Thomas Freer, though that was true: but more, he was embarrassed that Stephen and the others, not usually inarticulate, had stayed quite mute. There was something behind this allocution, meanings left unspoken: the Bishop liked young people to be carefree, he wanted to take away the strain. Until now, for him it had been an ordinary Saturday night: no, not quite ordinary, what he described to himself as a posh dinner was still an event. Nevertheless, it was a date like other dates. Dinner at the Registrar's. Saturday, 10 January 1970. Tomorrow, Sunday, first after Epiphany, the quietest period of the Christian year. But now the Bishop felt impelled to exert himself.

'It's a mistake to fancy one can foresee everything, Tom. We've got to do our best inside the situation. What they used to call the So Sein. That's all we have to play with.' The Bishop's accent rang oddly round that table: but he wasn't prepared to be out-faced and out-cultured by his host. In secret, the Bishop, who had his own modest pride, believed that he was a good deal the cleverer man. Then he said:

'Now Stephen. Tell us how those pulsars are going on.'

It sounded at the same time graceless and also very warm. It affected Stephen as both these things. On another occasion he would have been amused to hear his father's techniques brought to a dead stop: it didn't often happen. Thomas Freer was too evasive for most men. Curiously, however, the Bishop's interruption, well meant as it was,

produced an effect opposite to that intended. If Thomas
Freer had known, he would have been more than ever
satisfied. For the diversion made Stephen, not less tense and
impatient, but much more. His father's probing – the inaudible dialogue which only the two of them could hear,
though Mark had caught some echoes – that chimed with
his own thoughts. Now this kind man was distracting him
away from them. It was still a long time until the dinner
could be over. He had to force himself to produce a polite
reply.

'I don't think we're getting much further, sir.'

Stephen, as the Bishop knew, was doing research in
astrophysics. For the sake of lightening the party, the
Bishop would have been prepared to show interest in any
intellectual subject, but this one happened to be a favourite
of his. Stephen wished he had never heard of it.

The Bishop made cheerful noises about quasars and pulsars.

'It's wonderful how much we know, compared with
twenty years ago.'

Stephen made another effort, trying to liberate himself.

'Sometimes I think it's more wonderful, what we shall
never know.'

'That's very interesting, Stephen, that really is. What exactly do you mean?'

'I mean, if ever we thought nature was simple, now we
know for sure it isn't.'

Almost against his will, or his concentration, Stephen began to talk more freely.

'That is, if there are any universal laws for the cosmos,
they must be very difficult. So difficult that it looks as
though we may never know them –'

'Do you mean,' said the Bishop, sparkling, 'that our

minds are limited and the cosmos isn't? Is that what you're saying?'

'I shouldn't put it quite that way.' Stephen gave an involuntary smile. 'But I don't think the universe is going to look beautiful ever again. No nice beautiful simple generalizations like Einstein's. It's just a hideous tangle, and it's becoming more tangled every time we look. And, if you like, you can say that our minds are too simple to cope.'

The Bishop, ruddy face blushing deeper as he chortled, said:

'Well, you know, that doesn't come as altogether surprising to anyone in my profession. After all, what you're saying about the cosmos, theologians have sometimes said about the mind of God.'

The Bishop, indomitable, persevered, sure that he was bringing peace. He was so bright, so happy, that others were happy too. True, Thomas Freer wore a lugubrious expression, as though cosmology were not a suitable topic for a man of taste. But even he did not resist the Bishop's spirits, the Bishop's speculative joy – the hundred million stars in the galaxy! the billions of galaxies! the rim of the universe, to which the galaxies were rushing and rushing over!

Stephen was as disciplined as anyone there. He had to keep up his share of the conversation. Mark, who was reading history and was nothing like as knowledgeable as the Bishop, could come in only when he began to ask about the chances of intelligent life. Kate Freer's long-sighted eyes might be deceiving her about her left-hand neighbour, but she thought that he looked excitable and restless. She had an indulgent spot for that young man, so gentle as well as active, so affectionate to her. She didn't know that he and her son, and Tess Boltwood too, were all reckoning on the

Bishop going to bed early before his Sunday work: and then they would be released.

The pudding was in front of them and their glasses of sauterne. The candlesticks were reflected clear in the rosewood. It seemed a comfortable dinner party, one of many in that house, just as Thomas Freer expected his dinner parties to be comfortable. The Bishop continued to preside, amicably, joyously, over his seminar.

'There must be intelligent life elsewhere, I should be flabbergasted if there wasn't. There must be,' he said.

Mark and Tess emphatically agreed. With them, that was an article of faith. And some day we should get in touch with it.

'I'm not quite so certain of that,' said Stephen.

'But you don't doubt that there must be life, do you now?'

The Bishop was fond of them all, but it was Stephen he respected.

'It's beginning to look as though life may be a rarer chance than we ever thought.'

Stephen, with automatic competence, out of the front of his head with his preoccupation pushed deeper down, went through the arguments he could have reeled off in his sleep. Conceivably, though not very probably, life might be one preposterous fluke. We might be alone in an infinite silence, a random plasma of matter and energy, numberless billions of suns, burning away, billions already burnt away, progressing without anything that one could call meaning or purpose, all a prodigy of mindless waste, in the direction of entropy and thermodynamic death.

That didn't quell the Bishop, who possessed a remarkable gift for reconciling any idea with any other. Multitudes of planets with intelligent life, scattered all through the universe – yes, he liked that idea, he liked any prospect of life. He was perfectly prepared to reconcile that idea with the Christian revelation. On the other hand, if Stephen's scepticism turned out to be the answer, if human life was an extraordinary incident in the middle of infinity, well, that was marvellous too! Perhaps more marvellous! Meaning and purpose, said the Bishop warmly, those old theological proofs were nothing but naïve: but still, alone in the universe, that would be a special place for mankind, could anyone deny the exhilaration of that, could Stephen?

Stephen could not resist breaking into his curiously youthful, ironic, pleasing smile.

From the upright clock in the corner, the minutes ticked on. The party had not moved upstairs again. Thomas Freer remarked, in a formula all of them had heard before as one giving the final demonstration of his liberalism, that in this house there was no separation of the women after dinner. The Bishop behaved according to plan, or according to the plan of three people there. He announced, with amiable matter-of-fact humility, that it would soon be his bed-time.

At that Stephen was, for the first time at the table, fully alert.

'But you'll leave Tess with us for a bit, will you, sir? We'll get her safely home.'

'Oh, we trust you, Stephen,' said the Bishop's wife, with a smile which exuded confidence in her own judgement. She had discovered, or thought she had, that there was tenderness between her daughter and Stephen. Of which Mrs Boltwood whole-heartedly approved, and had already had delectable day-dreams planning the wedding.

Outside, a clamour of bells had started. 'Practising', said the Bishop. 'Good chaps, giving their time on a Saturday night.' He began to stir his short strong legs. 'Well, well.

Tom, it's been a very fine dinner, I must say.' Thomas Freer said:

'It's always good to see you, Bert.'

As the Bishop got up, he patted his daughter and, in homely fashion, told her not to be too late.

3

IN the lane, when Tess and the young men had at last got free, the bells were clanging: not a single bell, but the whole peal, shuddering out with mathematical solemnity. The night had turned colder, the sky was now brilliant with stars behind the spire, but none of them spared a backward glance. They were half-running to reach the pub in time. During the evening, Stephen had managed to give Tess the first sketch of the news: now he was telling her more. Tess's mother was right in thinking that there was a tie between these two: but she didn't know what the relation was, and she certainly didn't know that Tess, in addition to loving Stephen, was committed in another sense, and was one of the seven whom they called the core.

Their steps echoed in the empty street, past the school, the bank. Then the black windows of shops, one or two passers-by. The mouth of the market place, the lights of the Saracen's Head. There was Neil St John, waiting for them in the corner, coming towards them on his heavy cyclist's thighs.

'What's this in aid of?'

Quickly Stephen said no more than he had said to Mark four hours before.

'We can look after that,' Neil's squashed face was set, flushed up to the high temples, where the hair didn't grow.

'We've got to take it,' said Stephen, voice cool and biting, 'that someone's on to us.'

'Sod them. Sod the whole gang of them.'

Neil was exuding anger, all through his compact powerful body. His capacity for passion was no surprise to the rest of them, but it still impressed them and made him formidable. It would have been hard for an outsider, looking on, to guess whether he or Stephen had more authority over this group, or which was likely to be its leader. What was certain was that the others took for granted this young man's animal force, took his personality for granted and had ceased to wonder about him.

Earlier in their acquaintanceship, which had begun about two years before, they had done so. He was actually the youngest of them, only twenty, and a student in sociology at the local university, the one Tess was attending. He came from a family much poorer than any of theirs, poorer even than the Bishop's used to be, and from a slice of society that even the Bishop wouldn't have known first-hand. His father was a docker, their home was in Bootle, how they had acquired that grand-sounding surname no one knew, and Neil himself cursed it away as though he had been an American black loaded with a slave-master's name. His father and mother were both Irish Catholics, and that was another heritage which Neil cursed away.

He hadn't yet become an intimate friend of the other three, but he was one of their springs of action, and they trusted him. That was why he was the first person Stephen had asked for that night. In fact, it had been his initiative, more than anyone else's, which had started their present plan: the plan which, as they sat round the table in the pub, once old-fashioned, now tarted up, fairy lights and noise and all, with a juke-box conveniently blanketing all they said, seemed now at risk.

Mark, efficient, gentle with the barmaid, had bought pints of beer just on the call of time. They had no need to discuss the plan, which they all knew off by heart. Both as part of his field work and as part of his politics, Neil in the past year had been 'casing the joint' of the back streets in the town. Near his own lodgings, he had discovered a street of terraced houses let to West Indian families: in some the conditions were 'all right by Irish standards': in one section of three houses the blacks were being rack-rented as they might have been in a nineteenth-century slum. Those facts were not in dispute. All four had visited the rooms, and so had the other three members of the core. Two families to one room: a turnover of comings and going which defeated the local authorities: evictions of some immigrants who didn't know the laws nor whom to turn to.

If the victims had been white, that would have been bad enough. But they weren't white, and for all these young men and women, that brought them to a fighting-point. This Saturday night no one foresaw what was soon to happen: and when it did happen, some simplicities were forgotten. But there were real simplicities. Tess was concerned for sheer misery: Mark wanted people to be good: Neil was outraged by the helplessness of the poor: Stephen, who sometimes seemed the hardest and most sceptical, couldn't tolerate the sight of suffering. But though they were affected each in a different fashion, they were together about race. To them race, or rather the wiping-away of race and its effects, was as near a faith as any of them had, or as most pople ever had. So far it was simple. But the plan did not end there, but began. Neil had tracked down the sub-landlord of those three houses. He too was a West Indian, with the name Finlayson. He had been persuaded to talk (it was here that the first scruples had entered and been argued away). The chain of property led from him – that was true in law, and, anyone could persuade himself, in fact

– back to an agent: and beyond the agent to the ultimate owner of the whole street, who turned out to be an influential Tory M.P., a member of the Shadow Cabinet, and one who was proved to have interests in South Africa.

'That'll blow the roof off the bastards,' Neil had said.

This could be made a master-stroke against racialism. It had to be well-timed. Such a chance wouldn't come again. Anti-racialists in all universities, not only this one, would join in. This core had their contacts with others. So they had waited until all the 'presentation' was complete. They had plenty of advisers, public relations men, open politicians and secret ones: no one except themselves, though, had been told the whole truth: that was at the insistence of Stephen, who had the clearest mind among them. In precisely two weeks and three days from this Saturday, 'the balloon', to use Neil's exhorting phrase, 'would be ready to go up'. Now it was under attack. As they faced the news, they felt a cause endangered, faith denied, and anger, including moral anger: some of them felt also traces of guilty compunction, of secret knowledge driven underground, and perhaps of fear.

When they had to leave the pub and walked back towards the street, opposite the cathedral, where Mark's car was parked, they were still talking in low tones, although there was no one to hear.

'We can't stop now,' said Mark, fervent gaze traversing them all, 'that's the one thing clear.'

'I hope it's clear to everyone,' said Stephen.

'It'd better be,' Neil burst out, but he, as well as the others, waited for Stephen to go on. His temper was often below the surface, so were his patches of eloquence: and they had learned when they had to listen to him.

'This may not be pretty,' he said. 'They've all (he meant

the other three) got to be told. So that they can get out if that's what they choose. Tomorrow night.'

'If anyone gets out now,' said Neil, 'then we're finished with them.'

'In certain circumstances,' Stephen remarked, 'they might feel that wasn't such a deprivation as we think.'

Mark gave a chuckle, spirits high in the excitement, but Tess intervened:

'I don't think anyone will, you know.'

'They've had it bloody easy up to now.' That was Neil, suddenly as deliberate as Stephen.

'No, but Emma's solid, isn't she? And so is Bernard –'

'Lance?'

'We all know about him,' said Tess. 'But I think he has his pride.'

She was speaking unassertively, but with responsibility. And she had some: for it was through her, young as she was, that the core had come together. Meeting Stephen through the cathedral functions, and Mark as Stephen's friend, she had brought them in touch with Neil and the others at the university: as he learned about the local plans, Stephen had decided that here, on his vacations from Cambridge, was the place to act. But Tess was speaking not only with responsibility, but with a kind of modest vanity. In most things, intellectual and otherwise, she deferred to Stephen, and often to Mark: but about people she had a sense, which would some day turn into a maternal certainty, that her judgement was better than theirs, not least when it came to themselves.

The cathedral bells were silent now: so was the narrow street opposite, down which they walked, not often arguing but making contingency plans, walked to the end and back and kept retracing their steps while the clock chimed eleven, then the quarter and the half-hour. It was a street of Georgian houses, once elegant, such as might have suited Thomas Freer's taste, but all converted into lawyers' offices, not even a caretaker living there on a Saturday night.

How much did 'they' know? Who were 'they'? Stephen reported that his father hadn't been precise, and presumably didn't know: the information could have come from a colleague who might very well have political connections. It wasn't certain how much they knew, or what they intended.

'But we always under-estimate the other side,' he said. 'We mustn't make that mistake this time.'

What could the other side do? It depended on how good their intelligence was. 'It can't be all that good.' Neil, despite outbursts in which he was abusing them and all they stood for ('they'll never give in until we get rid of them, and that goes for everyone you know'), reminding the others that they came from that provenance themselves, was being realistic. 'Someone couldn't keep his mouth shut all the time, that's all.'

That was what it looked like. One of them must have let a word slip, perhaps after some drink, perhaps a vague euphoric threat against an eminent person, perhaps cheering someone up at a black and white party. Yes, in the narrow street, shut in by the tall houses, they said it must have been something like that.

'But that might be enough,' said Stephen.

It wouldn't need much insight to anticipate, not all, but some of their own moves. And the enemy's right course would be to get in first. That might not happen, but it had to be reckoned with. A counter-campaign, starting soon. What kind of campaign? Again it was a question of how good the intelligence was.

Stephen said that he would press his father to make inquiries. Those might have to wait until Monday. Meanwhile, they ought to consider hurrying up their own moves: once they were in the open, they couldn't be quite silenced, the important part of the job would have been achieved.

None of them seemed specially nervous as they walked up and down, up and down the street. They weren't anxious by temperament, any of them, not even Stephen, who had the most foresight. The adrenalin was pouring through them, the exhilaration of being near the point of action. And also, the more they talked, the more they listened to the hard realistic estimates of Stephen and Neil, the further the dangers receded. It was an alarm, but, the more they looked at it, it became less of an alarm.

'Well, that's all we can do tonight,' said Neil all of a sudden, not long after the half-hour struck. 'See you tomorrow.'

With that by way of good night, he turned out of the street into Friar Lane.

'Going to see Emma,' Mark observed, as the footsteps died away.

'Perhaps,' said Tess. 'Good luck to them.'

'He might have told us,' Mark went on, and the others smiled at him. Within minutes, they had returned to the car park, and there Stephen took Tess in his arms. While the kiss lasted, Mark was opening the car door: for here Stephen's authority had broken down, he didn't drive, he had to leave it to his friend to take the girl home. As he crossed the road in front of the cathedral, he waved back to the two of them inside the car.

When Mark was driving them up the London Road, he and Tess reminded each other of the plans. There was no more to say than had already been said that night, but it was a comfort to repeat themselves.

'It will be all right,' said Mark, like an older brother.

'It's got to be,' said Tess, like a sister, taking care of him in her turn.

Soon, past the gleaming shops, past the station, under the neon lights, they came to the park corner. Away to the left, in the back streets, was Neil's room, and, not half a mile away, the houses whose existence had set them going. Yet neither of them gave those houses a thought. They had become as abstract as the diplomatic causes of a war, or the origins of a family quarrel. Instead Mark was asking:

'How are things with you and Stephen?'

'Fine,' she said.

For Mark, the whole evening seemed to have passed out of mind, and that was genuine. If he had glanced at her, he would have seen that her expression was diffident, radiant, stubborn. She couldn't switch thoughts easily as he could, but memories and hopes were flooding within her and shone out of her face. And also she couldn't resist another half-thought flickering in the air. She wasn't at all vain, she was glad and rather surprised if a man was attracted to her, she was grateful that she had a little charm, yes, thank God, for Stephen. But yet, driving home late at night, she was ready for most of the men in their circle to (if she had spoken, she would have used an old-fashioned phrase) make a pass. Not so Mark. Not a sign or a touch of it.

'You'll have to be careful,' he was saying. 'He wants to be loved: and he doesn't want to be shut in. Somehow you'll have to find the way between the two.'

He really cares, she was thinking. He would like her to be good and happy, and Stephen too. No one else cared as much. And yet he didn't seem to want that kind of happiness for himself. So handsome, so kind. He was so sensitive about others' lives.

'Of course,' Mark went on, 'you're lucky in one thing. That's one of the reasons why he chose you, you know. You're quite different from his mother. She's the most unusual person in that family. I don't know what Stephen feels for her. I think he loves her, but she's scared him off. I don't believe hers has been a happy marriage. It couldn't very well, with anyone as much on her own – You won't be too much on your own for Stephen.'

They had come to the beginning of the comfortable, middle-class suburb, bushes catching the headlights, houses standing back from the broad road. Tess was feeling very fond of him. Yet, it was as innocent being with him as in a childhood friendship, perhaps more innocent than that. She was faithful to Stephen, she was born faithful, and yet she had a half-wish that it was not so innocent. Was she ashamed or not?

As for what he said about Stephen, she hadn't paid much attention to that. She was certain that she knew Stephen better than he did. Mark's lack of self-regard, or even his absence of self, that she could respond to: but she scarcely noticed his insight, and there, as it happened, she was wrong.

Soon they turned down a side road towards the Bishop's house, more comfortable middle-class houses, lights in windows, neat privet hedges defining the front gardens. As they said good night, he laid his cheek against hers, and said:

'You'll see, it will be all right!'

He had said that before, early on their way home: it might have been the same reassurance, or another, that he was giving her now.

4

As Stephen woke, the single bell was ringing. He didn't wake, as he had sometimes done, into well-being and then become invaded by disquiet: the strain of the night before had ceased, just as when he was walking with his friends. It was like a morning in childhood, the room still dark, no need to get up yet. The bell clanged on, it must be for the early communion, eight o'clock, the communion to which his father went.

It was luxurious, lying in the familiar room, half-awake. An idea about his work entered into consciousness. Neutrons packed together. No, the equations wouldn't fit.

People spoke and wrote, he had sometimes reflected, not now, there in the twilight between sleep and waking, as though their thoughts all came to them in words. It wasn't so for him, at least not often. Thoughts of sex were not much like sex itself. Thoughts of sex didn't come to him in words.

He had wanted to take Tess to bed the night before. There was nowhere to take her in this town. They would have to wait until she came to Cambridge. Pictures of the last time. Waiting in bed, watching her undress. Scampering to him, climbing in, pulling the bed clothes round them. Room colder than this. Face smiling beneath his, eyes going unfocused, rapt. Then he didn't see her face, just the rough sound of panting, joy, release and sigh, joyful sigh.

The first time, he had trembled until the unconscious took control. He had trembled before, the first time with a girl. Tess had taken it easier than he did. Now all that was past. Just the pictures of expectancy, comfort, lying together afterwards looking at the window, arms round her, the feel of cherished unmysterious flesh.

Other kinds of expectancy. He could hear her voice, as they were talking, one of those nights: 'We mustn't have false hopes, either of us, must we?' Direct, honest voice. But he thought later, when anyone talked of not having false hopes, it meant they had them.

He didn't know. She was more certain than he was.

Sometimes in her absence, he had tried to form the words, so that when they met, he could explain himself to her. The words never came out as they had been formed. Just as, when he made a picture of them next time in bed, it didn't turn out like that: as though bodies had their own will.

Now, nearer waking, he was forming the words of what he had to tell the others that afternoon. He mightn't think in words, but he knew that he was articulate, more than most of them. This time, though, it wasn't just being able to talk, he had to be precise. There mustn't be any responsibility left in doubt. Perhaps there had been too much left in doubt already.

Later that morning, when the full peal outside was making the windows shiver, he found his mother alone in the drawing room. That was like other Sundays: she didn't go with her husband to matins, his second observance of the day. Bifocals on her fine beak of a nose, she was reading a Sunday paper. With a quick snap, as it might be with a vestigial vanity, she had her glasses off. 'Hallo,' she said. Her voice was high and friendly, perhaps indistinguishable from what it had been in youth, sounding like a young woman's greeting a new young man.

When he sat down in an armchair opposite to hers, she said:

'How did you like last night?'

'Nice dinner.'

She grinned. It was a curiously urchin-like grin, incongruous on the handsome face, and from his childhood Stephen had always welcomed it.

'People do talk round the point, sometimes, don't they?' she said.

'I suppose so.'

'It used to embarrass me a little, once.'

All his life, Stephen had not heard her make a disloyal remark about his father. Maybe this was as near as she could come. Even now, she seemed to correct herself.

'Of course, it didn't take much to embarrass me.' She gazed at him. 'Do you ever get embarrassed?' She asked as though it were an interesting clinical point.

'Not terribly easily, I think.'

'Lucky,' said his mother.

With an air that was at the same time social and oddly youthful, she inquired if he would like some coffee. When he said no, she said, not altering her tone of voice:

'You're in a bit of a mess, aren't you?'

'Yes, a bit.' He had no idea how much she knew, or what his father had told her, or on what terms the two of them discussed him.

'I gathered as much.' After a pause, she went on:

'I expect you'll get out of it, though.'

'I hope so.'

'You will. You're pretty capable at getting out of things.'

It sounded bleak and brittle, it seemed all she had to say,

and yet Stephen, without knowing why, found it a support. Casually, she was reflecting:

'You remind me rather of a man I used to know. He was always walking into the most extraordinary situations. Somehow he always managed to pull himself out.'

'Who was he?' But Stephen realized that it was useless to ask. She was scrupulous and gallant about referring to men who had courted her. It was only through his father, who was by no means reluctant to admit that he had won in serious competition, that Stephen had caught hints of admirers, of passionate pursuers, in the past.

'No. You might have heard of him. He's done very well. I don't know what's happened to him now. I should think that he's all right.'

Then she asked, once more brittle, straight out:

'Are any of the others in this?'

'In what?' He knew well enough.

'In this mess of yours.'

'Yes, they are.'

'You needn't worry about Tess. She's strong. She can look after herself.'

Stephen was, not for the first time, surprised by his mother. She talked so little, gossiped with no one: she missed things which anyone round her noticed: phases of absence, then suddenly her eyes swathed through the darkness like a searchlight beam.

'What about Mark?'

Stephen replied, as candid as she was:

'Sometimes I worry about him.'

'Why?'

'He's more – fragile than some of us.'

'You may be right.'

Then her interest faded as though it had been switched

off. 'Your father,' as she always spoke of Thomas Freer to Stephen, would soon be coming in from service. This was the only day of the week on which he allowed himself a pre-lunch drink and so she ought to have it waiting for him.

5

As soon as lunch was over, Stephen made a journey which had become a habit: bus to the park corner, along the route where Mark had driven the night before, a walk into the back streets, Kimberley Road, Ladysmith Road, Mafeking Road, names of the imperial past, forgotten now. It was only a couple of miles from the cathedral, but it might have seemed, if Stephen had been visiting there for the first time, a different town. Not that the streets were squalid: the houses were terraced, built in the early 1900s, red brick, with a yard-long strip (in some of which there was grass gleaming) between the front room and the pavement, and sun-blistered railings in between. The streets weren't so squalid as that in which Neil St John had been born: and the room where he lived was better than anything he had known at home.

It was their usual meeting place. As Stephen entered, he saw it, and didn't see it, with blank accustomed eyes: just as his nose was accustomed to the smell of food in the little passage outside. Neil's landlady lived in the two back rooms and let off what would once have been the main bed-room and the sitting room. Another student occupied the bedroom, and Neil the ground floor sitting room. It was there that Stephen was now standing.

Outside, the afternoon was dark, one or two people passing by, close to the railings. In the half-light, the room itself stood bare. A camp bed along one wall, a couple of old armchairs, holes worn in the green velvet, padding showing through; several canvas chairs; a sleeping bag propped against one corner. The only decoration on the walls were posters of meetings. On a single shelf stood text books and pamphlets. Anyone searching through them, and knowing a little about Neil, would have found much that he expected, the standard left-wing literature of the period, Marcuse, early Marx: but he would also find some works not so much in fashion, including a collection of Mayakovsky's poems and a treatise on Sorel.

The solitary sign of self-indulgence anywhere was a record-player standing in another corner. For this room, Neil, whose fees at the university were paid, had to give a large slice, over half, of his student grant, which was £370 a year. Some of his protesting colleagues were protesting that this must be increased: as a sign of solidarity he joined in, but to the core he confessed or explained that that was 'playing at things' by the side of 'the real stuff'.

Most of the others were still to come: but already there, sitting on the bed, was Emma Knott. She greeted Stephen with a flashing smile, and said:

'Well, you were at it last night, weren't you?'

'You know about it, of course?'

'For Christ's sake!' she smiled again, this time at Neil. 'This is a silly bleeding business!'

Stephen had known her, as he had Mark, since they were children. Her father was a surgeon in the town, and a prosperous one. Their parents were all social acquaintances and she, who was up at St Hugh's, had also been drawn into the core through Tess as catalyst.

Emma was a strong-boned girl with the build of a tennis player, long back, long thighs. Her face, though, might have been an actress's: she had great deep-orbited eyes, big features, the coarse-pored skin which, as with some actresses, made her look more alluring in photographs than close to. Yet most people thought her good-looking and attractive. Most people also thought that she was a rich, spoilt and reckless girl who before long would marry and settle down and become a natural successor to her own mother and Kate Freer. Emma had a clear notion of such thoughts; they added to her scorn, which was considerable, for the class she had been born into. Much more visibly, or rather audibly, than Stephen or Mark, she had cut herself away: she had picked up as much as she could of Neil's accent, and that wasn't only because she was sleeping with him, but because it made her feel closer to the place where she wished to be. For her to have sat through last night's dinner at the Freers' would have meant self-denial, not to be contemplated except maybe in the way of cover. Even within the core, she was at home, not with her childhood friends, but with Neil – and that had added to his appeal and had driven her towards him, – and also with the poorest of them, Kelshall, 'little Bernie'.

Mark's car pulled up outside, and in a moment he and Tess came in. Quick unsecretive glance from Tess to Stephen:

'All right?'

'Yes,' he said. He added that nothing had happened that morning, there was no further news.

Over the railings passed a shock of fair hair, and unobtrusively Bernard Kelshall was among them. He was not specially little, though Emma, affectionately, half-baitingly, called him so. He did not look specially Jewish, though everyone there knew that his parents' name had once been Kornfeld, and that they had come to the town as refugees in the thirties. He had been born and bred there, and was the only person in the room who spoke like a midland native. His hair was as intractable as a Fijian's, but otherwise his whole appearance and bearing was subdued. Yet, even among the committed, he made an impression of his own: they talked of him as 'dedicated'. He did much of the staff-work for the core, and had done more political reading than any of them, which didn't prevent him being top of his year in the economics faculty.

Stephen was waiting for the last arrival. Meanwhile Neil and Emma broke the news to Bernard Kelshall. They had only to give him the first intimations: he nodded: he had understood.

'Where is he?' Stephen broke out, looking again at his watch. It had just gone half past two. They made, the whole group, an obsession of punctuality: if you were touching disorder, you had to keep yourself in order, someone had said: but it wasn't merely the breach of discipline which was fretting Stephen. For the absentee was the one who troubled them most, and who, to Stephen's mind as well as Neil's, though for reasons in which there was a shade of difference, should never have been let in.

The man, Lance Forrester, was not more than five minutes late. 'Sorry,' he said, but without being bowed down by chagrin. He was wearing a sweater up to his neck, and chestnut hair down to his shoulders: despite the youth-making effect of his hair, his face was adult, seamed, vulpine, and his glance matey and good-humoured.

'Now we can start,' said Stephen.

'It looks to me as though you had already,' said Lance, subsiding cross-legged on to the floor. Tess and Mark had sat themselves on the bed, and the others, except for Neil, still standing up, brought chairs so as to cut off half the room.

'No, everyone's got to hear it all,' Stephen replied, without expression. 'You tell him,' Stephen looked up at Neil. That was deliberate management, for Stephen knew that there was no sympathy between those two, and that Neil felt something like suspicion, or at any rate resentment, for the other man.

There had to be reiteration. Impersonally, competently, Neil rapped out a précis of what had been said in the pub and outside the cathedral the night before. Bernard, who had heard much less of it than the others, listened with attention. Lance swayed back and fro on heels and buttocks.

'That's about the size of it,' Neil finished, not wasting words.

'Well, you can't say life's entirely uneventful, can you?' said Lance, gazing round side-long, looking for an audience.

No, Neil wasn't easy with him. Neil had a grudge against people so well-off that they could waste their time; here was a man whose father had made money out of London property and who himself had a grudge because he hadn't got into Oxford; in this university, though nearly all the core took him to be intelligent, he was failing examinations. While Stephen wondered whether he was really only a façade. Stephen, as much as most, tolerated the way any of them elected to behave. Lance wanted girls: that was in the natural run of things: he had certainly tried to make it with Emma, with what success only she and he were certain. There were plenty of other girls calling at Lance's own rooms, much more luxurious than this, where the core sometimes, but not often, met. Partly because Lance, in spite of his air of conviviality, was curiously mean when it came to entertaining: but more because he was the only one of them who took to drugs. Not continuously, nor perhaps seriously: but Stephen had seen him in a state which he explained as 'over-liberated', the connections disjointed in his talk, much more boring than being with a drunk. That too they would all have tolerated, but for their purposes, so Stephen thought, it wasn't safe. That might have been a rationalization, for Stephen, unwilling to admit it and shaking it off in some of his personal life, was not free from a strain of puritanism or reserve.

Why, Mark had once asked, understanding his friend well, interested at seeing him for once so undecided, hadn't Stephen got rid of him? The truth was, he had an influence over them. He had daring, and they needed daring. Neil might have passion: 'little Bernie' devotion: the girls were brave and so was Mark: Stephen had control: but this man, who looked older than the rest though he was actually Tess's age, had, and gave out, the confidence of strong nerves.

It was not he who laughed first when Stephen, following after the exposition, made the formal offer. He was speaking directly to the three who had not been present the previous night. There was still time to draw out. Everyone was still bound by secrecy, that went without saying. But if anyone decided that they were better out of it, that would be accepted. No one but themselves could possibly know who had been involved. This might be the last chance to go. It had to be done that afternoon.

Emma did not wait until the speech was over.

'What in sweet Jesus' name do you take us for?' she cried. Then Lance joined in: 'Or just tell us, will you, what you expect us to say?'

Those two were laughing, Emma out loud, Lance with comradely sarcasm. Bernard did not join in the laughter and did not even speak, but simply shook his head.

Upon the whole group there seemed to have descended the air that they were used to. Likings, loves, antagonisms were all damped down; what they felt for each other didn't matter, nor did their egos; though they didn't know it, or might have been too embarrassed to admit it, that had been one of the rewards throughout the planning. They were being (the phrase of simpler people would have made them wince) taken out of themselves: the Bishop would have recognized what they were feeling, and how good it seemed.

It took an effort for Stephen to disturb that spirit. But as he had lain in bed in the morning, he had made up his mind what he ought to say, and he had to say it now. He began: 'This may not be the same for all of us. I don't know whether we're going to hear any more of this business. Quite likely it's a false alarm. The more I've thought about it, I can't for the life of me see how they've got anything on us. When we know a bit more, everything may have smoothed over –'

'Or it may get worse.' That was Bernard, very quietly, chin resting on his hands.

'What are you knocking at?' said Neil, bursting out in anger.

'Just that. We can't tell. It may get worse.'

'No one else thinks so.' Neil, turning in his chair, was threatening the other young man as though he was the bearer of bad news. But Bernard, not overawed, still quiet, raised clear eyes and said:

'We'd better remember, they're not fools.'

'True enough,' said Stephen. 'But I still don't see how they can have got much on us. Security's been as good as we could make it. I was going to say myself, though, we can't rule out the other possibilities. They're not probable, but it isn't sensible to assume they don't exist. Model A is that they can't touch us. But imagine Bernard is right. Model B is that they're able to. And that they feel inclined to play it rough. Well, in that case, and they go in for sanctions, they're going to penalize some of us a lot more than others. In practical terms we can't run away from that.'

'What do you mean by sanctions?' Emma asked.

'I should have thought it was obvious. They could get some grants stopped, just to begin with. And that's only the first step.'

'That's the sort of fucking dishonest thing the buggers would do,' Neil shouted, and Lance grinned at him:

'Do you think we've been the absolute prime specimens of honesty ourselves?'

'Stuff that,' Neil rapped back at him.

'No, I'm interested, anything we do is honest by definition and anything the others do we're right to get het up about –' Lance wasn't ruffled, but Tess put in:

'Please, Lance!' Her face was clouded, as was Mark's: that was something they didn't want to hear.

'Never mind that.' As the others had seen him do before, Neil had sunk his temper down, and was speaking to Stephen like a firm operator. 'What you're getting at is, isn't it, that Bernard and me, we're bloody paupers, and if they cut off our grants they can get rid of us for good. And some of you are stinking rich, and it couldn't matter less. That's it, isn't it?'

'We can manage –' Emma was saying, but Neil went on talking to Stephen:

'Forget it. I didn't come into this for my health. Nor did Bernie.'

'As far as that goes,' said Bernard, 'there are other things besides money. If this comes out. And they'll affect most

of us, won't they? What about your family, Tess? They're
not going to like it much, are they?'

Tess said steadily:

'No. It would be difficult for them.'

'So it would for mine,' said Bernard with a sudden surprising smile. 'I think we can forget about class, don't
you?'

'Good Lord, this is all in the game' Lance gave a hard
smile.

'They'll have to wear it,' said Emma. Stephen did not
comment. Neil said:

'The first thing is, you've got to forget about your
families. If you're going to do any good, you've got to
travel light.'

None of the others, not even Emma, had met his family
or had heard him mention them, except for their religion
and his father's job. So far as was known inside the group,
what he had just said applied most to Mark, whose mother
was dead and whose father, now retired, lived months of
the year abroad.

Soon afterwards, Neil put a kettle on the gas-ring and
brought out a teapot, a loaf of bread, and a large salami
sausage. As the water boiled, he was talking briskly of their
'presentation' in a fortnight's time, betting that the trouble
would fizzle out, detailing the pieces of organization still in
front of them. He poured out cups of tea, passed round the
plate with the bread, salami and knife. It couldn't have
looked more homely and prosaic, and so it was taken, for it
happened each time they met in that room. Only Mark had
guessed that it was the least prosaic thing about him, a piece
of romanticizing which no one would have suspected in
that harsh and bristling soul. For this was a ritual in which
Neil was, perhaps concealing it from himself, repeating

what occurred at another meeting – a meeting which had as it happened powerful consequences – in a menshevik apartment in Petrograd nearly fifty-three years before.

Arrangements for tomorrow. None of them were to make dates, Stephen said, they were to keep within reach of their telephones. If he received news from his father which made it necessary for them to meet, he would pass the word along. It might be – all he said was guarded, but he was suppressing his own hopes – that he would get 'positive' news. That would mean that they were 'in the clear'. In that case, the code phrase would be *no meeting until further notice*.

'It'll be nice, when we hear that,' said Tess.

'That's an original thought!' Lance was jeering at her.

She smiled at him. She didn't mind a sharp tongue, though her own wasn't, and she was fonder of Lance than the others were. Also she was thinking of next week-end in Cambridge, which she and Stephen had already planned.

6

THE following morning, Monday, was cloudless after the mist had cleared. It was one of those January days, not uncommon in an English winter, when there seems already to be the lift of spring. When Stephen took a stroll round the cathedral precincts, not wanting to be far from his own house, and at the same time trying to cheat expectations (if he were not present, then good news could have arrived), bells clanged indifferently into the warmish sunlight.

Back in his room, he tried to do some work. More than tried, for thoughts came to mind as indifferently, as naturally, as the noise of bells. One of the equations he had constructed appeared to make some sort of sense.

He wanted to telephone Tess, and shied away. He was being superstitious that day, more than he cared for. If he put off ringing, *then the news could come*. He had lunch alone with his mother, who inspected him with friendly curiosity and said nothing to disturb him. In the afternoon he took another walk, and then did more work on his equations.

It was after tea, he had returned to his room, when there was a tap on the door. His mother was standing there.

'I rather think,' she said, 'you ought to go and talk to your father.'

She was wearing a slight twitching smile. That told him nothing. He had seen that smile, and sometimes had tried to read its meaning, all his life.

'What is it?'

'I haven't the slightest idea. He's just come in.' The smile deepened. It might have expressed irritation, or concern, or even genuine amusement. 'I expect you'll find out what he wants.' She added: 'At least, I hope you will.'

Stephen went down one flight of stairs to his father's study. There, on the desk, the familiar green-shaded lamp. The smell of books. Leather-bound books all round the walls. In his childhood, not recalled now, Stephen had dipped among them. Biographies of nineteenth-century worthies, Lockhart's Scott, Forster's Dickens, Morley's Gladstone. Local histories. Thomas Freer's bookplate inside each of them.

Out of the window, which had the same view as from Stephen's bedroom, the sky was darkening. Thomas Freer was sitting, not at the desk but in an armchair on one side of the disused fireplace. He was sitting back, fingertips together, face in shadow, expression shuttered or obscured.

'Ah, do come in. That is, if you can spare a little time. Or would you rather wait an hour or two?'

'Have you anything to tell me?'

Getting no reply, Stephen sat down opposite his father, whose gaze, eyelids drawn down, was fixed obliquely on a corner of the room.

'I'm inclined to think that it's slightly too early for a drink, or perhaps you don't agree?' Thomas Freer spoke, not casually, but like an earnest seeker after truth, to whom the exact time of the first evening drink, or of the beginning of the interview, was of extreme significance: more significant, his tone suggested, than anything likely to be said. As a rule, Stephen, used to his father's cat's play, in which there was an element of the defensive, as though he were distancing himself from the present moment, would have been prepared to wait. Now he broke out:

'No, I don't want a drink. Has anything happened?'

Thomas Freer's gaze remained oblique. After a pause, he said:

'I think one has to say that. One has to say that.'

'Well then?'

Another pause.

'I should be the last person to want to worry you. It is always very difficult to judge when it's right to worry any-one. Sometimes it turns out to be unnecessary, and then one has done more harm than good. Sometimes one has given warnings which no one is prepared to accept. And then one has been crying wolf possibly in a useless fashion. Yes, wouldn't you say, it's very hard to know when to worry anyone –'

'You'd better let me decide that.'

Suddenly the circuitousness stopped. For an instant, Thomas Freer's glance, baleful and unhappy, flashed full upon his son. Then he looked away again, eyes once more hooded, and said:

'I should never have expected this to happen to you.'

He added, voice strained and loud:

'I'm getting old.'

That was a cry of self-pity, and also a cry for love. Stephen scarcely heard it, or else ignored it. For him, in the past few minutes, slightly before his father had finished being lanthanine, the day, his own state, had been utterly transformed. Up to then, he had been hoping, more than he realized – feeling, not that the trouble would be over, but that in reality it was. He had let himself be deceived by hope. Now all that was wiped out as though it were years in the past and as though he had known all along the news he was about to hear.

'You've got to tell me.' His voice matched his father's. 'What do they know?'

'I'll tell you. What appears to be known is this.'

Thomas Freer gave a summary, entirely accurate and in intimate detail, of the core's operations and plans. It was even known that they called themselves the core. Their names were known, including those of St John, Kelshall and Forrester, whom Thomas Freer had never met. So were the names of their contacts outside. Their manoeuvres with Finlayson were known, down to their fine structure.

'You were out to create a scandal, that's the least of it.'

'It was a genuine scandal,' said Stephen, in a hard un-yielding tone. He could say that to himself, it was true. It was true that the design had begun there: but that had been only the beginning, the design had grown, even now no one outside knew it all.

As he spoke, unconceding, Stephen nevertheless, un-known to his father, was already feeling a new apprehen-sion, darker than the others.

'One might be prepared to admit that,' said Thomas Freer. Stephen was too much possessed to recognize it, but his father, once he had made his disclosure, had been speak-ing with the precision of a competent lawyer. 'But – money passed to this man Finlayson?'

'Probably yes.'

'Probably?'

'Yes, it passed.' Stephen would not excuse himself: in fact, the excuse was frail: though, on the first occasion, he had heard after the event.

'That is, you were making up a story about –' (the M.P.)

'If he didn't know the facts, he should have done.' This time Stephen shouted, the skin reddening around his eyes.

'You were improving the occasion. That used to be known as framing, do you realize?'

'I realize everything we've done.'

'Well, do you realize that it's not only immoral, but also actionable?'

'I shouldn't be surprised.' The words were cold. The tempers were at breaking-point.

'It is fairly obvious that a charge of conspiracy would lie. To the best of my judgement, it is likely to be brought.'

'They're fools, if they want all this brought out in public –'

'They're not fools, but they want to make an example of people like you. And you've given them the best opportunity they'll ever have.'

The edge which was frequent in Stephen's voice was sharpening in his father's. As they quarrelled more deeply, they sounded more alike.

'I used to think,' Thomas Freer went on, 'that you weren't a fool yourself. What did you imagine you were up against? I suppose it didn't occur to you that if the man Finlayson could be bribed by your party, he might also take a little money from the other one? Who weren't so stupid and hadn't lost every conception of common honesty?'

Stephen's face had gone white with anger. Staring at him, his father said:

'No, I didn't mean quite that. I didn't know all this, of course, on Saturday night. But I think I was talking sensibly, you remember? I'll give you the credit, I believe you were doing evil so that good might come.'

He was speaking with a blend of affection and, as he recalled his own foresight, of something like conceit. Stephen's expression did not melt. For a while, in the doldrums of the quarrel, neither spoke. Then Thomas Freer said tentatively:

'I don't know whether it's possible for you to extricate yourself.'

47

Stephen, with the insight of family passion, didn't need an explanation of what his father meant.

'You'd like me to leave the others to it, would you?'

'So far as I understand the position legally, and I think I do, you're not involved in the sense that St John and Forrester are –'

'I take responsibility.'

'Legally, it's possible that you needn't.'

'You'd like me to do that.'

'It might be possible.'

'You'd regard that as a sign of common honesty, wouldn't you?'

At the bitter throw-back, Thomas Freer looked away.

'You don't think of me,' he said in a subdued tone. 'You don't think of my position.'

'Of course it'll be a nuisance for you. Round this place.' Stephen swung an arm in the direction of the cathedral. 'Of course it will be a nuisance. I'm sorry for that. It will soon be over. They'll get over it. That's all.'

Stephen had made an apology which wasn't one. In each of them, the feeling of reproach, outrage, affection denied, shading into contempt or hatred, was growing wilder.

'I can't understand how anyone with the ability you're supposed to have can have done anything so half-witted,' said Thomas Freer.

'No, you're not capable of understanding that.'

'Half-witted,' Thomas Freer repeated.

'I might listen to that, if you'd ever done anything at all.'

'If I'd ever done anything of this kind, it wouldn't have been crooked. You needn't have been crooked, that's the thing that I can't get over.'

'No, it isn't. The thing you can't get over is that you may be talked about yourself.'

'I still can't credit when you knew what you were doing that you hadn't the common decency to stop –'

'Can't you understand,' shouted Stephen, 'that it would have been less decent not to go on?'

One of their silences. Thomas Freer's hurt, miserable gaze upon his son.

Stephen spoke more steadily:

'There are times, and this is one of them, when the side one's on counts more than the steps one takes.'

'That's the justification,' said Thomas Freer, 'for a great deal of human wickedness.'

'Yes, you must have seen a lot of human wickedness. And you've never moved a finger to stop it, have you?' Stephen suddenly spoke with elation, almost with triumph. 'We're trying to fight some wickedness right in front of our eyes. What have you ever tried to do?' Stephen added, and his tone was light and dismissive: 'You're always on the right side when it's safely over.'

'Do you think that's fair?' But Thomas Freer spoke as though he had lost the initiative.

'Do you think your kind of liberalism is any good to me?' Stephen went on: 'If you'd ever been in any sort of struggle, you'd always have found good reasons why you should resign. That's why you've never been in a struggle, isn't it? Do you believe in anything enough? I've never been certain that you believe in anything at all. In any struggle that comes anywhere near you, and that's true here and now, all you're concerned about is yourself.'

Before Thomas Freer could reply, Stephen said, without emphasis or expression:

'That's been true in everything you've said tonight.'

'You ought to believe me,' said his father, 'I'm concerned for you.'

'No.'

'I'm proud of you. So is your mother.' That was the first time she had been mentioned between them. 'When we talk to each other, it's usually about you: and that's been so since you were very small. I'm proud of you. I've liked to think that you would make a name.'

'That's being proud of yourself,' said Stephen.

They had both spoken in low voices, as though exhausted by the quarrel. After a pause, in which the room pressed down on them, as they sat limp, facing each other, eyes not meeting, Thomas Freer made an effort:

'I don't want to leave it like this.'

Stephen stiffened himself.

'You'll have to. I've got things to do.'

His father's remark might have been a timid sign of love: but to Stephen, now the inflammation, the disappointment of his outbursts (in which there had been some echoes, inaudible to him, of chagrins long before) had died down, a sense, not just of danger, but of betrayal, had re-awakened: like a physical pain, as it might be neuralgia, which had been temporarily submerged in a sudden torrent of panic or desire.

'Oh, have you?'

Stephen rose, quick-moving.

His father looked up at him:

'I didn't want to leave it like this.' And, as Stephen left the room: 'If I can be any help to you –'

7

TELEPHONING. Neil, Mark. Pass the word round. Meeting at Neil's in half-an-hour. Arrange transport. Everyone provided for except Bernard Kelshall. Stephen himself would pick him up.

As the taxi slowed towards the Kelshalls' house, Stephen was wishing that he hadn't to go in. He had been there – in Walnut Street, in a house similar to that in which Neil St John was lodging, except that the front door gave straight on to the pavement – once before. He had seen the delight with which Bernard's mother welcomed him, joyful that her Bernard had such 'nice' friends. Meaning, from a richer class. It was bad enough having that setting one apart. It was worse, now that they would think he was taking Bernard out for a treat. Stephen, himself betrayed that night, felt like a betrayer.

He kept the taxi waiting, but he was not let off. Mrs Kelshall was on the doorstep.

'Ah, it is so good of you, Mr Freer. You must come in. Just for a minute. Just for one minute.'

She was a small woman, bright-visaged, dignified. Her husband and Bernard were standing up in the 'front room', all swept and immaculate, ready for a visitor. A plate, carrying slices of cake, was waiting on the table.

'You must have something before you go, just a little something.'

'I really would love to, Mrs Kelshall.' Stephen's own manner, he couldn't help it, was becoming effusive in

51

return, like that of a Lady Bountiful visiting a devoted tenant or an eminent industrialist making a presentation to a long-serving employee. 'But we're in a dreadful hurry. Another time –'

'No, please take your coat off,' said Mr Kelshall. 'We've had tea, yes we have. But our Bernard always likes a piece of cake, doesn't he?'

Bernard was their only child. They had picked up some of the local idiom, though one could hear the Yiddisher undertones beneath, especially in Mr Kelshall. He was bald with fringes of dark hair and a thin scholarly face, so that some of Bernard's friends, interested in Judaism, tried to get him talking about the Talmud and the Midrash. He didn't respond. Actually, he was a good craftsman. Much poorer than most of the thirties' refugees, he was ending now very much where he began in Berlin. He was a technician at the Infirmary, not far away from their house. He was earning a simple living, just as he had earned it in Germany nearly forty years before.

Resisting either sitting down or removing his coat, Stephen nevertheless had to make a concession, and nibbled at a slice of cake. It was good rice cake, but hard for him to swallow. Mrs Kelshall was talking away about her son.

'Of course, he has his examinations this summer, you mustn't let him waste his time,' she said.

'He won't do that, I assure you,' said Stephen, still over-hearty.

'We hope he'll do well, of course we do.'

'Yes. Yes. He'll do well. He'll do splendidly. You'll see.'

At last – measured on his watch, the time Stephen had been in that room was very short – at last Stephen got Bernard outside, into the taxi.

The Kelshall parents stood on the doorstep waving, in loving miniature dignity.

'Have a good time,' cried Mrs Kelshall after them.

They had not reached the end of the street before Stephen said:

'Things are very bad.'

'Are they?'

Bernard was as cool as any of them. Faced with that coolness, Stephen felt the need, known to any bearer of bad news, to thrust it home.

'We're likely to be prosecuted.'

'Oh.' Bernard reflected. 'There's an old politico's saying, isn't there, when you're chopping wood, the chips will fly.' He paused again. 'But I shall be a bit surprised if it comes to that, I really shall.'

'I believe it will.'

'Well, that would have publicity value.'

Stephen could make no more impression. He was tempted, to the edge of frustration, to bring out the darkest fact – the one which had been at moments possessing him, to the exclusion of all the others, since early in his father's exposition. But Stephen, even now, had the control to keep that back. It had to be reserved until they were all together.

'It'll turn out positive,' said Bernard. 'There are bound to be setbacks. It'll turn out positive in the end.' He said it clearly and intently, as the taxi drove past the gaol, up the rise towards the park: the park where, not so many years before, his mother used to take him for their Sunday walk. But he showed no sign of noticing anything round him: the present was shut out, much more so was the past. The broad and handsome road, the neon shadows, the domed hall on the skyline – happy Sundays as his mother promised him a treat – he spoke as though none of that existed, nothing existed but the future.

'Setbacks,' said Stephen, from his own thoughts.

'Two steps forward, one step back.' Bernard's tone was calm. 'We're bound to win. We've got to keep it simple. We'll go on telling them – the poor are always right in the end. Nothing can stop them. The blacks know that. So do the Arabs. That's why we have to do the same for the Arabs as we're doing for the blacks.'

Stephen was listening with only the surface of his mind. But this came as no surprise. Bernard used less words than any of them, but they were often precise and confident, just as they were now. He had clarified his anti-Zionism right from the beginning. Trained as they were to forbid any thoughts of race, the others took it naturally, although coming from a Jew: though in fact on that subject several wouldn't have committed themselves as he did.

Past the park gates, down the now familiar back streets: the lights of Neil's room rosy through the curtains. The other five were waiting for them, minutes late after the requirements of hospitality and politeness (and perhaps good nature) in the Kelshall's house. Greetings, hallo and hi. Greetings as at previous meetings, quick and casual. But they all knew something of what was coming.

They all knew. And yet, as they sat round, watching Stephen take his place on the bed next to Tess, there were intermittences of hope. Unlike Stephen in his father's study, one or two could not resist time playing tricks as though they were sitting in this room, not on this crisp and lucid evening (news irrevocable), but yesterday, in the dull, leaden, comforting afternoon, when everyone had wiped away the threat and was looking forward.

Stephen, leaning forward, elbows on knees, not describing any of his father's parabolas, said:

'We needn't waste any time. It's as bad as it can be. Or worse.'

There was a curse, unsurprised and habitual, from Neil.

'Two points,' Stephen went on. 'The first is, everything is known.'

'You can't mean it,' said Emma, with a defiant cry.

'I said everything.' Stephen was speaking, at this stage, without any stress. 'Everything that we've planned. And everything we've said to each other here. Or anywhere else.'

'This is quite something.' Mark's eyes were alight with excitement, excitement that looked almost like joy.

'I can't credit it.' Emma's voice was raised.

'You'd better. You'll have to soon enough.' Stephen wasn't looking up at her face, or at any other. 'I can tell you all the details that I've heard. But you'd better believe me.'

'Oh, cut that crap. We believe you,' said Neil, business-like, the quickest in response. 'And, you said yourself, on Saturday night' (to those who had been present, it seemed more than forty-eight hours before) 'we might have to hurry up. That's damn well certain now. We go on the attack. Blow up the whole bloody shooting match before they get us. This week.'

'And take the consequences?' said Bernard.

'We take the consequences whatever we do. That's it, isn't it?' Neil made Stephen raise his head, and fixed him with a glare, interrogative and impersonal.

Stephen nodded. 'We have to be ready for that.'

'Then we get in first. Jesus, we're not going to be caught like rabbits in a trap.'

'I'm with you.' Emma gave a great smile, complicit, comradely, respectful, straight at Neil. 'We'll have something to show for ourselves at any rate.'

Stephen was sitting very still. Suddenly he stirred himself. 'That may be right,' he said. 'But is it safe to talk about it? Now?'

Lance Forrester, slumped in an armchair, said in a knowledgeable aside:

'That's your second point, is it? Yes, I get you.'

Lance hadn't uttered before, except as an absent greeting. In the badly lit room, it was difficult for the others to see if his pupils were slotted down. His speech might have been a little slurred. Yet Stephen turned to him with something like relief.

Neil shouted ferociously:

'What do you mean?'

'It doesn't matter what I mean,' Lance had a lazy smile, 'but I know what he means.'

'What's that?' said Tess, but she, watching over Stephen's mood, had half-guessed.

'Oh, that the give-away must have come from inside, i.e. from one of us, dear Neil.'

'Sabotage.' Neil was on his feet. 'You're trying to break us up at last, are you?'

There was incredulity, rage, upheaval in the room. 'Take it back,' called out Emma.

Bernard added, in a cold quiet tone:

'It shouldn't have been said.'

Unmoved, Lance waved a hand in Stephen's direction.

'Just ask him,' he said.

Stephen did not reply at once. Then, without expression or inflection:

'I can't see any alternative.'

More angry murmurs. Neil had begun to shout. For the first time, Stephen raised his voice.

'Listen.' He had taken charge: he continued, with a depth of bitterness, coming out in harsh, clear words, that quietened them all. 'You might realize that I've thought of the possible ways out. It's just conceivable that they could have got hold of all our names – which they have. They just conceivably might have been tailing us from early on. Though in cold blood I suggest that that would be considerably flattering our own significance. They could certainly have discovered a lot of what you two (he gestured to Neil and Lance) did with Finlayson. They've bought him back just as you bought him to begin with. All that is conceivable. I should like to believe it. What isn't conceivable is that they should have somehow learned from outside exactly what goes on here. Exactly who does what. Not only what we've planned. But what we've discussed. The only pieces of paper in existence have gone straight into my bank. There's not been one word, so far as I know, certainly not by me or anyone speaking to me, over the telephone.'

'They could have bugged the room,' said Emma, suspicion brilliant in her eyes.

'I've even thought of that. Though it's flattering ourselves again. But we've met in other rooms. Most of the summer we took extra precautions and met in the open air.'

He added:

'We'd better all think about it. Without fooling ourselves.'

'We've been penetrated, anyway,' said Mark.

'Without fooling ourselves.' Stephen repeated. 'There's only one realistic method of penetrating a group like this.'

No one there could be certain of the climate of the meeting, it changed so fast. Protests jarred out, and arguments, chains of rational argument, were started: but some of the protests and arguments came from those who, maybe without admitting it, were convinced. And yet being convinced didn't become stable within them. The one certain emotion in the room was a miasma – shot with its opposite, a brilliance – of distrust. The miasma couldn't be shifted by anything that was said or felt: except that sporadically, in one or more of them, it cleared, as it had for Emma a few minutes before, into brilliance like a fog clearing, and showing a pattern of suspicion bright as a spider's web on a misty morning. It was distrust such as most of them had never known. Yes, they had known distrust of the forces, the people, they were fighting against: but that was abstract, but here it was, as it were in the flesh, in the central nervous system, within themselves. Before this, some hadn't been close to each other, there had been, if they had examined their feelings, elements of dislike, as between Neil St John and Lance. But those had been swept away, made irrational, or suppressed deep down, in the common cause – or in the group loyalty which had, deeper than will or personal relations, been carrying them along.

For Tess, who believed, who couldn't avoid believing, what Stephen had said, it was like hearing that someone she loved had been speaking of her with malice behind her back. Like hearing that Stephen himself had, when she wasn't present, been traducing her. She hadn't, not once in her life, been made to realize that kind of disloyalty. Ambivalence, the co-existence of affection and spite, the interplay of kindness and cruelty, or what her father would have called good and evil – those were discoveries she had still to make. And when she made them, she would not find them much easier to accept. Nor would others there. It was only the cold who learned that lesson lightly, or who knew it without having to learn it at all.

Mark, less self-centred than anyone in the room, living at high pitch in others' passions, had noticed that Tess was near to tears. He had not seen her in this state before, not in trouble or uncertainty over Stephen. She was as tough as any girl but now she would have to be looked after.

Time was passing. None of them could have told how long they had been there, in the midst of analyses of information (Stephen had been compelled to reproduce his conversation with his father), 'inquests' about innocent leaks, retracking so as to unconvince themselves: they were most of them orderly and used to business, but an outsider wouldn't have known it, hearing the spasms of conversations, the phases of incoherence, which were themselves a kind of defence.

Neil had not produced the ritual tea and sausage: though he kept speaking with angry violence, he seemed too far gone for that. After a while, Lance said he was going to the loo, and was a long time away. During his absence the others fell into silence, a silence so strained that the room appeared to have gone darker.

When he returned, and settled back into his chair, no one spoke. He looked round the circle, and with a smile, or at any rate a rictus, of jeering animation said:

'Well. We might as well give a thought to who did it, don't you think?'

The air was dense with hate. He was hated for saying it. Yet it had been thought.

It was Bernard who, after an interval, spoke first.

'We can't get any further without.'

Stephen said:

59

'We have to know.'

Neil broke out, with frightening fury:

'Whoever it is, I don't care who, whoever it is ought to be liquidated. It would be worth nine years' stir to get rid of a bastard like that.'

(At that time, a life sentence, which was what Neil was referring to, usually meant not more than nine years in prison.)

'That's no use,' said Stephen, with distaste that sounded like contempt.

'Speak for your blasted self.'

'I'm speaking for everyone –' Stephen glanced round the set of faces, some pallid, some as flushed as Neil's, excited, difficult to read.

'Christ, you might have done it yourself.'

'Yes, I might. For all that anyone knows.' Stephen's mouth twitched in a hard, nordic, fighting smile.

'How do we know,' Neil shouted on, 'that you haven't invented all this bullshit about your father –?'

'You don't know. You'll have to trust me, that's all.'

'My God,' said Emma, without her man's ferocity, 'but we don't know who to trust.'

'You'll have to decide for yourselves.' Stephen added: 'We shall all have to decide for ourselves.'

There was another patch of silence. Then Lance, who, without effort, sounded both airy and cool:

'Yes, that man's (he nodded at Neil) talking bilge. Where do we go from here?'

'The best that can happen,' Tess broke in, 'is that – whoever did it – just clears out of our way.'

'That's too easy,' said Bernard.

Stephen: 'I agree with Tess.'

Bernard: 'No, we can't forget as easily as all that.'

'No, we can't forget,' said Stephen, 'but we can't start reprisals. There's no end to that.'

'I should like to know,' said Lance, voice lively after Stephen's, 'just how this friend of ours is going to clear out.'

Miasma thickening, the argument went on. Distrust flickered from one to another, like static electricity leaping, pairing couples as it had paired Neil and Stephen. With all present in the room, no one could speak to one he trusted: though most trust had gone. They would have to meet tomorrow. No reprisals. The hope, the intimation, was that someone would be absent. Loaded words, intended for someone who should be absent. No reprisals. Then the rest of them could prepare themselves.

As it grew later, the exchanges became curiously formal. The bouts of rage had quite vanished. Innuendoes died down, and no one could ask who would be present next day. Remarks were made as at an official meeting, attended by members who did not, outside the office, know each other well. The only breeziness came from Lance, after another long visit to the lavatory (no one was free enough to ask, had he gone for a fix?). He said:

'If it's all the same to everyone, that is everyone who feels like coming –' he grinned – 'I suggest we make it my pad tomorrow afternoon.'

He grinned again, towards Neil:

'No hard feelings. We might have better luck.'

It sounded, and could have been, the remark of a gambler changing his luck, or a piece of sheer superstition. As they all – after what had happened, they still found it difficult to part – got up to go, Lance gazed round the room, and said, with the satisfaction of one dismissing a place where he has heard bad news: 'Well, we shan't come here again.'

8

As Mark drove his car towards the Bishop's house, on the back seat Tess was holding Stephen's hand. None of them spoke until, suddenly, Mark drew up by the side of the road, the house a hundred yards away, gate not yet in sight.

He said:

'I'm going to have a breath of air. Back in ten minutes.'

He walked away from them, beside the neat hedges. It was late, the road was silent, beyond one garden he could see a single light in a bedroom window. For an instant he wondered, with an indulgence that might have belonged to someone much older, what the two of them were saying to each other. He felt an elation so natural to him that he didn't examine it, though to others it would have seemed alien or disassociated. Yet to him life was going faster, and immersed as he was in the spectacle and thoughts of the evening his step was light.

When he returned to the car, he knew at a glance that Stephen hadn't a glimmer of his own mood. He had left Stephen to comfort Tess: but it was Stephen who needed comfort now. Of what he and Tess had said in privacy there was no sign: all that was left was prosaic, the time-table for tomorrow, who should see whom. The meeting had been arranged for five o'clock, to give 'someone' (who is it, Stephen said again, as he must have said obsessively to Tess) a chance to make a decision. For the rest of them, there were confrontations ahead of them, as well as other decisions to be made. It sounded matter-of-fact, like the routine of any crisis.

As soon as Tess had left them, Mark said:

'You're not tired, are you?'

'No.'

'Right.'

In fact, they each had the complete absence of fatigue that comes with any violent feeling: just as in an unhappy love affair one can go without sleep and walk for miles, or in waiting for news of a mother's illness.

Mark knew the town well, better than any of them, ever since, while he was still at school, he had gone on solitary, wilful explorations. Without asking, he began to drive fast down the London Road, away from the suburbs, into the city centre. Apart from a series of trucks clanking past, there was little traffic: the tarmac gleamed under the head-lights: in the darker streets, buildings closed down on them.

'Who is it?' said Stephen once.

'Wait a bit,' said Mark.

A little later, Mark remarked:

'It's turning out a long week-end.'

He had said it lightly, throwing back an irony of Stephen's in the cathedral precinct on Saturday night but Stephen wasn't fit for irony just then. Any more than he was fit for, or even noticed, another irony when they came to their destination. It was a lorry drivers' caff, open all night, which Mark had visited before in the small hours. They, and their friends, not only the core, entertained fellow feeling for the lorry drivers: but, as they made their way in, the lorry drivers did not entertain fellow feeling for them. It wasn't so much their dress: they were wearing sweaters and jeans. It wasn't their hair: some of the younger drivers grew hair at their necks and down their cheeks, much longer than theirs. It was something in their manner, though Mark's was gentle and Stephen's quiet. The lorry drivers recognized them at sight, and didn't like them. There was a barrier neither of them could have climbed. There were one or two curses, meant to be heard: more discontent, paradoxically enough, than if a pair of well-to-do young men had entered that same caff a generation before.

Stephen noticed none of that. He didn't lift his eyes from the formica-covered table, carrying rings of liquid still not dry, shining like snail-tracks under the naked bulb. He didn't lift his eyes until Mark brought mugs of coffee and sandwiches, thick bread, thin ham, edges of fat protruding. Neither of them had eaten, apart from Stephen's slice of cake at the Kelshalls', since midday, and they found themselves – appetite having its own tactless way – shamingly hungry. Then Stephen said:

'Who is it?'

'It might be me.' Mark looked at him with bold, affectionate eyes, catching precisely the tone in which Stephen had replied to Neil St John.

Stephen said:

'It might be. But I tell myself it isn't.'

Mark was left with a smile, but the discomforting smile that isn't shared. To him, that answer had been totally unexpected: he had perceived much about his friend, but not that he had been going through one of those states, almost emotionless, in which everything seemed as likely, or unlikely, as anything else. In Neil's room Emma had not been the only person who was staring open-eyed with the brilliance of suspicion. Even with Tess: there had been an instant, repudiated now, not to be remembered, when

Stephen – it flashed on him like an illumination, not different in kind from an illumination of sense – wondered. Meeting her gaze, candid and devoted. Could she have had a motive – perhaps a loving one?

That dismissed, he had had, among other thoughts (though they were not so much thoughts as coronas of suspicion), one of Mark. Only half-an-hour ago, driving through the free night streets. He had remembered Mark acting at random, walking out of an examination because it was all too stupid: acting as though he didn't care about past or future, just moved by pure free will. He had often shown a strength of resolve, and no one could tell where it came from.

For the first time in his life, Stephen had been plunged into one of those paranoias, paranoias of secrecy, which come to some, perhaps to most, in crises, especially in claustrophobic crises: when one can read anything into anyone around one, including those one has loved for a life-time: when one has no faith in one's instinct or one's mind, or when they seem not to exist.

With an effort he had controlled himself. How much an effort he had made, Mark, trying to reach him across the smeared and shiny table, did not realize. As it was, he felt compassion for what the other man was going through: and also, but that he was used to, respect for the nature underneath.

'No,' said Stephen roughly, as though cutting off someone else's useless thoughts. 'We must find out who it is.'

For Mark, it would have seemed silly, and also unfeeling, to mention Tess's name. Or to make more jokes about themselves. The sooner they had some ground solid beneath them, the less helpless they would be.

'So there are four possibilities,' said Mark, with flat

common sense. 'Just four.' Stephen gave a nod of recognition. After a moment, he said:

'That includes Neil. Is he a possibility?'

'What do you think?'

'Could anyone act as well as that?'

'Whoever it is,' said Mark, 'someone is acting pretty well.'

Yet each of them found it difficult, or perverse, to concentrate a suspicion upon Neil. They didn't so much like him: he was a colleague and ally, not a friend: but in two years they had never seen – not even Mark, so observant of people round him – the slightest sign of deviating from his commitment. In fact, that was for some the forbidding thing about him. And also both Stephen and Mark were with Neil at a moral disadvantage. It was an old story, which other middle-class young men, taking part in a rebel movement, had known long before they did. In a sense, they were lucky: but they were also on their own: they had only their own will or conscience to impel them: while Neil – so they felt and so did he – had the force of his own people behind him. When he talked about the poor there was nothing artificial about it. He could harangue them about class hatred, and it wasn't pretended: it was the hatred that he felt for their own class. In theory they had learned, long before they met him, that you could change nothing without the Neils and the masses for whom the Neils were speaking. Were the Neils really speaking for the masses? In detachment that might appear romantic. When they met Neil in the flesh, it seemed true. Stephen, much less than Mark, wasn't at all humble: but there was no doubt that, working in their cause alongside Neil, he had sometimes felt more humble – or more awkward, with an outsider's inferiority – than he had ever done.

It was the same with 'little Bernie'. Bernard, much colder

and more intellectual than Neil: he didn't talk about any personal suffering, yet he must have had it. In this home town of Stephen's and Mark's, there had never been many Jews, nor, so far as the two of them knew, much anti-semitism. They could only guess what it was like to be a poor Jew in the local back streets. Had he had his share among 'the insulted and injured'? He gave no sign of it. Except by being so impregnably on the side of those who were. Stephen and Mark were thinking at the table (at the next one, drivers had been cursing, not at them, not at anything in particular, but so that they heard 'fucking' as often as at a smart artistic party) – he was acting from an experience different in kind from theirs, perhaps richer, more firmly based. Stephen could not allow a realistic suspicion about him, any more than about Neil. Occasionally Mark, less consistent than his friend, found a thought drifting back (could one rule out anyone?), but both of them found their attention narrowing, to the two whose origins were like their own.

Emma? Lance? Emma – they couldn't believe it, except, as happened at moments, when universal suspiciousness flashed bright again. Not Emma. They had known her since she was a little girl. She could do almost anything, said Stephen, but not this. She could go to bed with anyone, and had with a good many. *But not this*. Mark, arguing against his intuition, said she might be getting tired of not conforming, she might be trying to find her way back. 'I don't believe that,' said Stephen. 'Do you?' Mark shook his head. No, she might hanker after the past, in the long run, but it wouldn't stop her. She'd be prostrating herself in front of progressive heroes, until her life's end. To Stephen that sounded over-fanciful, but he said something simpler. She was an honest girl. Whatever she did, she didn't lie.

She had her own code. It might be a curious one, but she abided by it. She was a hundred per cent honest.

'Yes,' said Mark in complete acquiescence. 'Which seems to leave Lance.' In fact, except in fugues, it had been Lance of whom Stephen had been thinking all that night. He was no good, he said with savageness. It had been folly, blinding folly, ever to let him in. Stephen blamed himself. Lance was a layabout. All he wanted was sensation. They ought to have known that from the start.

It rang strange to hear themselves speak bitterly of a companion: not only of one of the core, but even of an acquaintance of their own age, they hadn't spoken like this. They could plan violent things, they could take risks: but among themselves they were curiously gentle in passing opinions, loth to criticize. But now that pattern, that protective and tender prudishness, had broken.

'Why would he do it?' asked Mark.

'Does that matter?'

'He could be looking for another sensation, that might be enough.'

Stephen was not ready to discuss his motives. He had to be seen tomorrow – no, today, for it was already two o'clock in the morning. Other people had to be talked to: some of these arrangements had been settled with Tess, and now Mark would take on others: they must have the whole operation clear by the afternoon: Stephen himself – as he had all along intended – would, in the morning, interrogate Lance. Yet even the clarity of decision, the prospect of action – Mark, himself borne up, was observing with concern – hadn't settled his friend. Stephen's voice had been firm, but the resonance had gone. Once more he was staring down at the formica, and the skim of milk on the cold coffee.

Even Mark, who was no sort of coward, had to screw himself up to intrude. 'It needn't be so bad,' he said, half as though it were a question. Under the bleak light, the two heads, fair and dark, the two faces, one unlined and one indrawn, faced each other across the table.

'If you mean what we're in for ourselves,' said Stephen, 'that's the least of it.'

He said it as if brooding to himself, with something like tired contempt. He might have been deceiving himself, or softening the truth. It was often the simplest and most selfish thoughts which weighed the most. Professionally, Stephen could have thought, he would live this one down. A decent scientist wasn't going to be put out of action for ever. But he had never lived with a scandal. He didn't know what it would be like. Perhaps he was more frightened than he recognized.

Still, there was something else. Mark was searching for it.

'You're not worrying about Lance, are you? Or whoever else it is. He doesn't matter. He's not worth worrying about. One person's not worth worrying about.'

It was not what Mark expected, but all of a sudden, as though a key had been turned, Stephen began fervently to talk.

'Are any of us worth worrying about? Is he any different from the rest of us? I mean, from the rest of blasted human beings. You know, there are times when it looks as though everything is a nonsense. Quite likely, humanity is a nonsense. Do you see any answer to that? Men are just clever animals. Not all that clever, but the cleverest that have appeared so far. Just clever animals, with no good in them.'

Stephen was speaking to someone whom – though he had never said so – he thought good.

'Is this man any worse than the rest of us?' Stephen's eyes, dark and penetrating, didn't leave the other's. 'We're cruel like animals. We're worse than they are, because we get enjoyment out of it.'

For an instant, Mark's expression lost its innocence, and he interrupted:

'I think there's something worse than that, those who are cruel without feeling anything at all.'

Stephen rushed on:

'My father talked to me this evening. As you know. I tell you, I was cruel to him. Quite needlessly. There was no good in either of us. He was as bad as I was. That doesn't make it better, don't you see?'

Stephen added more slowly:

'He doesn't believe in anything. He goes to his cathedral, and he doesn't believe a word of it. Or perhaps he cheats himself with words. If they didn't cheat themselves, could anyone believe? Any faith you like. Most of the questions men have asked since they learned to talk haven't any meaning. If we haven't learned anything else this century, we've learned that. What does man live by? We'd all like the answer to that. But I ask you, does it mean anything at all?'

Mark's face, which during some of Stephen's outburst had been shadowed with pain, regained its radiance. He said:

'When you talk of your father not believing, aren't you talking of yourself?'

'Maybe.' Stephen replied with indifference, as though he were for the moment spent.

'But you do believe in something, you know. I can tell you what you live by, if you want.'

Stephen did not utter.

'Why have you been doing what you have?' Mark said. 'You needn't have. You could just have sat pretty and let everything go by. Very few people have had all the luck you've had. But that wasn't enough for you, was it? You weren't ready just to enjoy your luck. So you've got into danger and you'll pay the price.'

Mark gave a fresh smile:

'Well, would one of your clever animals have done that? I don't care what you've done it for. Or where the motive comes from. "Killing your father", as they say, or from anywhere else. It's the same with the rest of us. We haven't been content with what we've got. And that's something to build on. Have you ever asked yourself, why you got mixed up in this at all?'

Stephen hesitated, and then answered awkwardly:

'I suppose I should say I don't like seeing intolerable things. If there's a chance of shifting them. Perhaps it's a distaste for injustice, if you like.'

'It's more than that. It's a kind of love.'

Mark spoke without inhibition. And Stephen became un-inhibited as he answered:

'No, I doubt that. I wish it were true. I haven't much love to spare. I wish I had.'

Now it was Mark who was fervent:

But, don't you see, whatever you call it, there is enough to build on. There will be enough people who aren't content. For all sorts of motives, I give you that. Not all love. But there'll be enough to eliminate the intolerable things. It won't go smooth, perhaps we shan't see the best of it. We shall need some martyrs. There'll be plenty of those. Perhaps Neil would make a martyr, if he got rid of this chap. But it will all happen. Somehow or other we shall finish off the worst things.'

71

'Now you really do have faith,' said Stephen, speaking with unusual intimacy, and a touch of envy, to his friend.

'Oh,' said Mark casually, 'I should have made a decent religious, once upon a time.'

Late as it was, they didn't wish to sleep. There would be time for a few hours in bed before their missions in the morning, said Stephen: time for one more coffee – was it their fifth or sixth? – before they left. Then, with his obsessive concentration, Stephen came back to a first thought: who had it been? were they sure it was Lance? why should he, or anyone else, have done it?

'As for that,' said Mark, 'I can think of several reasons, can't you? Sheer nihilism. There's plenty of that about, but usually it's a pretty name for something cheaper. Like getting on the right side, meaning the side that's going to have the power for quite some time. Or just a liking for money.'

Mark was thought of as an idealist: but no one could have been more unsentimental than that. He continued:

'No, don't let's go in for psychological double-talk. Ten to one it's as simple as that. There'll always be those who can't resist. Never mind. I keep telling you, there is enough to build on. You mustn't stop believing that.'

9

THE following morning, Tuesday, about half-past nine, Tess arrived in the largest of the students' common rooms. She had, before breakfast, telephoned Neil to make an appointment: this was her part of the division of labour, agreed on with Stephen and Mark not so many hours ago. At that time in the morning, the room was already half full of students, giving the illusory impression that they had been sitting there for days and were unlikely to move. It was a spacious room, broken up by columns, furnished with leather sofas and deep reclining armchairs, altogether more luxurious than students at that university would have known in a previous generation or than Stephen and Mark had ever found at Cambridge. It could have been a concourse in the V.I.P. section of a peculiarly lavish airport. Although it might be luxurious, however, it didn't show a sign of old-maidish tidiness, or any other sort of tidiness. Someone was using a transistor radio in the middle of the room, and no one thought of objecting: on the floor were scattered loose pages of the morning's newspapers. From where Tess was sitting, she could see a copy of *Le Monde*. It might not have been that day's, she wasn't curious: they were all used to the European papers flowing into the room, and no one inquired if they were ever read, or by whom.

On time, Neil pushed through the translucent doors. Behind him came Emma, taller than he was, moving in her rangy athletic stride. Her Tess had not reckoned on: she had a moment's set-back, she had been preparing to speak

73

to the man alone. She made herself settle down. This wasn't the time to show impatience, there wouldn't be a worse time.

They drew up chairs close to hers, near to the window, in an aquarium-like corner of the room.

'What do you want?' Neil began, even less conciliatory than usual, as though he sometimes made too many concessions to fine manners.

'I think we ought to talk a bit, don't you?'

'Is there anything to talk about?'

'Well, there might be, mightn't there?' Less than any of them, Tess was not put down by Neil's force. Unlike some other women (Emma was not the only one) she did not find him attractive: her own taste, which she was too young to define but which she knew well enough, was for men finer-nerved and subtler on the outside, however hard they were as one went deeper: which really meant only one man, for she had chosen him already, and though she might have talked in generalities, she wasn't moved by anyone else. That set her free to deal with Neil as a comrade: and yes, that morning, as a suspect.

'It can't do any harm to talk, anyway, can it?' she said in a firm but gentle manner.

'Oh, cut it out,' Emma broke in. 'We shall soon know who this bleeder is.'

'Shall we?' Tess asked, in the same gentle tone.

'What are you getting at?' In reply, Neil's tone was nothing like gentle. 'Do you mean, he'll come and bluff it out this afternoon.'

'That's what I should do if it was me. Wouldn't you?' She gazed at him, not at all a piercing or even an investigating glance, her eyes warm, chestnut-brown with a trace of amber flecks.

'I don't know what the hell I should do.'

Emma said:

'I should cut my throat.'

'He won't do that,' said Neil.

They sounded defeated, more so than on the previous evening. And they sounded lost, as though they didn't know where to look. If that wasn't genuine, it was a masterly piece of dissimulation. Yet, Tess had to tell herself, as Mark had told Stephen a few hours before, whoever had done this had to be good at dissimulation.

Whatever their own condition was, she was certain of one thing. They didn't suspect her. They weren't even pretending to, which, if either or both were guilty, they presumably might have done. Or perhaps they were more ingenious than that. Quietly, she got them talking about the question which, if they were innocent, must be as insistent, as brilliant in their heads as it was in hers. Who was it? There they differed. That could have been another piece of dissimulation. Or else they could have been arguing, without any settlement, all through the night.

In a rough and grating voice, Neil took an impersonal line. Whoever had done it, he said, must have access to one of two channels. One was to 'respectable' people in the city – the people who were out to 'get' them. That would have been possible for the 'bourgeois characters' in the core. 'Any of you could have dropped a word in the right quarters, it would be as easy as filling in the pools. That goes for all the rest except Bernard. They're the ones who could have done that particular operation as quick as kiss your hand. Leaving you out of it. Well, I'm ready to leave out Stephen and Mark. They're not exactly my cup of tea, but they didn't do this. That would be ideological nonsense.'

As Tess listened, she felt dislike in return for the equivalent dislike which, underneath the words, was simmering towards Stephen, but she also felt something like admiration for the strength and detachment of his mind.

'No, if it went that way, it was Lance, he's the one.'

But there might be a second channel, Neil went on, obsessively. He began to inform her about the operations of MI5. In fact, he knew nothing at first-hand about the security services: it was unlikely that anyone in that room had ever met an agent, or that the Bishop had, or even Thomas Freer. Nevertheless, Neil had read a good deal about secret police. He had a conviction, half paranoid, half-intellectually worked out, that he understood them. If MI5 or 'anyone else in the same blasted filthy business', wanted to penetrate them, what would they do? 'Obviously, they'd pick an agent provocateur or a double agent or an informer, or whatever you fucking well like to call him.' That was how it was done, Neil had no doubts. Who would they pick? As a rule, it would be someone of 'good family' (Neil brought out the phrase with violence), who talked the same language as themselves, whose loyalties they could rely on. 'I bet all these organs are packed stiff with chaps like the Freers and the Robinsons and Uncle Tom Cobley and all.' That was how the C.I.A. were recruited, Neil informed them. And that would lead back to Lance by another route. But suppose that the people here were a bit cleverer. Neil's smile wasn't a smile, it was bitter and grim. 'What about slipping down a couple of layers below the beautiful bourgeoisie? Getting hold of someone right out of a different drawer.'

He stared at Tess:

'Well, there's only one who meets the specification. What about a nice Jew-boy from the working class? Little Bernie. That would be clever of them. It might be over-estimating them, but that's where they'd look if they were up to their job.'

It was all curiously abstract, despite his detestations, despite even the atavistic jeer from the Catholic slums. There was no indication that he had any feeling against Bernie, or even that he really distrusted him or believed in his own chain of reasoning.

Still, that name seemed to have come between him and Emma during the night. She couldn't take it. She'd as soon believe it of her own brother, she said. Sooner, because her brother had been born on the wrong side – while Bernie had had everything against him from the start, he was the sort you wanted, he wasn't just a hanger-on as she was herself.

'I haven't much use for plushy hangers-on,' she said, expression bold, spreading out strong arms.

'You've got plenty of use for the workers, though, haven't you?' Neil gibed at her.

'Of course I have.'

'You don't credit that the workers can rat as well as your crowd. My girl, I shall have to introduce you to some of the chaps at home. It's time you learned the facts of life.'

Listening, Tess could hear exchanges that sounded like a worn tape, as though they had gone over them times before and hadn't anything new to say. That was how they must talk to each other, meeting head-on, without any softening or give, a kind of masochistic sparring. Emma passionately respected him, in her own fashion – she had proclaimed it herself. She adored him yet he hadn't ground down her opposition or even made her doubt. No, she insisted, more vehement than he was, they'd been 'sunk' by someone she'd known all her life. 'It's one of the hangers-on. I tell you, we're a no-good lot. You'd better stick to the workers in future.'

She was caring less than any of the others about her own fate. She didn't seem specially protective about Neil: he would survive and so would she, and this might be a rehearsal for the future. Did she ever like mothering him, Tess had a random thought. Perhaps if he was ill. She'd be realistic, she'd do her duty.

She added to her scorn for the hangers-on, the bourgeois contingent. 'I've known Stephen longer than you have,' she said to Tess, 'ever since we went to the same frightful kindergarten. I don't want to say anything against him to you,' she went on, with the righteousness of one about to do just that, 'but he's been no good to us. No, I don't mean he's done it, of course he hasn't, but we should have been better off without him. He might make a respectable spectator, with moderately decent opinions, so long as he could keep his private income.'

'That's not fair,' cried Tess, blushing down to her neck.

'You'll find out whether it's fair or not.' Emma looked at Neil. 'If you'd been in charge and we'd kept the others out, we should never have got into this mess. I tell you, it's not Lance who's sold us—'

Once more the worn tape, the repeated conversation, tired words coming out as in a scene gone over.

'Lance's several kinds of a shit, but he's not that kind of shit,' she said.

'You've got nothing to go on,' said Neil, echoing her mechanical and listless tone.

'It must be Mark,' said Emma, emphatically, knowing that it came as no surprise to Neil, indifferent to Tess. But Tess was astonished. It came easier to make some defence of Mark, after being aphasic over Stephen, but yet what she said sounded to herself fatuously limp.

'Oh, it's not Mark. He's sweet.'

'If that's being sweet,' said Emma, 'give me a bit of sour.'

Tess found herself hurt, angry, baffled, trying to speak in Mark's favour, as though she were explaining the colour blue to a couple born blind. Neil wasn't so much as interested: he brushed off Emma's accusation, but because 'the man hadn't got it in him': he was an amiable do-gooder who (and here he supported Emma) never ought to have been involved: but he hadn't done any harm, and could be forgotten. While Emma, with the histrionic force of which she was capable, and also with the respect for solid virtue of the family she had renounced, piled on the charges: he was irresponsible: he didn't stick at anything: he didn't even apply himself to a professional career: he wasn't serious about a job.

It was the most pointless of psychological discussions, and Neil soon got tired of it.

'Well, we're not getting any further,' he said, and, with the rudeness that had become part of his style, got up and left Tess without a goodbye. Emma, who had come to copy that same style, did likewise.

Tess sat there in the corner, flushed, hating them for what they had said of Stephen (and also of Mark, for mysteriously that had wounded her as much), feeling that she had hated them all along. Nevertheless, she hadn't lost touch with what she came for, and she could separate her own responses. Despite Neil's contemptuous parting words, Tess knew that she at least had got some distance further. She was by now certain that neither of those two had done it. She was, as often, trusting her own judgement. She was quite sure that Emma, whom she now thought of with open dislike, was innocent in all she said: innocent if detestable, and she and that man were close together. A pair as close together, Tess was convinced with her own kind of wisdom, lived in complicity: neither could have kept a secret, not of this magnitude anyway, from each other: it would be unthinkable that she and Stephen could. That pair might in the future do things, and do them together, which Tess couldn't tolerate: but they hadn't done this.

Whether that was a relief to her or not, she couldn't have said, or perhaps have admitted to herself. Instead, she was taken over by another thought, or something like a wish. It was vaguer than her thoughts of Stephen, but it included those, and gave her some of the same well-being. Although she didn't know it, it happened to many in any kind of danger. When all this was behind her – as she thought, it seemed as though it already was – she had a sense of how promising and rich her life could be. She felt, tingling within her, a fulfilment of all she could do with it: nice things, good things, all blended with pleasures to come. This was a moment of mercy such as a prisoner felt before trial. To her, it was utterly fresh and uplifting, as fresh as – in her childhood not so long before – a moment before sleep, when she was looking forward to her birthday next morning.

For a while, all trouble was done with and over. She didn't even bring to mind that there were the next twenty-four hours to ride through, and longer than that.

10

WHEN Tess was listening to those two in the common room, Mark was walking with Bernard Kelshall in the university garden. Mark had fixed that meeting-place because he was as security-conscious as any of them: it was safer to talk in the open air. Even so, Mark was soothed at being in a garden – though it was January, only the English grass to impress the eye, the green of the soft damp weather. Still, for Mark any garden was better than none. Not that he was a horticulturist; in this one, maintained by the botany department, he couldn't in summer have named one flower in ten. But Mark, so easy with all people, men and women, often got out of their way: he spent much time alone, he sat about for hours, sometimes in sight of foliage, before he went and expended energies on a friend.

He wasn't tired that morning, although he had had only four hours' sleep: he would have been glad, though, to be strolling in that place alone.

As it was, he was devoting himself to Bernard. Mark was using his own spontaneity to loosen some in the other, but without producing much of a response. Bernard was composed and civil, as Mark had found him all through their acquaintanceship: the stabs of pessimism, just discernible at last night's meeting, didn't show themselves again. As Mark looked down at the intelligent face, under hair as blond as his own, there was nothing forthcoming there. All he said was considered, as though he had hardened himself and become implacable.

'Well,' Mark tried again, 'what's going to happen this afternoon?'

'That's out of our control.'

'Perhaps there'll be a vacancy in the party.'

'Perhaps.'

'That would tell us –'

'It's not significant,' Bernard interrupted, quietly, in a manner half-academic, half-fanatical.

'It's significant to the rest of us.'

'No. The damage is done. For serious purposes, it doesn't matter if we never find out who did it.'

'We all want to.'

'It's trivial,' Bernard continued in the same cool tone. 'There's never been a movement in history which didn't have its traitors. We've had ours, and it's going to finish us temporarily. That's all. The only lesson is, how to avoid it in the future.'

He reflected and said:

'No, that isn't the only lesson. It isn't even the main lesson. We're amateurs, and we have to become professionals. We've got to re-think what we're aiming at. This was wrong from the beginning. When we get the purpose right, we shall recruit the correct cadres.'

Bernard proceeded, as calmly as though he were at a seminar, without either deference or patronage, to give a lecture on revolutionary theory. Mark was astonished, no, more than that, for the moment disoriented. It wasn't that he was unaccustomed to theory. He had listened to plenty of it, and had taken part, long sessions in Cambridge, long sessions in this town. Himself, though he was intellectually as capable as Bernard or Stephen, he had no great taste for it. Still, it was what their minds were digging into. But now, that morning, walking in the garden –

It was a platitude, Bernard was saying, that all intellectuals could do was to act as a stimulus to the workers. The workers had to be induced to smash the social relations, and transmogrify the relations of work. It was another platitude that the relations of work were intolerable: that was the sickness of capitalist society. But the difficulty was, to persuade the workers that the relations were intolerable. Capitalism in advanced countries was much stronger than anyone thought. The real root of the problem was that it had far more hold on the workers – and, in a strict sense, a deeper understanding of them – than anything the revolutionaries had so far told them. That is where all of us, all the intellectuals, said Bernard without inflection, were stupidly romantic. Including the bodies their associates were linked with, the I.S. and all the rest. How do you influence and grip the workers in Western Europe, or, hardest of all, in this country or the U.S.?

That was where the analysis didn't exist, or had gone wrong. It was accepted that the workers in this country wouldn't get roused about the relations of society without examples from outside. That was the intellectuals' faith: they had all subscribed to it, he had himself. But only intellectuals were interested in examples from outside. They talked about the exploitation of the underdeveloped countries: only intellectuals without any theoretical grasp could believe that that had the remotest meaning for workers in an advanced country such as this. In their own effort, the core had made an identical mistake. Even if all had gone according to plan, they would have got nowhere. They were concerned about race. They expected their example to be picked up by the workers. That was poor thinking. The workers weren't conceivably concerned about race. Except possibly in a negative sense. They wouldn't react to it as well-meaning intellectuals did. Capitalism understood that. As before, capitalism had more social insight into the workers: that was why it was so strong: that was why they would need a deeper theory before it could be shaken.

Mark had anticipated anything but this, as they kept turning up and down the lawn: one could see their footprints on the winter turf. It might have been (though Mark was existing in the here-and-now, not distracted by analogies) like listening to a revolutionary in exile, detached from the point of action or his own present, utterly set upon the future. In all that Bernard had said, there had not been one word of personal experience. Mark, brushing free from his mystification, decided to intrude. As gently as when he questioned Tess about her love for Stephen, but also as directly, he asked:

'How much has race mattered to you?'

'That doesn't enter.'

'Are you sure it doesn't?'

'Subjective considerations only distort the picture.'

'How much,' said Mark, 'have you suffered through being Jewish?'

Politely, with absolute control, Bernard answered:

'That's not relevant.'

Judaism was a negligible factor in the modern world, he said. He went on with his exposition. What wasn't negligible were the relations of work in advanced society. That was where the theory had failed. They had to analyse the relations under monopoly capitalism and under socialism. It was no use being utopian or anti-industrial. How much of these relations was determined by technology? How much were they independent of the social structures? When they had better solutions of that analysis, then they could begin to speak to the workers in a meaningful language –

Impatient, springy on his feet, Mark went on listening, and, except casually, did not intervene again.

I I

THERE was a good deal going on that morning. Somewhat later than the others, Stephen left home to pay his own visit. In case he was wanted (there might be any kind of news) he told his mother, who didn't eat breakfast but had just come down, that for the next couple of hours he would be with Lance Forrester.

'Oh, that one,' she said without more comment.

It wasn't often, not more than two or three times, that Stephen had been inside 'that one's' flat, which was on the fifth floor of a converted Regency house, in what had once been a private road, half-a-mile from the university. This was a place were only an affluent young man could have afforded to live, and in fact, as Stephen saw him there, drinking coffee at a table by the window, the setting, with some qualifications, was not so very different from that of an affluent young man's at a university forty years before. True, it would have been necessary to clip his hair. The dressing-gown and sweater hadn't been touched by fashion: forty years before, the posters might have been erotic, but probably wouldn't have been so enthusiastically Hindu. The books, granted that an affluent young man was also raffish, hadn't changed much: Fanny Hill, Casanova, a translation of the Satyricon, the old stand-bys – pornography had a survival value of its own. So had the texts which he was supposed to be studying, *Middlemarch*, *The Mill on the Floss*, *Mansfield Park*, *Sense and Sensibility*, collections of Matthew Arnold interspersed with Anglo-

Saxon grammars, standing passively on the shelf beneath. Near the book shelves was a portable bar, doors open, displaying bottles of whisky, gin, curaçao, fruit essences – nothing that had changed with time, except for the introduction of Coca-Cola. A squash racket had been thrown down in one corner, together with gym shoes, a scarf and shorts.

Among all that, there were however two things which would have struck unfamiliar to a revenant from the thirties. Lance had, as Stephen knew, a set of rooms, this one, a bedroom, a bathroom: this window, by which he was sitting, looked over a side street and gave an airy view, across the roofs of lower houses, towards the park. It was an expensive flat. But nowadays he had no one to look after it, or to cook a meal. All that he made for himself was the morning coffee.

After finishing which, he went to a cupboard beside the bar. This was the second innovation. He brought out a reefer, saying to Stephen:

'No use to you, I suppose?'

Stephen shook his head. So far he had said nothing but a greeting. Now, at the same moment as he caught the first whiff of the sweet and decomposing smell, he said:

'I want to talk to you.'

'I thought perhaps you did.' Lance gave a matey, nonchalant grin. The skin, leathery for so young a man, was tight round his eyes and made them appear flat and saurian against his head.

He had returned to his seat at the window, and exhaled. Stephen brought up a chair and sat down opposite to him at the table. 'Was it you?' he asked. On the way up the New Walk, he had decided that fencing, or even watching and listening, was useless. Lance stared at at him, still with a grin:

'What's the correct answer to that, now?' he said.

'Never mind whether it's correct or not. As long as it's true.'

'This is all a bit sudden, you know.'

'Just tell me, yes or no.'

'Oh relax, man, relax.' Lance's tone was capricious, teasing, friendly.

'For God's sake, this is serious.'

'I suppose it might be serious for anyone who says he's done it. If that man Neil means half what he told us. Once upon a time, I shouldn't have put it past him. So we're in the cart whether we say yes or no, aren't we?'

Not much missed Lance, high or not high, Stephen was compelled to recognize. He hadn't failed to note Neil's threats the night before, and apparently hadn't dismissed them. Further, Stephen had a sense, maddening, tinged with envy, that Lance was keyed up by the double danger – not precisely happy nor excited because his life was running faster, but glad to have it occupied, to have nothing in front of him but the short term, with boredom, or the tasks he couldn't or wouldn't perform, all removed.

Stephen himself was very far from being an adventurer, and his imagination could have been taking him too far, either in feeling that that would be any adventurer's state of mind, or that this man really was one and was existing so. 'Mind you,' Lance said, with an air of dispassion, 'if we're talking about who did it, I should be inclined to have an eye on that chap himself. I'm not quite certain, but I think that for my money he's the one.'

Stephen said:

'Was it you?'

He was calling on all his force of will; the other man was

gazing away from him, out of the window. Stephen repeated

'Was it you?'

'Oh, if you must have it,' said Lance, 'the answer's no.'

He went on:

'It wouldn't have occurred to me, as a matter of fact. Would it to you?'

The conversation became loose, almost random, as though Stephen, having come resolved not to fence, was compelled to now. He felt quite unresolved, with nothing settled and fulfilled, jangling as in a sexual episode which had gone wrong. They talked like that, desultorily and without contact, for some time: until there was a ring at the flat bell. Lance spoke down the tube, asked who it was, pressed a button, said he was opening the door, just push and come upstairs.

'Friend of yours,' he said.

He couldn't even come clean about this, Stephen thought, with another jag of irritation. Who was it, he had to ask.

'Sylvia Ellis.'

Yes, she was a friend, Stephen had known her as long as he had known Mark or Emma. So long that, when she came in he did not see her quite as a stranger would have done. He had, somewhere in his eye or mind, a remembrance of her self-consciousness as a young girl: and, as she entered, he saw it again, while a stranger might have seen a young woman poised, firm, almost assertive. Also Stephen had watched her grow up: people now said that she was a beauty, but that wasn't the little girl he had once played with. People of his parents' generation went on to tell Stephen that she looked something like his mother at the same age. To an outsider, certainly, she was something of a beauty. She had a sculptured fine-drawn face with great luminous grey eyes: and there was an asymmetry or incongruity between that sensitive and nervous face and her unflimsy body, full-breasted, wide-hipped, which to some was a taunt and an attraction.

'Sorry if I'm breaking in,' she said.

'Come any time,' said Lance, with off-hand gallantry.

'I shan't be a minute,' she was speaking with urgency. 'But they told me at your house –' she had turned to Stephen – 'that you'd be here. I'm really looking for Mark, but I can't find him.'

Stephen said that Mark was probably at the university, and that he would go along with her and help search for him.

'But I'm interrupting something, aren't I?' Her eyes, as well as being luminous, were shrewd.

'I think we'd about finished,' said Stephen, in a dulled and unresilient manner.

'It doesn't signify a little bit,' said Lance, whose manner by contrast was perky and free.

By this time the room was redolent with the smell of pot, and Sylvia fugitively wafted a hand in front of her face.

'Don't you like it, duckie?' Lance, who hadn't met her often, was grinning at her.

'Not all that much.'

'You really ought to try it some time.' Lance began to talk to her, not so much seductively as earnestly. 'Under careful supervision. I promise you that. It'd make all the difference in the world, you'll find it will. You don't know what you're missing.'

'What you haven't had, you don't miss,' she said, as though practised in repartee with men like Lance.

'But really. You ought to try. I'll take care of you, I

guarantee. I've got everything here.' He went and opened the little cupboard for her. 'Nice acid.' He tapped a bottle. 'L.S.D. to you. That can be wonderful. Sometimes one gets right outside of space and time.'

It wasn't often that Lance was moved to eloquence. Once more, equably, she put him off.

'I think I'd prefer to stay inside, on the whole,' she said.

'Oh well. No 'ard feelings?'

'No 'ard feelings.'

Lance was still regarding her with a vestige of hope.

'Sweetie,' he said, 'I suppose it isn't your scene, really.'

'Perhaps it isn't.'

'But,' he went on, 'we should all like to know what is.'

'Well then,' said Sylvia unfussily, 'we shall all have to wait and see, shan't we?'

12

As soon as they got outside the apartment block, Sylvia
said to Stephen:

'You're a pair of bloody fools.'

She meant himself and Mark, and she said it in a brisk
comradely fashion. She continued:

'Getting mixed up with a man like that.'

'He had his uses –'

'You needn't explain. I know it all.'

Stephen looked sideways at the sculptured profile, eyes
gazing steadily ahead, wondering who had broken security
and confided in her. But immediately she told him that she
hadn't received information from any of them, but through
her job. Her father, like Mark's, was a manufacturer, by the
town's standards a wealthy one: she had been to a smart
boarding school and to Switzerland: and then, as though
not liking to compete, she hadn't gone with the others to a
university but had been trained as a secretary. She wasn't a
bad secretary, she said. As they all knew, she worked in the
office of one of the town's leading solicitors – who handled
the business, so she told Stephen, of leading members of the
local Conservative Party. That was how she had picked up
the news. 'I know it all,' she said. 'No, not quite all. But
more than you possibly can.' What was more, she had come
to tell them. That meant betraying confidence, and Stephen
assumed that it had taken moral effort, for she was an
honourable girl. Now that she had made her resolve,

though, she was doing it straightforwardly and without finicking.

Stephen had no doubt why she was doing it. It wasn't out of regard or affection for him, though in a temperate way she had a little. It was out of love for Mark. This girl was a puzzle to most of them. She had her looks, money, intelligence: to the Freers, she would have seemed an admirable match for Stephen, far more desirable than Tess, and there had even been colloguing between the families. Sylvia had had numbers of men chasing her: Lance was one of a dozen who had tried to take her to bed, and had failed. At twenty-two (she was a few weeks older than Stephen) she was, her friends believed, still a virgin. Emma, who had been at school with her, regarded her with a mixture of derision, contempt and an element of reverence. She's so upright, Emma jeered, as she told the others, exuding incredulity, that Sylvia didn't 'do that'.

Whatever the result was going to be, Sylvia was lost in love for Mark. Her self-possession, which impressed all those round her, had to herself utterly failed. It was a love more innocent, younger, purer (despite the fugues of her imagination), less organically warm than Tess's for Stephen, but still total. For his sake she was behaving dishonourably – which she didn't like, though she was so exalted about Mark that it cost her less effort than Stephen thought – in order to protect him. She would have done much more than that, to serve him much less.

Sitting in her car, before she started to drive them to the university, she said:

'I tried to get Mark out of it. Last week.'

That had been, Stephen was thinking, before he himself had had any warning, before the hints from his father on Saturday afternoon. In everything she said about the

93

imbroglio, Sylvia was firm, efficient, authoritative but apparently, in her first approach to Mark, she had been more tentative, and now was taking the blame for that.

Stephen had enough friendly feeling to try to console her. 'Whatever you'd said, you ought to know him, it wouldn't have made any difference,' he remarked.

The severe expression didn't soften.

'I didn't do it properly,' she said.

'When he's on the move, nothing in the world will stop him.'

'I don't understand,' said Sylvia. 'I don't understand the lot of you, as far as that goes.' She gave a sharp-edged, deprecating smile. 'I've never been one for causes, though. I just sit back.'

'There's been someone else who wasn't one for causes, hasn't there?' said Stephen, probing into what she knew.

She replied, quick on the point:

'Yes. Someone's given you away, of course they have.'

'Who? Can you tell me?'

'I'm not certain. I can tell you one thing. It wasn't that man up there.' She waved a hand, with a gesture of dislike, in the direction of Lance's flat.

'You're sure?'

'I tell you, I'm not guessing. I've seen some papers. That I really know.'

Stephen had been confused during his interview with Lance, at one moment convinced jet-clear of his suspicion, at another finding it wiped away. Even now, though intellectually he believed what he had just heard, some of the suspicion was still whirling round, the crystallization wasn't complete. 'Well then,' he was attempting to shake himself free, 'who was it?'

'I'm not certain. I'd tell you if I was.'

There wasn't much on paper, she explained: at any rate, not much that had come to her. Nothing at all that dealt with the real security operation: she was sure there had been one, though there was nothing on paper about that, or if there were, it would be kept on secret files. But Lance happened to be marked down – as the most vulnerable. His case didn't need any professional security work, or much in the way of information from inside. They might get him anyway. If other things were too delicate to touch, they might get him for drugs.

Stephen left behind at the university to share the morning's news with Tess, Mark duly discovered, alone in the garden, Sylvia drove him into the town. They entered an old-fashioned restaurant in Granby Street, and as they passed to their table business-men's heads turned to watch them: anywhere, they would have been a handsome couple.

In an alcove, while they were ordering (the crisis would have made Stephen austere but Mark was ready for a solid meal), Sylvia spoke across the table. Her tone, instead of being severely brisk, had turned soft and loving. She said:

'I once waited for you a couple of hours here, do you remember?'

'It must have been someone's fault.'

'Oh yes, we got it straight on the telephone that night –'

Mark, usually so spontaneous, so natural at leading others to say what they were truly feeling, for once gave an embarrassed smile. Yet he was affectionate with her, and for Sylvia, who hadn't seen him for several days, that was enough. She didn't wish to break the peace of the moment. She could feel that he was preoccupied and fervent, but she loved it when he made the exertion to break out of himself and said something to please her. She had to make her own exertion: it was very hard: why weren't things placid, why couldn't they sit on like this? She kept delaying. She made some chit-chat. She recounted brightly how Lance had demonstrated his stock of L.S.D. and tried to recruit her.

'Can you imagine it? Aren't people extraordinary?'

It was not until Mark had mopped up his steak-and-kidney pie that she said, in a voice that sounded constrained and hard:

'I've been talking to Stephen.'

'Oh, have you?'

'I've told him that Lance Forrester isn't the one you're looking for.'

'No?' To her bewilderment, Mark, expression radiant, broke into a happy mocking laugh.

'You knew?'

'I obviously don't know as much as you.'

His expression was radiant: but as so often, except when he was being kind and perceptive about others, she found it difficult to read. Sometimes it didn't matter, it only made her think of him, wonder about him, more. But now it did matter: had he made some resolve, hidden from her? Why was he so – excited, no, more than excited, lit up from inside?

In the same hard voice, which she couldn't control, she said:

'Please, be careful.' And then, almost in a whisper, she shyly added: 'Darling.'

'I don't see what use carefulness is going to be now. Do you?'

He made it sound matter-of-fact, like one sensible and prosaic person talking to another. She said:

'Anything you do, will only make it worse. The same

96

with the others. All you can do is sit it out. You must be patient. Please.'

'Don't worry.'

'There's nothing you can do.'

'I expect that's right.'

'What are you thinking about?' she cried.

'Oh, there might be one or two little things to put straight, that's all.'

She was being fended off, that was the one thing she was certain of. She set herself (self-consciousness and pride didn't matter, she scarcely realized how, alone with him, she threw them away, nor what a release that was) to be sober and accurate.

'You can't get anything straight with these people. They hold all the cards. They have it neatly stacked up. I can give you the details if you like.'

'I'll take your word,' said Mark lightly.

'You've offered them the opportunity of a life-time. They're not philanthropists, they're pretty hard in their own fashion. They're going to take you on. Believe me, there's not a chance of putting things straight with them.'

'Not a chance in the world.'

She was more disconcerted by that reply than by anything he had said so far. She had re-shaped her own words, but she didn't expect and understand this agreement, casual, easy, unperturbed. She had to hack on.

'Well then. At the best they're going to make an example of you. That means they'll expose you. At the worst they'll prosecute, and that's more likely than not. Very much more likely,' she said, speaking straight to him and slowly. 'It's going to be very dirty. And all you can do is take it.'

'Oh, I'll take it.'

'*Can* we ride it out?' Suddenly, the emphasis, the realistic assessment went out of her voice, and she sounded youthful and pleading again.

'There's not much else to do, is there?'

A pang of disappointment for her: she had hoped for more than that.

She went on:

'Darling. Do take it quietly. Resign yourself as much as you can. That's the best way out. And then –'

He looked at her with a brilliant smile. When she saw that, there were times, as now, when she didn't know whether he cared about himself at all: and she, self-bound, felt melted and lost.

'Don't do anything now,' she said. 'Get away from them, and let it wash over you. It'll pass, you know.'

She said:

'Please don't do anything now. Come and see me tonight. We'll have a quiet time.'

'I'm not sure that's possible.' He was making a gentle apology. 'There's a meeting of the others this evening.'

'Must you go?'

'If I didn't, they might think I'd done the damage.'

To her astonishment – used as she was to his spirits, so high and (as she thought to herself) so lonely – he began to hum. She recognized the Jemmy Twitcher song. She couldn't resist a smile herself: 'You are absurd.'

Then, pressing him again, she said:

'Then come and see me afterwards. It doesn't matter how late it is. It'll be restful. I'll play you some music.'

Mark said, as though to soothe her, that he had no idea how long the meeting would go on or what would happen there. In any event, when it was over he would ring her up.

13

THAT afternoon, while Stephen and the others were waiting for the crisis, only a handful of people in the town knew anything of their affairs, or gave them a thought. There were a quarter of a million people living round about; no one has ever done a survey of what is happening, on such an afternoon, to so many human lives. For many of course, it wouldn't be much different from the day before or the day after. For a few, the anxieties of any of Stephen's companions would have seemed trivial beside their own. If statistics are any guide, there must have been, in the homes and hospitals of the town, something like six or eight men and women who were nearing their deaths that day, as on any other day throughout the year. That was in the nature of things, just mortality: but to some close to them those words would have been no comfort.

Nearer home, that is nearer Stephen's home, the fates were less evident and the goings-on more domestic. The Bishop had come away from a Rotary luncheon, and was for once slightly depressed about his fellow-men. It wasn't his daughter who was on his mind, or at least not heavily. He had noticed that she was preoccupied, but assumed that that was on account of a young man: since his wife was not a silent partner, he hadn't been left in doubt who the young man was. Well, that would be more than satisfactory: anyway, for the Bishop was a hearty man, he hoped and expected that his daughter would marry someone soon enough, enjoy herself, have children and be happy. He was very fond of her, and he thought of her marriage as being as happy as his own.

So it wasn't she who, that afternoon, had lowered his spirits a few points. It had been some of his hosts at the luncheon. The Bishop could get on with anyone, and in his ascent through the Church he had got on with many business-men. Yet in some deep, private, inadmissible recess he didn't really like them. That was un-Christian, and the Bishop didn't approve of forming an attitude to groups of people, instead of to separate human beings. Nevertheless, when he did meet business-men as a group, and listened to their back-chat and exchanged his own, he found them discomfiting. If this was how men thought about the poor, or those who worked for them – he was used to it, and yet, each time it happened, he was never used to it. The Bishop was a Christian socialist, in what was by then an old-fashioned but also a rooted sense. He was not deluded, he didn't expect business-men or anyone else to talk or behave like St Francis or Beatrice Webb. But that they could talk as they did: that they could blissfully believe that these opinions were still permissible: it made the Bishop absent-minded, inattentive to his timetable, which usually he adhered to with the dutifulness of a Cabinet Minister, distracted him for a quarter of an hour, a long time for him, from the sermon he ought to have been preparing for a parish church next Sunday, the second after Epiphany.

In his office, Thomas Freer, more apprehensive by nature than the Bishop and informed of matters of which the Bishop was still totally ignorant, had phases of worry about his son. He had not spoken to him since the evening before. Some of those words were still wounding. Thomas Freer took more blame, and felt more sadness than others, including maybe his wife, would have imagined. Despite his self-indulgence and self-protectiveness, he could be candid with himself. He knew that he was very selfish, but he also knew, and couldn't help knowing, that he wasn't sufficient to himself. It wasn't entirely for his own esteem that he worried about his son.

He had received no more news. He couldn't decide, he had no means of knowing, when either side would take action: or even, for he was still capable of a surreptitious hope, if they would. That day did not seem specially significant, or at least no more than any day that week.

As the afternoon went by, Thomas Freer spent the time drafting a letter to the Chancellor of the cathedral. It was a standard business letter, such as he wrote several times a month: however, as he became engrossed in the draft, his thoughts – for minutes together, and then for longer than that – left him alone. He enjoyed writing in his stylish italic hand. He enjoyed the process of composition. It was more of a nepenthe than one might have thought.

There were other activities that afternoon. The Bishop's wife, who still behaved as she had in their first living, was visiting sick West Indians in a street not far from Neil St John's room. Mrs Kelshall was preparing the pastry for chicken liver patties, a luxury for her husband which they couldn't often afford. Sylvia Ellis sat staring at her typewriter, wondering whether Mark would keep his promise to ring her up that night. Could she find an excuse to get access to more papers? Even that would be a relief.

Some of them were thinking, couldn't keep the thoughts away, of what was going to happen: but none of them that afternoon was thinking what had happened. Just as Sylvia, who had as much conscience as most girls, could push out of mind the fact that she had been disloyal to her employers, so could Stephen, Tess and Mark push out of mind some of their own behaviour: and they had done worse than that. They hadn't been continuously complacent, or merciful to themselves, about it. When Stephen had said to his father that the side one was on counted more than the steps one takes, that would have been self-evident to Neil: but to Stephen it was a rationalization which (if he hadn't been swamped by the revelation of betrayal) wouldn't have been free from guilt. But he had found – it wasn't a new discovery – that moral affronts against oneself drive out the moral affronts one has oneself committed: and so, more overpoweringly, do hopes and dangers.

As a matter of record, they had moved from step to step with something like the logic or escalation of action. Neil's initial find about the rack-renting was both innocent and genuine: so was their indignation: so was their realization that they could use it in their cause. The chain of tenants, culminating in the ground landlord, the Shadow Minister, was quite authentic.

What was not so innocent was the connection they had made between these finds. Simply – and for different reasons with no qualms – Neil and Lance Forrester had persuaded, using a straightforward bribe in the process, the man Finlayson to implicate both agents and the landlord. Stephen and Mark had known of this soon afterwards. They didn't like it, but Stephen hadn't stopped it, or tried to. It stiffened the case, it enriched the cause. There was a price to pay in scruple: which had allowed Lance to make his jeers about prime specimens of honesty, that last Sunday night in Neil's room.

But it had escalated further. Through their contacts, similar groups in other universities, they knew they were on to a big thing and, in a phrase they kept hearing, 'something real'. Journalists, press and TV were drawn in: 'we'll blow this up,' they said. So were one or two politicians. This was a chance to bring down the Shadow Minister for good. With a bit more trimming, his character could be killed off. This was not directly political, in the English party sense. Most of those involved would have been just as happy, or more so, if they could have done the same character-killing of a Labour front-bencher. The most ardent adviser was, in fact, a journalist of the irregular right. To him, it would be a stroke against what he called 'the system'.

To Stephen, that kind of thinking was crassly simple. But the machinations weren't. They led into what became a conspiracy of defamation. It was that which Thomas Freer had heard of, as a ground for legal action, though his informants couldn't at that time have learned the full story.

One interesting thing was, none of them knew, or gave a thought to, the man whom they were aiming at. To themselves, among themselves, they could be sensitive: but they didn't, not even the most imaginative of them, even when they were coming frank about the ethics of situations (or what the Bishop would have recognized as the theology of cases), speak of him as though he were a man.

In that, they made a practical mistake. For the Shadow Minister was an unusual man for a politician: not because of his dangerous or attacking qualities, but the reverse. He was a gentle soul, with a touch of defenceless paranoia. Like others with that kind of temperament – so rare in politics that people in Whitehall couldn't understand how he had got so far – he inspired protectiveness in others. That was why, so inexplicably to outsiders, security officers had been devoting what seemed a disproportionate amount of attention to the activities of the core. Neil's picture of security resources was exaggerated, a conspirator's image in reverse.

Stephen had been correct in observing, at the Monday meeting, that they would be flattering themselves to think that they were worth much in the way of professional security surveillance. The security service wasn't without its intelligence in universities. There was a shortish file on Neil in a London office, since he had for a time carried a party card. Lance's drug purchases hadn't passed unsuspected by the police. Normally, that would have been all.

But, owing to the Shadow Minister's personality, things hadn't proceeded normally. In his previous term of office, he had been on close terms with a couple of security chiefs. They liked him: they saw he was in trouble: they discovered why: they set their apparatus going. As a matter of duty, they would have done something for other politicians in trouble. But here they went rather beyond the line of duty. As it happened, they had some help from inside.

14

NEARLY twenty minutes early, it was not yet a quarter to five, Stephen and Tess stood outside the New Walk apartment block. After Stephen rang the bell, they heard the buzz and Lance's jaunty voice down the inter-com.

In his sitting-room he looked to Stephen as though he hadn't stirred out since the morning. He had, it was true, taken off his dressing-gown and changed from pyjama trousers into jeans: otherwise he might just have got up, not precisely sleepy but not ready to recognize that the day had begun.

'Hi,' he said. 'I thought you two would come.'

Just as in the morning, Stephen couldn't match that tone, and Tess set herself not to be provoked.

'Plenty of time to wait,' Lance went on. 'It will be interesting to see who comes, won't it?'

Neither of them replied. Stephen, who didn't often smoke, lit a cigarette.

'Oh, hell,' said Lance, 'you can't say it won't be interesting, can you?'

'I want to get this over.' Stephen spoke impatiently and sternly, and for a moment Lance stopped gibing. Then he began again:

'Did you ever play last across?'

'No.'

'Nor did I. Too carefully brought up, that was the trouble. Very precious we were, weren't we?' He looked at Tess. 'Were you precious too, duckie?'

She couldn't tell whether he was lit up. He sounded quite coherent, maddeningly and indifferently so. Suddenly her unassertive manner fell away, and she said, with firm flat authority:

'Drop it. We're not playing.'

Lance gazed, eyes hooded, at the two taut faces. He wasn't put down. He said: 'It isn't going to be a bit like last across, you know it isn't.' He drew no response at all, and the room fell quiet. Then the bell rang, and even Lance, quick on his feet, appeared glad to hear it.

It was Neil.

'Welcome,' said Lance. 'I'd have liked a bet on the next arrival.'

Neil nodded to the others. He didn't pay special attention to Lance, as though unsurprised that he was present and the meeting going according to plan. Dislike, even suspicion, much nearer the nerve of living than dislike and so much more ineradicable, seemed to have become neutralized by now: or at least there were neutral intervals, curiously lacking in personal exchanges, as they sat there while their watches ticked on towards five o'clock.

Another ring of the bell. It took between twenty and thirty seconds for someone to push on the outside door and climb upstairs. Twenty seconds is a long time. When Emma entered, all their eyes were already watching: and immediately she looked round, counting who was there.

'Well,' she said trailingly.

The next to come was Bernard. Some of the greetings were louder by now, and it would have been difficult to tell whether they were heartier or more strained. He said good afternoon and went over to a chair. Everyone else was sitting unoccupied, but he took out a small writing pad and began to make some notes.

Five o'clock had just passed. No one said it, but Mark had not come. Several of them, Emma first, without a word spoken, had begun to walk about the room. Although it was a January evening, there was light enough to see from the windows people in the road below.

All of a sudden, Emma, standing by the side-window close to which Lance had drunk his coffee that morning, cried out:

'There he is!'

It was a strong cry, but the excitement had died out of it. Stephen gazed down to the pavement, five storeys beneath, and saw, in the last of the sunset, Mark's hair shining like an oriflamme.

As soon as he entered the room, he said:

'I'm so sorry I'm late. I had a bit of trouble with the car.' He apologized with an embracing smile, with the manners that were both first and second nature.

Neil said:

'We're all here, then.'

There was a pause, until Lance gave a creaking yell of a laugh.

'What else in Christ's name did anyone expect?'

Others were laughing, as though the let-down was a re- lief, as though they had forgotten the moment in which they stood – or perhaps as though they wanted it to linger. Tess watched Stephen, unable to restrain, for an instant, a sardonic smile, which she had seen when he was happy. Emma said:

'Have we got it all wrong? Is there a chance we've got it wrong?'

She meant, could they all have been loyal after all. She asked like one grasping at a new hope and wanting to believe. Not quite at once, but after an instant's silence, Mark said:

'I'm sorry.'

He said it gently but with certainty.

'What are you getting at?' Emma asked harshly, but she knew.

'We've not got it wrong.'

'How can you tell –'

'No. I know.'

'We don't believe in bleeding clairvoyance,' said Neil. 'You'd better explain how.'

'I can't. But I know.'

Stephen was certain who was Mark's source, and Lance could make a guess. In fact, though, the others were convinced. The moment of hope – and it had been a moment of hope – had vanished. They were back with the harsh clarities of the night before. Even though Neil had started to argue, his tone had been tired and resigned. Now he said:

'Oh, have it your own way. Then where do we go from here?'

In the high room, all lights switched on, faces had become guarded once more. Again each was hesitating before he spoke. Until Lance shouted:

'I'll tell you where we go. We're going to have the hell of a good party. If it's the last thing we do.'

He added with a sidelong grin:

'Of course it may be.'

Astonishing as it seemed afterwards, their mood had swung, wildly swung, and they were to remember afterwards that none of them said no. More than that, Lance, that odd-man-out, had touched a trigger releasing unknown forces.

There was one level voice. Unobtrusive, matter-of-fact, Bernard said:

'Isn't there work to do?'

As they looked at him, quietened, he went on:

'We ought to settle the contingency plan. Plan B2.'

That was the plan which they had argued about, which Neil had pressed, on the two preceding nights. If the exposure was coming within days – still none of them knew their enemies' timing, nor whether it was fixed – then they should get their own attack in first. Some of it would be ragged: their political contacts weren't ready, though most of their press was. It could be mounted within seventy-two hours, by Thursday afternoon. It wouldn't be the operation they had planned for. Nevertheless they wouldn't have been silenced.

Although Neil, with his ally Emma, had demanded a decision the night before, they hadn't made one. For a reason which didn't need saying, and had, with the curious delicacy of distrust, not been said. They could name a date – but then security would be broken again. All they were arranging, there was someone to listen to. The realization had the crystal sharpness of paranoia, except that it was true. They assumed – certainly Stephen assumed – that this talk of the contingency plan had already been reported.

That would be so with what they decided that night. Yet did it matter? Either/or. Either wait, and the other side got in and stopped you. Or mount the plan, knowing it will have been leaked by next morning: in which case you might still be stopped. But there was a finite chance that way, against a certainty.

'That may be right,' said Stephen, in answer to Bernard. But though Stephen's intellect gave a clear answer, he had to control himself to sound positive and give a lead.

'Of course it's right,' said Neil.

At once they began to take part in a committee meeting.

In the future some of them recalled it as the strangest committee meeting they had had: on the spot there was nothing outwardly strange about it. The sense of a spy among them flickered in and out of minds but it may have been more omnipresent in retrospect than there, in the prosaic well-lit room, discussing in the business-like fashion they had used so many times before.

By this time they were all trained to business. When the others applied themselves, so did Lance. They were as competent as a meeting of officials – probably more so, certainly less long-winded, than a meeting of executives at Mark's father's firm. The standard of relevance was high. The proceedings were quite short, all over in less than half-an-hour. At any meeting of decision, as opposed to theorizing, they had always taken secret minutes, kept by Bernard, and deposited in a safe at Stephen's bank. The minute of that meeting had its own terse eloquence.

Moved To put plan B2 in operation by 6.00 p.m. Friday, 16 January, 1970.

In favour: St John, Forrester, Knott, Kelshall.

Against: Boltwood, Robinson.

Carried

There hadn't been a vote on paper. Stephen had asked each of them where he stood, for or against, and had then, with what seemed to others like uncharacteristic indifference, not cast a vote himself.

'That's all,' said Lance, after Bernard had read out the minute.

'Perhaps that's all for tonight,' said Stephen.

'We can't do anything tonight,' Lance looked round. 'Right?'

'Right,' said Neil.

'Now it's a party,' Lance proclaimed. 'Anything you like.'

Again the mood swung. A good many people, including some of those in the room that night, elected to face a disaster, and even more an issue hanging undecided, stone cold, without any softening to the nerves. As a rule, that was so with Stephen. But not this time. He too, before he began to drink, had already been taken into the collective mood. When he did drink, the mood – it was something like well-being – ran through his blood-stream and his senses. A first whisky wouldn't usually affect him like this: in the fashion of his kind of family, he had been used to alcohol since he was a child. Yet, after another whisky, he was gazing round at his companions with euphoria, with yearning, with hope. There was Bernard, across the room, near the side-window, sipping at a glass of beer: he had never seen Bernard with a drink before. Closer at hand, Lance was standing by the sofa, and Stephen listened to him exhorting Emma: 'Come on, girl. Take a trip.'

Any other night, Stephen would have told her not to. Now he watched, the sight was sharp, the sounds were pleasant, as Emma answered: 'Oh, I don't mind if I do,' and Lance picked up a bottle and poured a few drops into her gin.

Stephen wasn't drunk, or even getting drunk, nor was anyone there. Yet excitement, strain, perhaps even lack of sleep, blended with alcohol, had brought him – and this was true of others – into a state of synaesthesia, in which the senses were confused, bright lights clanging like noise, cries, laughter approaching and receding like light and dark. So that the room was a riot of confusion, sights and sounds clashing and bringing pleasure, resonating with each other as from the interior of a telescoping cave. Together with that synaesthesia, there was another confusion, as though feelings had become blended too, so that, more soothing than at any time since last Saturday night, it seemed simultaneously that nothing would happen and that all that would happen would dissolve into ease.

He was later to regard that interval with incredulity and shame. He couldn't believe that all his caution, his concentration, had – for no reason, on that special night – evanesced. And yet he couldn't deny his own experience: he had to recollect that, for a couple of hours in that room, he was basking on an island of peace. Later, he knew that it lasted for a couple of hours, but then he had no sense of time passing. No one had mentioned eating: some must have been in a condition like his own. Time too had its relativistic shortening. Once he looked at his watch, and noticed that it was 7.55.

Not long afterwards – he was listening to Lance, whose face was softened with Stephen's own benignity – he heard a shout. No, not a shout, a bark of exclamation.

It came from Neil.

'Bernie.' That was all he said.

They looked to the end of the room.

Neil, stiff-armed, pointed to the side-window. It stood wide open. That was nothing new. It had been opened long since, to waft away the smell of Lance's reefers.

'Bernie. He walked out.'

Neil said it without expression. For an instant, others gazed without expression at the open window. The rectangle was innocent, a curtain stirring gently in a draught of air. It was an instant of dead blank. Shock hadn't reached them, it was the vacuum before the shock. When afterwards they tried to explain what they saw and felt, the accounts contradicted each other, but all were reconstructions after the fact. Tess believed, and held to it, that she had heard the smash on the pavement: but that was almost certainly an illusion. She was sitting near the front window, talking to Mark, some distance away, with her back towards where Bernard had been sitting and nothing to draw her attention. Neil was close to him. His story, from which he never departed, was that he watched Bernard get up, stand quite straight, take two steps and then another over the sill and through the window. Others began to think that they had seen the same sight, but that might have been in retrospect.

15

NEIL was the first to act. 'Come on,' he said, and vanished out of the room. Following him, from the top of the stairs Stephen heard the footsteps clattering below. It was some distance, perhaps a hundred yards, round the front of the building, along the New Walk, down the side street under the window. Along that street there was no one in sight, but only, near a lamp-standard, a heap on the stone flags.

Neil was there first, and had already turned away when Stephen joined him.

'I think he's had it,' said Neil.

There was no inflection in his voice: and, as he told Stephen that he would ring the ambulance, he might have been making efficient arrangements with a stranger. His quick footsteps departed in the direction of the apartment, and Stephen knelt down beside the body.

He had not seen a corpse before (he had been born at a time curiously sheltered from the sight of death), nor a man dying. He hadn't seen wounds.

Bernard's right shoulder was twisted under him, but his face was looking upwards. In the lamp light the skin shone a livid blue. His eyes were open, pupils dilated: but Stephen was looking at the black courses, three or four almost in parallel, running from the side of his head down to his temple and cheek. From two of these a flocculent mass had issued, and could, like ectoplasm, still be seen ballooning out: Stephen thought of it as white, for he knew that was the colour of brain tissue, but on a colour film, taken under the lamp, it would have been nearer green. There was a lake of blood percolating over the flagstones, more on his clothes, missing his coat, darkening his trouser legs below the knees. As Stephen stood there, he was, without being conscious of it, shifting his feet to avoid two disjected pools. There was the sweet thick smell of blood.

Afterwards Neil said that, when he first arrived, he had heard the sound of quick pulsing breaths. Stephen heard nothing. He felt nothing, not pity or remorse or fright (all of that came later), except the hollowness of not knowing what to do. Perhaps he felt how un-human death could look.

Mark and Tess had come beside him. Tess gazed down at Bernard, and said:

'We mustn't move him.'

The three of them stood silent. Very soon, from the other side of the quiet street, two or three passers-by stopped and crossed over. 'What's happened? What's happened?' said someone in an officious, kind, inquisitive tone. 'He fell out of a window,' Mark replied.

'Poor chap.' Their interlocutor, who was wearing a bowler hat and carrying a brief case, made his own inspection and then faced them with a brisk glance: 'You must send for an ambulance.' 'That's been looked after,' Stephen said. All this sounded a long distance away.

'In that case,' said the bowler-hatted man, 'I'd better go and find a policeman.' He jogged off towards the main road – from which, only a minute or two later, blue light flashing, siren hooting, the ambulance arrived. Neil had returned by now, and two ambulance men were asking the same question as the passers-by, and getting the same flat reply.

As the two men, quick-handed, laid Bernard on a stretcher, Tess asked:

'Is he dead?'

'Can't tell you, miss. They'll let you know about him from the hospital.'

Stephen had written down his own name, Bernard's, and the telephone number of Lance's flat (that was the first time that any of them thought of how to tell Bernard's parents), but before the ambulance drove away a policeman half ran down the road, the organizing man behind him.

The policeman had some whispered words with one of the ambulance men. As the flashing and hooting started again, and the vehicle swirled round the corner, the policeman asked Stephen whether he knew Bernard.

Hearing the reply (or really the tone which Stephen, in trouble, couldn't subdue) the policeman changed his manner.

'I'm afraid it looks bad for him, sir.'

The policeman, whose name was Shipman, was a local lad, quite young, fresh-skinned. His questions were unassertive. Where had he fallen from, did they know? Who lived there? Had anyone seen him fall? It was Stephen who told him that they had been in the room themselves.

'I see,' said Shipman. Tentatively, soft-voiced, he thought they had better go up there again: he'd have to take statements, of course they knew that.

On the way upstairs, Shipman asked Stephen:

'What were you all doing there, sir?'

'Just a party.'

A very small party, Stephen added.

'A bit of drinking, was there?'

'A bit.' Stephen recollected that his breath must be obvious enough. 'I've had three whiskies myself. Maybe four.'

'That's all right, that's all right.'

Stephen was utterly alert, not numb but chilled, chilled into control, as much by fear as shock. Fear, purely selfish fear, or rather a set of fears, one replacing another. What would this man notice? Would Lance have had the wit to get his drugs away? What state would they be in?

As soon as they entered the sitting room, light brilliant after the dark landing, cold air blew in their faces. The side-window, to which Stephen's eyes were compelled, had been left open, untouched: but so were the other windows open, over-bracingly for a January night. Lance at least had been active. He was standing up, explaining hospitably that there had been too much of a fug: his speech was connected, the synapses were working, he was cool, serious, not too facile. As for Emma, her head lay back in the arm-chair, but she gave a half-smile which might have meant distress.

Shipman took off his helmet, and appeared younger than before, hair as fair as Mark's, nearly as low on his neck, and trimmed in the same style. He was shown the window, and Neil began to re-tell how he had seen Bernard walk across towards it and then out –

'I'd better talk to you one at a time, if you don't mind.'

Pulling out a note-book, he sat with Neil in the corner, asked low-voiced questions in his soft midland accent, and wrote as carefully as, much more slowly than, Bernard had written the minutes two-and-a-half hours before.

While he was compiling Neil's statement, the telephone rang. Lance answered it, and called to Stephen. 'It's the hospital. They want you.' A woman's voice said:

'It's about Mr Kelshall. The ambulance gave us your name. D.O.A. Dead on arrival, I'm afraid.'

'Yes.'

'There's a police officer here. He'll want –'

'We have one here already.'

'Oh. Will you put him on?'

As Shipman spoke, inaudibly to the rest of them, Stephen said:

'He's dead.'

'We knew that,' said Neil.

'Yes, we knew that.'

Not shifting her head, Emma said:

'It's a shame.'

So far, they had said nothing to each other. They had asked no questions, those who had stood by the body in the road, and no one had asked questions in this room. Some of them, coming out of shock as though it was an anaesthetic, watched each other to identify (it brought back some feeling) the lineaments of their own fear. They watched the young constable, now sitting with Lance at the coffee table, close by the still open window.

In a short time – Lance looked casual, but wasn't spreading himself on lawyer-like diversions – Stephen had replaced him at the table. It all seemed so unclimactic, so simple. Once or twice Shipman gazed at him, as though in puzzlement, with light-blue nordic eyes. In holidays years before, Stephen had played village cricket in the county with boys who looked like this.

Bernard's name, his address, Shipman had written down already. Stephen didn't know his date of birth; he wasn't much over twenty.

'Did you see him go out, sir?'

'No.' Stephen pointed out where he had been sitting; he had been in conversation, and hadn't noticed what Bernard was doing, for some time past.

'What was the first you heard of it then?'

'There was some sort of noise. I think it came from Neil St John.'

Shipman wrote carefully away.

'Then you went down into the street, did you?'

All simple, like all actions.

More writing: Shipman stared down at his composition.

'Should you say that he had anything on his mind?'

Suddenly a jangle of suspicions, fear renewed, fear breaking out in a new place.

'Do you mean, to make him kill himself?'

It was a half-evasive answer, but Stephen's reactions were quick, it would have taken an observant man to pick out the change in tone.

'Well, he threw himself out of this window, didn't he, so I'm told?'

'Did he?'

It wasn't precisely what Stephen had been told.

'You don't believe he meant to do away with himself, sir?'

'I think it's very unlikely.'

That was an honest answer. It might have been wiser, he thought later, to have been less positive: the trouble was, in the shock, in the presence of the fact, nothing else had entered his mind. He hadn't wondered about suicide, or any other motive behind the fact. To an extent, his caution had returned, enough to be anxious about what a policeman might suspect in Lance's flat. But, for the first time since Saturday night, his intelligence hadn't been working. He might have comforted himself that he was more sensitive than most to the sight of death: but in fact it was a source of self-reproach for a long time after.

'That's as maybe,' said Shipman, a frowning line between his eyes. After a pause, he said:

'Had he been drinking, did you notice?'

'I saw him with a glass of beer. He didn't drink, less than anyone here.'

Shipman, writing, muttered: 'They'll find out what was inside him. Well, sir,' he said to Stephen, 'I think that's all for the time being.' He asked for Stephen's address. 'You'll be at home until the inquest, will you?'

'When will it be?'

'Two or three days after, as a rule, when it's an accident.'

Stephen was getting up, beckoning to Tess, as Shipman said:

'Oh, there's the matter of his family.'

Mark, as well as Tess, was coming near. Glances met.

'Yes,' said Tess. 'Someone's got to tell them.'

'We can do it for you, if you like,' said the policeman.

For an instant, Stephen was craving to agree. Tess was watching him, her face frigid with concern.

'No,' he said. 'I've met them. I'd better do it myself.'

'Shall I come with you?' cried Tess.

'I'd better do it myself.'

'Thank you, sir,' said Shipman. 'You can go as soon as you want.' He added, in an off-hand fashion. 'A colleague of mine will be coming along here from the station. We don't want to keep anyone too long.'

Once in the street outside, Stephen for the first time felt active fear (what was this going to mean?), and an edge of remorse.

Then he had another feeling, less selfish than either the fear or the remorse, but just as much like a physical sickness, oppressive, emptying him inside: so heavy, that he would have chosen to have the fear back instead. Rear lights of cars glowing and cheerful down the slope to the gaol: against the sky, the bright circle of the fire-station clock. The heaviness wouldn't leave him, now it was all he felt. Just as he had never seen a dead body before that night, he had never seen others grieving over death. Now he had to bring the grief with him. He would have liked to turn back and ask the police to go instead. He felt unavailing, impotent. As he walked on, down by the drill hall, his legs dragged as though gravity had doubled itself, or as though this was his first outing after weeks in bed.

16

THERE was no escape. Light shone through a chink at the side of the street door. They were at home. He made himself press the bell.

He heard steps along the little hall, and, as the door opened, music from the back of the house. They must have been looking at TV in the kitchen. Mrs Kelshall stood gazing up at him, with a smile of welcome.

'Good evening, good evening, Mr Freer. Please come in.'

'It's terrible. Bernard has been killed.'

The words had been prepared, he had to get them out: there was no way of breaking this news. His voice sounded harsh, almost angry. For an instant the smile remained, not yet wiped out, on Mrs Kelshall's face.

'Please come in,' she said.

She called out 'Hyman', and opened the door of the front room, as tidy as on the evening before, but, with no fire lit, smelling dankly cold. Mr Kelshall followed them, pulling his jacket over his shirtsleeves. Without a word, his wife inclined her head towards Stephen. He said, this time quietly, to Mr Kelshall: 'Bernard has been killed.' In the silence, he went on: 'Nothing I can say is any good. I'm dreadfully sorry for you both.'

'I don't understand,' said Mr Kelshall.

'What has happened, Mr Freer? Please, you must tell us.' Mrs Kelshall was polite, and spoke as though belief hadn't touched her: and yet, there was hate and accusation in her expression, hate and accusation towards Stephen because he was the bearer of the news.

They were sitting round the parlour table.

'He fell out of a window. Fifth storey window.'

'Bernard is a careful boy.'

'We were having a small meeting after tea. I don't know how it happened, but he fell out. He must have been killed instantly. He can't have suffered.'

He said that in the hope that it would be a comfort: as she heard it, Mrs Kelshall gave a loud, prolonged, passionate cry, not a wail, more violent, more harsh with pain than that. She hadn't begun to show tears, though they were running down her husband's face.

As the cry exhausted her, she said:

'What have you done to him?'

'I wish I could tell you something,' said Stephen. 'He was one of us, you know.'

'I know.' She had replied quite gently, and now she was crying.

Prudish about emotion, and nevertheless emotional, Stephen was near crying himself: as though the meaning of that night had suddenly caught up with him, and overwhelmed the blankness. Mr Kelshall was muttering his son's name.

Mrs Kelshall began to show feelings that contradicted each other. She said to Stephen, with a tentative maternal care, that he was looking very tired: then, only minutes later, flashed out with suspicion. Was something being kept from her? Had there been an accident? Had there been some fighting?

Stephen told her, no. It occurred to him that she knew almost nothing of Bernard's companions or of his political life. Stephen said:

'I think I ought to warn you, there'll have to be an inquest.'

'Inquest?'

For the first time since they came into the room, she spoke directly to her husband in what, so Stephen took it, was Yiddish. They had an exchange, soft-voiced. Mr Kelshall, eyes filled, was nodding his head.

'It is necessary. We wish it,' he said.

'I ought to warn you of something else,' said Stephen. 'The police seem to think that he committed suicide.'

Just as his attempt to give comfort provoked an outburst, so this, which he was timid about saying, had a surprising result. Mrs Kelshall actually smiled, a curious proud smile. She said:

'That is not true.'

She and her husband gazed at each other, with what seemed like understanding, and he repeated:

'That is not true.'

'Do you believe it, Mr Freer –'

'No,' said Stephen. He would have said it anyway: but, as to the constable, he was giving an honest answer.

'You are quite right.' She spoke with politeness, but with dignity, not gratitude, as though she were congratulating him.

Then she was asking him questions and he had to repeat what he had told Shipman. There wasn't much to tell, he tried to persuade her. There had been a short discussion in Lance Forrester's flat (she didn't recognize Lance's name) in which Bernard had taken part, and then they had sat round. Was there drink? Yes, there was some drink. Not for Bernard, she said. Her glance was alight with suspicion. She had no idea what a drinking party was like. At instants Stephen's quiet answers melted her, at others she

believed that he was covering up. Someone had pushed
Bernard or hit him, wasn't that it?

'No,' said Stephen, 'I'm almost sure that wasn't
it.'

'They are your friends.'

All Stephen could do was repeat: 'I'm almost sure that
wasn't it.'

He had heard a shout, he said, and someone crying that
Bernard had gone out of the window.

'He couldn't do that,' Mrs Kelshall said.

Mr Kelshall was too far gone to find any release in
blame. For her, it was a help, though one that flickered in
and out. When she was doubting him, reproaching him,
facing him like an enemy and a detective, Stephen could
keep his own control. It was worse when the room fell
quiet. Once, he was wondering, if one were drunk enough,
one might confuse a window with a door: but Bernard
hadn't been in the slightest drunk, no one had mentioned
his even having a second glass of beer.

There was another curious thing, in the midst of pain
such as Stephen had not witnessed before. Mrs Kelshall and
he himself were sometimes speaking – almost without emotion – as though the facts of Bernard's death were all-
important in themselves, irrespective of what had caused it,
as though the facts of a violent death had their own magic.
How far open was the window? How high was the sill?
What was the distance from the pavement? To himself,
though not to her, Stephen could give the same importance
to the nature of Bernard's injuries. His skull had been
fractured. He had gone on breathing. How many minutes
before clinical death? It might have been the same obsession, which doesn't seem to have been morbid or clinical,
that recurs throughout the literature of fighting men: as

though it was essential, and in some manner magical, to know precisely how a man met his death.

There was a long silence. Their mourning had been very quiet. Mr Kelshall sat, head bent over the table. Mrs Kelshall was crying again.

At last she looked at Stephen. 'Please can I make you a cup of tea, Mr Freer?'

'No, thank you very much, Mrs Kelshall,' said Stephen, finding himself match her politeness, which seemed an easement to them both. 'But do you mind if I have a cigarette?'

'Please. Please.' But then there was a commotion. The Kelshalls neither drank nor smoked, and she couldn't give him an ash-tray. He said apologetically that she wasn't to trouble, he would use the packet, it made no difference.

Silence again. In the little room Stephen saw, on the wall to his right hand, a framed certificate. Bernard's A levels.

Mrs Kelshall had followed the direction of his glance.

'Yes, he did very well, they all said so.'

'Of course he did.'

She had to take only one step to fetch something from the sideboard.

'He always keeps his album in here,' she said, putting it in front of Stephen.

'Are you fond of stamps, Mr Freer?'

'Well, I used to –' Stephen opened a page, annotations neat, stamps accurately aligned.

'He's always been fond of his stamps. Ever since he was little.'

'Yes.'

'Of course, he hasn't been able to do so much with them this last year or two. Because of his work.'

'Of course.'

In the next silence, while Stephen was riffling through the album, she was dry-eyed. When Stephen (she wasn't asking any more, for the time being, there mightn't be an easier time to leave) said that he ought to be going, she once more offered him a cup of tea, but as a matter of courtesy, and didn't press him. She told her husband that Mr Freer was saying good-bye, and he raised his head and half-stood up. It was Mrs Kelshall who took Stephen to the door, shook his hand, and said: 'It was good of you to come, I'm sure.'

17

AFTER taking a bus into the town centre, Stephen called
at a pub. He did not want to drink, he was allowing himself no anodyne, but he was all of a sudden hungry, rapaci-
ously so. The bread was dry on the sandwiches; he got
through them and went to the bar for more. His mind
wasn't clearing, he was looking at the faces round him as
though through smoked glass.

Then he walked through the market place towards his
home. In sight of the cathedral, all was dead quiet. There
were no stars, the spire lifted away vague, assimilated into
the dark. As he entered the familiar hall, so familiar that for
years he hadn't noticed the little Varley, chaste reminder of
Thomas Freer's predilection, he saw a note on the letter-
table. It had been written by their housekeeper, and said:
'Mr Robinson rang, 9.20. Will Mr Stephen ring him back at
10.15?' There followed a telephone number which wasn't
Mark's and which meant nothing to Stephen.

Time had elongated since Neil's first shout, but it was
still not ten o'clock. Stephen went up to his room, lay on
his bed, picked up a book, even glanced at an equation.
Seconds before 10.15 he was dialling the number.

A woman's voice answered.

'Who's that?' asked Stephen.

'It's me. Sylvia.'

'Is Mark there?'

'Yes, he's here.'

'He's told you?'

'He's told me.'

In the background Stephen could hear music, too faint to identify, maybe Bach, maybe a fugue.

'It's pretty awful,' Sylvia was saying. Her voice sounded brittle, strained but friendly.

'How is he?'

'He seems fine. More than I do.' She added: 'He has something to tell you.'

'Hallo.' That was Mark.

'What is it?'

'Well. Another policeman came. And someone in plain clothes. They went through the place fairly thoroughly. They took away some stuff.'

'Didn't anyone stop them?' Stephen heard his own question, so violent, so lame.

'It wouldn't have been much use, would it?'

'Did they get anything?'

'He can't have got rid of it all. They must have done.'

Mark's voice was urgent and constrained.

'Did they do any more about Bernard?' Stephen was beating about, unable to let go.

'There wasn't much more to do, was there?' Then Mark went on: 'This is it, I think.'

Stephen replied, harsher, less evenly:

'It looks like it.'

'There's nothing we can do. Nothing in the world. We have to sit through it, that's all.'

Mark spoke as though he were consoling and encouraging his friend. When Stephen said that they would have to meet tomorrow, Mark said of course, but like one humouring a wish that wasn't real.

He said 'We can't do anything. We can't really. You'd better accept it. Try and rest.'

In his intellect Stephen might be accepting it, but the intellect didn't reach deep. There was nothing to do, but that made rest less attainable, not more. When there was nothing to do, one wasn't self-sufficient. He went downstairs. Before he reached the drawing room floor, he caught the sound of more music, Mark was not the only one listening that night. But this Stephen could recognize: it was his mother's favourite Schoenberg, she would be listening to it alone. That relieved him. Not that he would have gone to her for comfort, not that he had ever done: directly, that is. But, more than he knew, he had looked up to her coolness, her sarcastic style: they had been welcome on Sunday morning, they had always been welcome: more than he knew, he modelled some of his manners upon them.

Lying back on the sofa, one of the standard lamps behind her, she smiled as he came in, and waved a hand. He brought a chair near to her, and waited for the piece to end. She was rapt, cheekbones shadowed, the lines on her forehead smoothed out. After the final note, she said:

'You're in, are you?'

'As you see,' said Stephen.

'Nice,' she said, gazing at the record-player.

'Do you mind talking?'

'Not a bit.'

'As a matter of fact, things have gone worse than they reasonably could.' Stephen was speaking – it came naturally just then, it didn't take an effort – with scrupulous care. He went on to give an account, lucid, quite brief, of the last two days, of Bernard's death, and of the police searches. He was looking in front of him, not at his mother, like one concentrating on leaving nothing out. He and his friends, he said, would for certain be involved in the inquest: there would most likely be drug charges against Lance, and suspicions against the rest ('which happen not to be true,' he remarked evenly): after that, the other consequences neither he nor anyone else could foresee, 'but it would be an error to think that they're going to be pretty'. Before he had finished, his mother broke out:

'This is unspeakable!'

The cry, high-pitched, was angry; so, when he turned to her, in disappointment that was emptier than disappointment, was the expression on her face. The fine features were ravaged: her mouth was open, she might have been a football fan shouting at the referee: the remoteness, the coolness, had gone, all gone.

'Unspeakable. How do you expect us to get through this?'

'We shall have to, shan't we?'

'It's going to mean a public scandal. I can't bear living in public. I never have done. I wasn't made for it. I got out of it from the start.'

'It won't last for ever.' He had to supply the strength, he didn't wish to. To take command would have been the last of his choices, when he came to see her a quarter of an hour before.

'Why in God's name did you let me in for this?'

'It will pass, I tell you.'

'Don't talk to me about things passing.' She was speaking loudly, almost stridently: he hadn't often heard her raise her clear county voice.

'This isn't mortal.'

'You've ruined everything for me. All I wanted was to be left in peace.'

'This isn't mortal. I might remind you, someone died to-night.' He said it sternly: perhaps because there was a comparison lurking (unwittingly, vestigially) between her whom he admired and the other mother whom he had recently left in Walnut Street. Perhaps because Bernard's death, to himself, went in and out of mind.

'I didn't know him,' she said.

They looked at each other; neither of them spoke. At last she said, as though attempting to get her distance back:

'Will you ask your father to come down?'

Thomas Freer was in his study, and Stephen, outside in the passage, talked to him on the internal telephone. 'Mother would like you to join us,' he said, and added: 'I'm afraid that I have bad news.'

Carpet slippers flopping, smoking jacket glowing, Thomas Freer entered. Before he could ask a question, his wife said: 'He may as well tell you himself.'

Thomas Freer pulled up another armchair, so that he and his son faced each other, flanking the sofa on two sides. Once more, this time in a rougher manner, more alienated and also seeming older, Stephen went through the story, but didn't end with a sarcasm or an understatement.

Thomas Freer had tented his fingers together as he listened.

'I knew it,' he said. 'I knew it.'

'You can't have known it.' His wife broke in, temper edged with impatience and contempt. 'You can't have known that this fellow would get himself killed.'

'No, not that.'

'That's what's blown them all wide open.'

Thomas Freer said, shaking his head:

'I knew the rest. I knew the rest.'

That seemed to give him some obscure consolation. And yet, to Stephen, far less than other darknesses of that night, but still pressing on a nerve, the reversal of roles between his parents was striking inward. From infancy his mother had been immaculate, above the battle. If he had asked himself, he would have expected her in a crisis to be brave. Long since Stephen had accepted that his father slid out of trouble and gave nice reasons for behaving like a coward. But, in the future, Stephen was to think his mother was an accomplice, tacit if you like, in just that cowardice. Maybe that was one of the secrets of this marriage. 'I can't bear living in public.' Maybe, as a courted girl, that was why she had elected for Thomas Freer. It was possible that, with a different wife, he might have relapsed into fewer indulgences, or have been less satisfied with them.

That night he was making an effort – not strong-willed, but with a tinge of conscience or concern – not to add to pain. He wasn't angry, he was genuinely sad.

He said:

'This is bad, Steve.' (It was years since he had called Stephen by that name.) 'This is very bad.'

'It couldn't be much worse.'

Thomas Freer was reflecting.

'Poor chap,' he said. 'Poor chap.' Then he added, with an air of interested curiosity:

'Will he be buried according to the Jewish rite, should you say?'

His wife exclaimed:

'What in God's name does that matter?'

Stephen also had been shaken by that bizarre irrelevance. He didn't perceive – though if she had been calm she might have done, for she had lived with those defences for so long – that this was the device of a timid man, trying to slow himself down, trying to control his nerves.

'Don't you realize that this is going to be a public scandal?' cried Kate Freer, voice unsteady.

'Yes, I realize that. I realize that.'

'Do you?'

Once more tenting his fingers, he began speaking circuitously to Stephen:

'I suppose that in circumstances of this kind you have to be prepared for an inquest?'

'Of course.'

'I suppose that it mightn't be a pure formality, don't you think? There might be certain questions about these police inquiries, isn't that a possibility?'

'Of course it is.'

'I'm inclined to suggest, I don't know what you think, I'm inclined to suggest that you might consider employing a lawyer, just to watch over your interests, as a precaution, you understand.'

'That sounds sensible.' Stephen's reply was impatient, hard.

'As a matter of fact, I'd already had a preliminary word with Hotchkinson. Not old Hotchkinson, of course, he's getting beyond it now, he must be in his eighties, but his son isn't bad as we provincial solicitors go. Yes, I had a preliminary word with him before this happened, just on the chance that you might be getting into troubled water.'

Again, Thomas Freer, in the midst of his labyrinth (which to himself contained feeling which it concealed from others), derived some consolation from his own foresight.

'Thank you.' That was formal manners from Stephen, not more.

'What's going to come out of this?' Kate Freer's glance moved from one to the other.

'I can't tell you that. I can't tell you that.'

'What's going to happen?' This time she was interrogating Stephen direct. He replied without inflection:

'I hope, nothing too uncomfortable for you.'

He wanted to get away. There was no surcease for him here. Quite politely – strange how politeness survived – he said good night to them both, and went upstairs to his room. It was not eleven o'clock, but he undressed and got into bed although he didn't expect to sleep. Before he had switched off the light, the telephone rang.

'Darling. Tess here.'

'Yes?'

'This is dreadful for you.'

'Dreadful for everyone.'

'Worse for you. I'm thinking of you. I wish I could come to you straight away.'

'I wish you could.' (Did he mean that? Did he want her with him, then?)

'Look, let's meet tomorrow morning.'

They arranged that she would call for him. Then she said:

'Darling. There's something else.'

'What is it?'

'Everything's going to be public property soon, isn't it?'

'Nearly everything.'

'So I think I ought to tell my father. Tonight.'

'He'll hear soon enough.'

'No, I think I ought to tell him myself.'

'What good will that do?' She must have heard his tone, more insensitive than she was used to.

'No, I think I've got to. Do I have permission?'

Even now, habits of secrecy endured, were hard to break. It was after a pause that Stephen said: 'I suppose so. If you must.'

18

STEPHEN woke out of a happy dream. He had gone to sleep at once, and it was the middle of the night, no, later, the cathedral clock was chiming, he hadn't counted, five or six. He had been dreaming of someone, presumably himself, though in his memory, already fading, it didn't look like himself, sitting by the bank of a stream, fishing (which Stephen had not done since he was a child). The bank of the stream was very close to, or subliminally coincided with, the foyer of a luxurious hotel. Curtained, warm, with, as appeared entirely reasonable, bright lights flashing. Flashing in colour as he remembered it, if one dreamed in colour.

The aura of the dream had been of utter tranquillity and bliss. So, when he was first awake, was its after-glow.

Stephen's body stiffened, his brow was furrowing, into the sense of loss, the primal deprivation, which comes from moving out of bliss (all beyond one's will) into misery. The first thought that took charge wasn't of the danger, though that was just below consciousness: it wasn't regret or responsibility or a picture of the Kelshall parents the night before: it was the recollection of his own. The drawing room, what they had said, what he had said, it wasn't a true memory or a record, more like a momentary film-shot. He felt a stranger. Sharper than that, he was projecting the estrangement on to them, he was feeling angry and quite cold.

Round the edges of the window, the sky was black. He

switched on the light and looked at his watch. Ten past six. The morning was a long time off. He tried to sleep again. He couldn't use the spell which he had used while there was still hope: wishing time to stay still, to linger just as it was, letting him sleep in peace. He would have been ashamed for others to know that he had been wishing that, those past nights: he wasn't easy-natured enough to guess that other active and strenuous men had often wished the same.

He couldn't sleep. He couldn't capture the hypnagogic faces that sometimes came before one slept. There was the realization – not like a photograph or film, not like the physical fact – of Bernard's shattered head. Was that more shaking than the physical fact? The sight of the open window. He had a thought which in confusion hours before he had pushed out of mind: now he didn't want to admit it, it came back. As with the detective-work of jealousy, it wouldn't leave him alone. Shut out one answer, convince yourself, another returned.

He switched on the light again. Only ten minutes had passed. Time had expanded. He could get up at 7.15. The housekeeper (she had looked after him since he was a baby: how much did she know now?) would give him breakfast. That way he would miss both his father and mother. He did not choose to see his mother.

Tess would be here. He didn't want to be alone. It startled him, how much he didn't want to be alone. He could talk to her about those thoughts. Perhaps to Mark.

At last, at procrastinated last, a single bell began to clang, over in the cathedral tower. Early morning communion. What the Bishop in secret (gossip, quite irrelevant, flooded back to Stephen) would like to have called Mass, but the Provost wouldn't have it. Just before seven.

Although he had disciplined himself to wait in bed until a quarter past, he was down in the kitchen five minutes before. The housekeeper, wearing an expression worried and kind, gave him scrambled eggs. With the disrespect of the senses, indifferent to anything he felt, they tasted very good.

Back in his room, insulated from the household, he waited, as though waiting were a condition in itself. Tess could not be here for hours: it was not sensible to pretend that he was waiting for a ring from downstairs: yet he was, he was waiting. The cathedral bell again, nearly eight o'clock. Soon afterwards he telephoned Mark, who sounded unconstrained and fresh. They ought to meet today, this afternoon, said Stephen. If you like, Mark agreed. Where?

'Not here,' said Stephen. 'This is out.'

Mark recognized the tone of voice, and didn't inquire why: though any meeting-place was open now, there was no need for security any more. Instead Mark said that Stephen had better come to him; he would drive in and pick him up. There would probably be Tess too, said Stephen. Good, said Mark, as casually hospitable as they had always been among themselves, as though nothing had changed.

Another service, the bell was ringing. Sounds of childhood. He used to hear them on holidays from school, as he went down to breakfast. One grew accustomed to bells, one came to like them, one didn't fret about what they were ringing for, the noise was jolly and secure.

It was half-past nine before the housekeeper spoke from below. Miss Boltwood had come. 'Tell her I'll be down,' said Stephen into the telephone. He was not going to invite her into the house, any more than Mark. He was being more unreasonable than he let himself admit, now that reason wasn't helping any more. Once he had been proud of the house, with a token sarcasm about the signs of privilege. It wasn't token sarcasm that shut the house behind him now.

'How are you?' asked Tess, as they walked in the lane, in the chilly wind.

'All right.'

'Are you really?' She studied him with a candid, protective gaze.

'As well as might be expected.'

He said it off-handedly, but it seemed that he was not holding back from her: she gave a smile of relief, and, when they turned towards the market place, let herself slip her arm into his, and felt him press it. But he was paying a price, a matter-of-fact price, for unreason, and so was she. It was bitterly cold in the streets, and they had nowhere to go. He might be a well-to-do young man, but once he felt his home was alien he had no other place to take them. There wasn't even a café they could go to, at that time in the morning. Tess trudged uncomplainingly at his side.

In the Market Street the shop windows were shining bright. Where could they go? Where could they talk? There was a bookshop not far away, but it was so small, they would be overheard. Tess, who knew how obsessive he could be, began to talk to herself, in the breath-catching wind, outside the taunting windows.

'Haven't you heard of people doing weird things, if they've been taking L.S.D.?'

Stephen didn't reply at once.

She said:

'Could they go out of a window, could that happen? I don't know, I seem to have an idea –'

She looked up at Stephen. He gave her a recognizing smile.

'I might have got in first,' he said. 'I had exactly the same thought. During the night.'

'I suppose –'

'I've kept thinking round it. I can't get anywhere, can you?'

'The trouble is,' she said, 'Bernard would never have taken it. Any more than we would.'

'Maybe less.' Actually Stephen, with his share of puritan reserve, had smoked marijuana exactly once in his life, and neither he nor Tess had touched any hard drugs.

'It wasn't his thing.'

They walked along, gazed absently into another window.

'I did just wonder –' Stephen began.

'Yes.'

'Some fool might have thought it was a bright idea to slip him some.'

'Yes.'

Could it be done without Bernard noticing? The stuff had no taste, Tess believed but wasn't sure. It didn't require much, judging by the drops which Stephen had watched Lance add – slowly, hieratically, one, two, three – to Emma's gin.

'It might be easy. If someone was giving him (Bernard) another drink.'

'I didn't notice anyone doing that,' said Stephen.

'You had a fair amount yourself,' said Tess. She added: 'I wouldn't put it past Lance, would you?'

If they ruled out suicide – then what? Was this it? It wasn't just blind chance. Tess said her father had said something like that, last night.

'It makes it worse,' said Stephen.

'Yes,' said Tess. 'It makes it worse.'

With an effort, shaking himself from his thoughts, Stephen asked what else her father had said.

'He was pretty quiet. For him,' she said. She went on: 'He took it very well.'

'I'm glad.'

She could feel enough, she had already felt, what his own home had been like. She had had a purpose before she met him, stronger since they had been walking.

'Look here, darling,' she said, 'wouldn't you like to talk to him?'

'I don't see the point of that.'

'Underneath it all, you know, he has a lot of sense.'

'I'm afraid sense isn't going to get us very far.'

She said:

'Listen. You oughtn't to be quite on your own, now ought you?'

It was a risk. She knew how proud he was and in distress how difficult to reach. But it was a calculated risk, at any rate a calculation of hope. Sometimes he couldn't be persuaded, certainly not flattered, but curiously (she had found that her will was as strong as his) he could be budged.

After a silence he said:

'Oh, if you like.'

They retraced the way towards the cathedral, by now repeating their moves on the past (by this time so innocent) Saturday night. She didn't say anything more, except that her father had volunteered to be ready for them, if they decided to come. As they crossed the cathedral yard, Stephen did not look up towards the windows of his own house. They passed round the church itself towards a small red-brick building, not more than fifty years old. There was nothing grand about the Bishop's office, any more than there was anything grand about the Bishop himself. In fact, it really was an office, consisting of three rooms, one for the archdeacon, one for the Bishop's secretary, sharing it with his chaplain, and one for the Bishop himself. For a few minutes, Stephen and Tess had to sit in the secretary's room, nothing to see except charts pinned up on the green baize notice boards, one picture of Highland cattle. The typewriter tapped. Then a young clergyman emerged from inside, and the Bishop called them in.

'Come in, come in. Here you are then, I'm glad to see you. I am glad to see you.'

The comfortable vowels rolled out.

'Sit you down,' said the Bishop as they entered. There wasn't much room to sit, a couple of chairs in front of a small table, at which the Bishop was already installed, short legs tucked under, so that he looked a more reasonable height than when on his feet. His face was roseate, his eyes gleamed brightly through his spectacles. Behind him on the bare, dun-painted, schoolroom-like wall stood a large crucifix. Despite his oecumenical fervour, the Bishop was orthodox both in liturgy and theology. The crucifix was a complete cross, not a tau, I.N.R.I. on the top limb above the head, nails through the centre of the palms and the doubled feet. Stephen scarcely noticed it (he was meeting the Bishop's glance, sharp, appraising but not mournful) and didn't recall how at school he had speculated about crucifixes of that kind. Didn't anyone realize that they were impossible, mechanically and anatomically? How did anyone think they got the cross bar into place? No human body could have been supported like that, there was nothing to take the strain. Strange how the early Church (when did they first use the symbol of the cross, fifth century or was it later?)

had forgotten what crucifixion had been like. Strange how the most powerful symbol there had ever been should have lasted all these years and been so wrong.

These discursions didn't come back to him now. He was listening to the Bishop, who said in a strong voice:

'This is a bad business for you both. Of course it is.'

Stephen was jolted, he hadn't seen the Bishop behave like this, no small talk, none of his touch of knockabout, no preliminaries at all. And yet it was a relief to go straight in. Stephen glanced at Tess, and they each muttered something.

'I'm going to tell you straight away, you have to put first things first. The first thing is, you mustn't take to your own account any more responsibility than you really have to. It isn't your fault that this poor boy's been killed. My girl has told me you don't know anything about it.'

'I expect she's told you everything we know.'

'Of course she has.'

In reply to that brisk tone, unsentimental, not even over-kind but stiffening to listen to, Stephen mentioned their exchanges about the possibility of the drug.

'Could be. Could be. There's a natural explanation somewhere. But neither of you had anything to do with that?'

'No.'

'Well done, well done. That's not a way to expand consciousness. We ought to listen to people your age about most things, but I'm not inclined to be permissive about drugs. Well then, that's the first thing. You have to take responsibility for some of the things that have happened, of course you have, and that's going to bring you suffering. But so far as any of us have genuine responsibility for someone else, you haven't any for this boy's death. I want you to get your consciences clear on that.'

Stephen didn't reply. Often maybe, he had thought of the Bishop as a comic little man, but now it was mystifying (yes, partly a reassurance, but the kind of reassurance that leaves one at a loss) to meet someone so robust. Tess said:

'That's easier said than done, isn't it, though?'

'No, no. We mustn't let things fester. That does no good to anyone. It makes you worse to yourselves and worse to other people. You'll have enough weight to carry without that.' His colour was growing higher, his eyes still brighter. 'You're not going to forget this whole business in a hurry, are you? It will stay with you for a long time, it will leave its mark. So far as I can judge, you've done wrong, very wrong. There aren't any two ways about that, as far as I'm concerned. And yet you're both serious. I hope you are. I know you are. I only wish you could find something good enough to be serious about.'

Stephen was beginning to speak, but the Bishop interrupted:

'I only wish you were both Christians, you know.'

He said it as a wish, not as propaganda, simply, directly, like everything he had said that morning. With one fraction of an English privileged ear, Stephen noted that he pronounced the 't' in Christian, which wouldn't have happened among Thomas Freer's friends: but Stephen replied, and Tess heard with pleasure that he was just as simple and direct:

'I'm afraid that the words mean nothing.'

'What words?'

'Resurrection. Atonement. Redemption. Immortality. Or even God.'

'Of course the words aren't adequate. They're only shadows, they're the best we can do. We have to try and reach what lies behind the shadows, that's what it's all about.'

'I'm afraid that amounts to adding more words without meaning – to cover up the first set.'

Another day, the Bishop always ready for a discussion, might have plunged into epistemology, linguistic analysis and their theological correlatives. As it was, he said:

'Ah well. Faith exists somewhere beyond all that, you see.'

'You don't want him to pretend, do you?' cried his daughter.

'He'd never do that. He couldn't do that if he tried,' said the Bishop, looking at Stephen with a curious respect. 'Not in a month of Sundays,' he added, breaking into incongruous laughter, gratified by the homely old phrase. Then he said: 'But I should like you two to tell me something. I think I know what you're living for. You want to see a more decent world here-and-now, isn't that it? So do we all, so do we all. Don't give that up, oh no. Yes, I think I know what you're living for. But I really don't know what you're living by –'

Oddly, he was using terms which they had used themselves: or perhaps it was not so odd, for those terms, ordinary enough, might have filtered into their speech from his, or even the other way round. In asking the question, the Bishop wasn't so naïve as he seemed. Hopeful as he was, he wasn't naïve. He knew, as well as any man, that people had found codes, aspirations, moralities, humanisms and creeds in every community under heaven, whether they believed in heaven or not. He would have said that men were sinful creatures but – they might profess any religion or none – with a possibility of grace. But about these two he was puzzled, puzzled more than hurt. Both of them had been born right in the heart of the Church. Stephen had lived all his life within sight and sound of the cathedral: Tess's childhood had been spent in a town vicarage, before they moved here. It wasn't that they had rebelled against Christianity – the Bishop could have understood that, it would have been no problem – but that they had quietly, without conflict, friction, or apparent loss, let it drop. True, Stephen mightn't have been attracted by his parents' example (the Bishop, in the depth of his soul, which wasn't so uniformly affable and outpouring as it seemed, had a certain lack of charity towards Thomas Freer), but Tess had always been close to her father. He didn't know all about her life nowadays: perhaps he didn't want to know, or knew-and-not-knew. That didn't matter, they were still close. And yet she had let her religion fade out as effortlessly as Stephen. Just as though it were in the nature of things.

The Bishop was disturbed as much as puzzled. When he was puzzled, he had to find a name for it. 'I take it that that American – what's his name – would call you inner-directed, wouldn't he? Well, it's a good thing to be inner-directed, I hope we all are, part of our time. But can anyone be totally inner-directed for ever? That's what I wonder about you two. You'll have to discover that yourselves, won't you? We shall see. We shall see.'

Suddenly, as though coming to attention, he broke out:

'Have you prepared yourselves? I mean, have you prepared yourselves for what's in store? Very soon. You must have thought about it, you must have.'

'I don't suppose we've thought about anything else,' said Stephen.

'That isn't the same as living it, Stephen.' It was the first time he had called Stephen by his name: perhaps it was the first time that he spoke as an older man, or looked on them as very young. 'You'll find that public shame is very difficult to live with. It's going to mean that, there's no avoiding it. There are some things you wouldn't mind being pilloried for, of course there are. But that won't be so this time, you know. You'll have to be ready to see your names in public and hate the sight of them.'

'I think we're ready for that,' said Tess, as firmly as her father.

'You won't know, I've got to warn you, you won't know until you've been through it.' He added, with feeling, with strength: 'I think we're all going to need each other.'

In the midst of the selfishness of dread, Stephen had not had the free energy to imagine how the Bishop was himself involved. Yet he too was exposed, wide-open. A radical bishop, who had his enemies – now to have a daughter implicated like this. Apart from that one remark which seemed more comradely than reproachful, he did not obtrude himself again: and (so Tess told Stephen later) he had not done so, not once on the previous night. Perhaps they still did not realize how much he had subdued his own concern. Training, tenderness for their futures, certainly a knowledge that his daughter loved this man – they all helped him: but Stephen, if not distracted, must have observed that the Bishop was triumphing over his nature.

Public shame, that was bad enough: private doubts, for, though he was a sturdy, he wasn't a complacent man: but also there might be practical consequences. It would have been hard for Stephen, even in cool days, to guess how much they weighed. Stephen had heard plenty of ladder-climbing talk at his father's table: Thomas Freer, himself a non-competitor, had a remarkably beady eye for the ambitions of clergymen: it was assumed that the Bishop wouldn't stay for long in this diocese, and that he had a pleasurable expectation of a call to higher things: a call about which, Thomas Freer remarked, he would scrupulously examine his conscience, while his wife was packing the bags upstairs. Now, it might have seemed to the Bishop, that call was not likely to come.

Stephen got no hint at all that those could be among the Bishop's thoughts. It was true that he mentioned the practical consequences for Stephen: but he had a shrewd assessment that there at least Stephen was already protected, partly by his trust fund, partly by the nature of his profession, and didn't inquire much further. Instead, he told them that there might be occasions when his own presence would be useful. Whether he meant at the inquest, or with the press, or at any possible trial, he didn't say. As he made the offer, though, he and Stephen appeared, almost for the first time that morning, embarrassed with each other.

It wasn't long before he was muttering 'Well! Well!' like one seeing them off at a railway station. When they got up, he did so too, and accompanied them through his secretary's room out into the open air. He wasn't wearing his overcoat, his face went purpler in the January air, he walked between them, only an inch taller than his daughter, not up to Stephen's shoulder. They passed round the west end – nineteenth-century gothic, nothing there of the original church. The archdeacon hustled by, the Bishop shouted a hearty good morning. In front of the cathedral porch, in sight of a trickle of people, all elderly, coming out of matins, the Bishop kissed his daughter and shook Stephen's hand.

19

As Tess and Stephen were getting near the outer gate, he said that he would have to call at his house, in case there were any messages.

'Shall I go on ahead?' said Tess, with candour, who had still not been told about the night before but who was not in ignorance.

He hesitated. 'No,' he said peremptorily, 'come with me.'

When they went into the high, warm, pot-pourri-smelling hall (the house had always smelt fragrant, it was part of Stephen's memory), no one seemed at home. According to habit, Stephen's first glance was to the telephone pad. Yes, a number, would you ring? The number was Neil's. As soon as Stephen got through, he heard the unpropitiating scouse.

'It's me. I'd better see you.'

'Can you say?'

'No.'

Stephen said that he and Tess were going to lunch in the town.

'No good for me.'

Well then, they were moving out to Mark's house: they could collect him.

'I'll make my own way. See you there.'

The telephone clicked down. Turning away, Stephen met Tess's glance, anxious, inquiring. 'Something's happened,' he said.

'What is it?' she asked.

He shook his head. After he had made one more call,

telling Mark where to pick them up, they went, preoccupied, back in the kaleidoscope of care, into the lane.

The sun had come out, low winter sun, dazzling on windscreens. The shopping crowds went by, anonymous, busy, unheeding. The town was bright and burnished, prosperous, the pattern of a consumer's town. Tess cried:

'It's a pretty dark tunnel to be in. I can't help it –'

'Yes.'

'Shall we get out of it?'

She knew that the best way to give him reassurance was to ask for some: and also, though in some ways braver than he was, she was frightened.

'Perhaps,' he said.

Unlike Mark, Stephen and Tess didn't use the one or two old restaurants, or the smart ones, in the town: partly because Tess wasn't brought up to them, partly because Stephen had once felt easier 'living like everyone else'. So they made their way to a wimpy bar in Granby Street – where they did not recognize a single face and had (this might have given Stephen, before trouble fell, a sarcastic amusement, as a jab against himself) very little idea of the lives behind those faces. Men and women mostly of their own age: clerks, secretaries, shop assistants: what did they want? What, to ask the Bishop's question, did they live by? Most of them seemed cheerful enough, there was plenty of casual mateyness. People talked of the loneliness of towns: claptrap, Stephen used to think, before he found Tess, on solitary excursions: there was a metaphysical ultimate loneliness all right, but the people he watched, in places like this, were no more lonely than human beings had to be.

They sat at the further corner of the bar, backs to the light, drinking cups of coffee, ate hamburgers, had more coffee. Sometimes they watched the stools fill up: occasionally, the repetitive unanswerable worries broke out. Were they right about Bernard's death? Could he have killed himself, after all? Could he have been drugged, would it have worked that way? What had happened to Neil? What was he going to tell them? When – and this came back often, unsuppressible now – would they hear something about themselves?

In a patch of silence, Stephen said:

'Your father was rather good this morning.'

He said it without any preliminaries, harshly, almost grudgingly. But neither he nor Tess was pretending to the other, they weren't acting as though stronger than they were, or less afraid.

'I think he is, when he's up against it. I wish I was.'

'You're not bad.'

Stephen could be eloquent, making love. That wasn't eloquent, but it was naked, and gave her warmth.

'I suppose parsons get plenty of experience with people's crises, don't they?' she said.

'No. Most of them would be no more use than –' He didn't finish and then went on: 'No, he's just got more spirit than I have. Or you either.'

He gave her a slight smile, hard-edged. He could sometimes put on humility, but she hadn't heard him speak so humbly – nor in that sense so intimately – before.

They had returned to the treadmill-recurring questions, faces close, when Mark stood behind them. He said: 'Ready to move?' He was looking fresher than they were, the whites of his eyes were as milky blue as a child's: but, without showing the tightness of strain, he was quiet. He had eaten at home, he said, he didn't want anything more. Leading them to his car, putting Stephen in the back seat and Tess beside him, he began to drive fast up the London

Road towards the country. They weren't past the railway station before Tess reverted – she couldn't keep it quiet, she couldn't make any other conversation – to the question of drugs.

'Have you ever heard of anything like that?' she asked Mark.

'Oh yes,' he said. Yes, didn't some people get deranged on L.S.D.?

Driving by the side of the park, he said:

'Of course. They're said to find themselves in odd places. Without remembering how they got there. Like being drunk.'

There were reports of hallucinations, said Stephen. Someone might walk out of a window, it was conceivable.

'It doesn't seem very likely. But we can't think of anything else that makes any sense at all. Can you?' He was speaking to Mark's back.

'The trouble is,' said Mark, 'none of us knows much about drugs, do we? You don't. I don't.'

They were at the beginning of the suburbs.

'We're not switched on,' said Mark.

'I wasn't so sure this morning,' said Tess. 'But now I am. He was doped all right. Someone doped him.'

In a moment, Mark commented:

'He could have done it himself, couldn't he?'

'Not him. No, not him.'

Jerky, spasmodic, sometimes desultory, the interchange went on until they were entering the drive of Mark's house. It was half-a-dozen miles out of town, in the placid, neat-hedged, domesticated midland countryside (romantics thought that countryside was sempiternal, but it would have been unrecognizably more unkempt only two hundred years before). The house itself was shining red brick, whitesilled, white-gabled, all shining spick-and-span red and white, a pretty 1920-ish version of Queen Anne, bright and sparkling like a children's picture book. It was a good deal larger, as well as more comfortable, than the neighbouring manor houses which manufacturers like Mark's father had a habit of renovating for themselves. Mark's father, though (whom Stephen had met only once, since he returned to England so rarely), was an independent man, as independent as his burgher predecessors. He was self-made, and he made his own comfort and prescribed his own house. Mark was not just an only child, but a child of old age: his father was over sixty when he was born, and the fortune had been well started during the first world war. This house had been by way of one of its first celebrations: and there Mark's father had lived, quite alone, improbably serene in the big establishment until he married in his fifties.

In the middle drawing room, windows giving on to rolling pasture, a copse in sight (a view as tranquil as, and less anaemic than, the watercolours round the walls) – in that drawing room which Mark had reserved years before for his own use, Stephen had sometimes wondered (not that afternoon, there was no free thought to spare) how much richer was Mark's father than his own. Several times over, he thought. But he hadn't much notion how rich his father was. It was third-generation wealth, not first: it had probably been shrewdly handled: it could have accumulated. Also Stephen's mother had some money in her own right. Maybe there was less difference than one imagined as one walked through the three drawing rooms at Thurlby, the dining room, the breakfast room, the billiard room, which was never used, the music room, which in Mark's father's bachelorhood often was. Mark's father took a simple pleasure out of looking opulent: Stephen's father's pleasures weren't so simple. Maybe there was less difference, if one had access to their holdings. But Stephen was not likely to know until his father died. Thomas Freer's gift for labyrinths of secrecy was in most matters very great, but in matters of money it became not only a gift but a dedication.

They hadn't long arrived before Neil was shown in.

'How did you get out?' said Mark, composed and host-like.

'Emma's car.'

'Is she here?'

Impatiently Neil shook his head. 'She's out on her feet. Blasted fool. She's had a bad trip.'

Neil wasn't noticing the house, which he hadn't been inside before, not even to record anger that the bourgeois could still live like this. More than ever indifferent to environment, he sat there as unaffected as in his own room. Yet he was seething with anger of a different kind, anger churning from inside.

'They came with a warrant this morning,' he announced, not wasting time. 'They went through everything I've got. Damn them to hell.'

'What were they looking for?' asked Stephen. Since the telephone conversation, he and Tess had wondered, but had not expected this.

'What do you think? Acid, grass, the lot.'

'There was nothing there, though, was there?' Mark said. Neil had always been as little indulgent as they were themselves.

'Nothing that they didn't put there.'

'They haven't, have they?' said Tess.

'We'll see. Do you think that we're going to benefit from the splendid impartiality of English law?'

He asked:

'Have they come round to any of you?'

The others said no.

'I thought as much.'

He was seething with bitter fury, more abstract than anything the others felt, more morally outraged. He was one of those combatants, such as Lance had jeered about on the Sunday night, to whom the right is on his own side – the right, the moral justice. One had to be his kind of combatant to be rigid with that moral certainty. It was his strength. One had to be capable of that unambiguous anger. It wasn't the fair-minded, much less the reflective or ironic, who were made to survive in conflict, and in the end to have a chance of winning. Anger, total anger, was the prime necessity.

Stephen said – his father's advice sifting unwillingly back – that Neil must have a lawyer. Neil, capable of sustaining his emotion and being simultaneously practical, agreed. Who should he go to? Stephen replied that they might as well all use Hotchkinson: he was said to be competent. Neil nodded: he knew when to take advantage of middle-class know-how.

Then Stephen said:

'About Bernard.'

'What about him?' Neil's voice was level.

'We've been thinking.' Once again, Stephen brought out their explanation. Neil sat without moving a feature, and remarked:

'You've got it.'

He was quicker to accept than any of them had been, and more positive. He was more positive also that someone, not Bernard himself, must have done the drugging.

'Yes, it was that shit Lance. His idea of a nice party.'

'That's what we think,' said Tess.

Stephen added:

'I don't see who else it was likely to be.'

'We may as well find out.' Neil broke out. 'Christ Jesus! If it hadn't been for that bastard, we should have got away with it all.'

'I doubt it,' said Mark. 'I really doubt it.'

'You've doubted everything, haven't you?' Neil turned on him. There was hostility in the room: Neil had no affection for Stephen, but he was less hostile to him than to Mark. Business-like again, Neil said that they needed to cut out the talk and ask Lance the straight question, yes or no.

'I did that yesterday. About the other thing,' said Stephen.

'You didn't get anywhere.' It wasn't a question, though Neil hadn't heard in precise terms that the others had information – over and above Stephen's impression – that Lance was not the betrayer.

Neil went on:

'Trying again this time?'

'If necessary.'

All of a sudden Neil stirred.

'No,' he said. 'I'd better do it myself. It's a chance to have it out with the bleeder.'

He stood up, exuding purpose, glad to be moving, light on the balls of his feet. He would ring them up if he had news, he said: he would find his way out, he said. He left without any kind of good-bye.

It was still early in the afternoon. The others returned to the condition they had known before, but instead of wearing it more lightly, they felt it worse: it was that special blend of boredom and dread which, they were later to realize, took up in terms of time so much of any crisis or any

156

period of action: it was the anxious ennui which was an occupational affliction of a soldier before battle, or a politician when his future was being decided by others, himself as powerless – and preferably as silent – as a giraffe in the zoo.

The longer it lasted, the less they got used to it. That afternoon there was even more waiting to do. They were waiting – for what? Well, for Neil's telephone call. That wasn't decisive, it couldn't matter much: and yet it was something to wait for. Once Stephen rang up his house, to ask if there were any messages: none at all. The three of them, so used to talking to each other, could find nothing to talk about. There were extensions of silence. Mark began playing records, and that came as some kind of relief.

At last the telephone. That must be Neil, some news. Mark went quickly to answer: the others saw a frown cover his face.

'Oh,' he said. And, a shade less easily than usual, 'Oh yes. That'll be all right. Yes, I'll expect you.'

He came back to his chair saying:

'That was Sylvia. She's coming out here. After the office.'

Neither Stephen nor Tess commented. More records. The maid brought in tea. It was half-past four before the telephone rang again. Again Mark answered:

'Hallo, it is you, is it?'

He nodded to the others: this was Neil. He didn't summon Stephen to conduct the talking. It had been part of their discipline that personal relations were submerged, that each of them was interchangeable with any other.

'I've had a session with him,' Neil was saying.

'Well?'

'He didn't admit a thing. He says, of course he gave her

157

(Emma) a dose, she asked for it. He says, he nearly tried the effect on Stephen, it might have been interesting, he says. But he wouldn't have done it to Bernie, it wouldn't have crossed his mind, Bernie wasn't anyone you wanted to try it on.'

'Well?'

'I don't know. I don't know why, but I feel inclined to believe him.'

Objectively, said Neil, it might be true. Oh, and Lance hadn't denied the possibility of Bernie acting under the influence of L.S.D. It happened often enough. He had actually known someone who, during a trip, had been certain that he could levitate.

To the others, Mark reported Neil's end of the conversation something like word-for-word. They were disappointed, disproportionately so; they had expected, they had been curiously certain, that one anxiety would have been clinched. Once more restless, Stephen telephoned his home: once more no message whatever.

'Do you want us to go?' he said to Mark, not referring directly to Sylvia's visit.

'No, don't go.'

Both Stephen and Tess assumed that Sylvia was making an excuse, this was another of her pretexts (she was so importunate, at the same time so haughty and so meek) to be with him. They also assumed, knowing that Mark was for once embarrassed, that he would be glad of their company when she came. They had nothing else to do, there was nothing to do but wait, and so they stayed.

20

THE last of the light faded over the fields, Mark drew the curtains. With a grin towards the other two (quieter than usual, he was still livelier than they were) he put on a record from *Fidelio*. The cries of liberty swelled and mounted, waves of hope fulfilled surged through the room. Stephen, more depressed as he listened, was blaming Mark, it was one of his lapses of feeling – his abandon, as though he didn't expect anyone to care – to make them hear the sound of such a joy.

'She'll be free soon,' said Mark, letting them see that Sylvia was on his mind. 'She's very dutiful about not leaving the office early.'

Music and time lingered on, they weren't sedated, they had the night to get through. Six o'clock struck from the clock over the fireplace. Minutes passed, and then Sylvia made an entrance. Yes, she made an entrance, for in her extreme self-consciousness (perhaps sharpened the instant she saw Mark was not alone), recalling to Stephen the time when she was much younger, she couldn't walk in naturally, she flounced from the door, head bent forward and then thrown back, like an old-fashioned music hall comedian projecting himself on to the stage. It wasn't comic, it would have been jarring on the most peaceful of afternoons, to see the absurd and put-on smile on the severely beautiful face. 'Here I am,' she cried.

She expected to be kissed, and yet wasn't certain how to make him. Though he had his own unease, Mark couldn't let her remain in hers. He put an arm round her, brushed her cheek (awkwardly for him, his physical grace failing him as though copying hers), and said 'Come and settle down.'

He led her to the sofa, asked her to have a drink. 'Good idea,' she said over-brightly, and then, as he brought a tray, poured herself a large-sized gin. The others took more modest ones, their first that night. It wasn't simply however that she was accepting comfort which they wouldn't: despite her nerves, she was a strong girl with hearty hunting tastes, and was used to drinking more than any of them.

'Hallo, Stephen,' she said, greeting him for the first time. 'Hallo, Tess.'

Tess, who had met her only occasionally, watched her as she became relaxed, though still she had one leg entwined in the other. She was wearing a plain black-and-white office dress, and looking singularly beautiful, with the kind of beauty which is much rarer than very high intelligence or olympic-class ability at the 400 metres. Tess felt a pang of jealousy. She needn't have. Stephen had noticed her looks since the two of them were grown up, and like everyone else admired them: he liked her much more than most people did: he thought she was clever and fundamentally kind. But, almost without consideration, he – like other young men with their share of sexual confidence or intuition – knew that she was not for him.

'Well!' she said, gulping at her glass. 'I have some news for you.'

'What?' asked Stephen, but she was talking, eyes staring, straight at Mark.

'On the whole, it's good news. Yes, I think it is. I hope you think so too.' Her tone was clear and competent, and also submissive: she was issuing bulletins, and also so anxious to please him.

'What ever do you mean?' Mark broke out. He was astonished, so were the others. It was absolute astonishment, so complete, so instantaneous, cutting across the grain of their mood, that, though they felt surprise like a physical shock, their original dread – the apprehension, the fear of that afternoon, even the ennui – continued to weigh upon them, even to go on developing new disquiet.

'It is more or less all right. For you anyway.' She had a thought for Stephen and Tess. 'And you two as well. It's more or less all right.'

'That can't be.' A mechanical response from Stephen.

'Listen. It's turned out better than anyone imagined. It may have turned out better for the wrong reasons, but you'll have to put up with that.'

In fact, though her belief hadn't sunk deep, nevertheless Stephen and Mark had believed her straight away. She was happy to bring Mark good news, radiantly happy: but they trusted her sense, she was as competent – and more legally minded – than they were. While to Stephen there was a half-conscious thought: investing so many hopes in her love for Mark, so brilliant, so fragile, she would never have dared raise false hopes in him, or even any hopes that stood a chance of proving false. More than that, underneath the shrinking nerve-ends, underneath the classical façade, Stephen accepted her as someone solid, and trusted her as he might have done the lawyer Hotchkinson. The day before, he had concealed nothing from her, accepting that she was discreet. Although he did not know it, she had been discreet that afternoon. Mark's explanation for her late arrival was ingenious, true to her character, but wrong: she wasn't so punctilious that she wouldn't have slipped out of the office to transmit news like this. The reason was much more business-like: until all was over, she didn't want to draw attention to herself.

'They're letting you off the hook. You three and Emma,' she said, voice high and crisp. 'It makes sense, so far as they're concerned,' she went on. 'They've got you exactly where they want you. After what happened last night, they can kill your plans stone-dead. They never did want to come out in the open, if they could avoid it. The less fuss the better, so long as they could shut you up so that no one would listen to you. Well. They'll take Forrester and St John for drugs, that's all they needed. If there's any evidence that Kelshall took drugs too, that's a bonus. What with an inquest and a couple of drug charges, they're untouchable. So they're playing it cool. They can't see any reason for bothering about you.'

Most of this explanation she delivered, not to Mark, but to Stephen, and her tone became changed into one friendly and astringent. She was being quite lucid: so much so that on the plane of intellect Stephen could already predict – and accurately – a good deal of the practical future. As he was listening, Tess was in his field of vision: she had blushed dark: was she, like him, suffused with cowardly relief? Relief which swept through him, taking control like an anaesthetic. Shame that it could be so cowardly: there were liabilities in parallel, that he couldn't miss. Yet the relief was overmastering. Cowardly relief and shame.

'Plan B2 can't work now,' said Sylvia. She wasn't asking them, she was informing them. Stephen acquiesced. If any-one tried it, their allies, such as they were, in politics and the press would be frightened off. Maybe their enemies had already done the frightening. Their intelligence (Sylvia had just used one of the secret operational terms) was exact. Whoever had been a traitor had been an efficient one. 'It's all right, I tell you.' Sylvia gazed round with great eyes, happy to be looking after them, happy to be in command. 'It's cut-and-dried. They won't worry you any more.' She fixed her gaze, suddenly diffident, on Mark and said, tentative and like an adolescent girl offering a gift:

'Is that something nice for you? I hope it is.'

Mark said gently: 'You've been very good.'

At another time Stephen would have wished her luck, troubled that she was so defenceless. But that night in the drawing room it was too incongruous to be borne, splintering the respite and the shadows beyond it, utterly incongruous with the authority she had brought them. She sat there, the bones of her face sculptured, body composed by now, the fine skin blooming. In a brusque impatient manner, Stephen told her:

'You said that they were going to take Neil St John for drugs.'

'I did.'

'That's nonsense.'

'Is it? You'll see.'

'He's as innocent as we are.'

'They don't agree. Of course I don't know him.'

'That doesn't completely eliminate him from the human race, you know.'

It wasn't an unfriendly gibe: it took her back to dances two or three years before, when she was too shy to meet young men outside her own acquaintances. She gave an indrawn, apologetic laugh.

'I've only met him once. With you,' she said to Mark. 'I must say, I thought he was pretty awful.'

'He's not.' Tess was angry, ready to dislike her, ready to

believe her snobbish. But she was sisterly to Tess, at ease with her as she wasn't with men.

'Well, you know him and I don't. I take your word for it. That doesn't affect the issue, though. They've got him.'

'This can't be right,' said Stephen.

'You'll see,' she repeated.

'Sylvia dear, you'll have to spell it out,' said Mark.

'It's very simple.' As before, she was incisive about facts. 'They collected enough stuff from Forrester's place last night to fix him. That's laid on. They're hoping that the post-mortem will show some signs in Kelshall, but they're not putting too much faith in that. As for St John, they made a search there today –'

'We've heard that.'

'I couldn't find out whether they'd picked up anything. But they have another string. That Jamaican of ·yours, what's his name, Finlayson is prepared to swear –'

'What do you mean?' Tess cried.

'Just that the pair of them, Forrester and St John, were flogging marijuana in that precious street.'

'Would anyone in his senses believe a word,' said Stephen, 'that that crook said?'

'I thought you were all willing to. Not so long ago.' She spoke without malice, but firmly, giving her first hint of scruple and distaste.

'I think that's fair comment,' said Mark very lightly.

'This is a filthy business,' said Tess.

'Yes. You walked into it pretty deep, though, didn't you?'

Stephen interrupted (echoing an old-fashioned term of his father's):

'You're telling us that Neil St John is going to be framed, that's what it amounts to, isn't it?'

She had by this time more control and poise than any of them.

'I'm not in a position to be certain of that. I can tell you, they have some security information about him. They can't use that –'

'That's his politics.'

'Maybe. It doesn't make them less anxious to get him. And they will.'

'He's absolutely innocent in this drug business. You must believe us.'

Stephen's voice was strained and harsh, hers cool in reply.

'If you say so, then I think I do.'

'We can't let him go into this alone. We shall have to say so.' In the middle of the first blaze of relief, this had been a shadow, sharp-edged now.

'That's your responsibility.' Then she said, with a curious awkward softness: 'But please, please, don't stretch it any further than you must. Please don't stretch yourself too far.' With the same awkwardness, injected now with humility, she spoke to Tess, as though the other two were not present: 'You can say things to him I can't, perhaps you can influence him. Please don't let him stretch himself too far. He can't be responsible for everything.'

Just for the moment, Sylvia seemed more concerned for Stephen than for Mark: perhaps understanding him better, because loving him less. In the medley of the wealthy, untasteful, indifferent room, in the confusion of moral impressions, Tess was half-recollecting that she had listened to two people that day begging Stephen to define the limits of responsibility – both of them speaking with the same insight, the same kindness, her own father, whom she loved, and this cold superior young woman, whom she envied and didn't wish to like.

'That sounds too easy,' said Stephen.

'I didn't mean it that way.'

'If you'd like us to let everything happen –'

'Yes. If you can't do any good.' She went on: 'I'm trying to think how you feel. I'm not much of a one for having comrades, you know. I couldn't have got into your kind of game. But still – if you can't do any good? That doesn't seem serious. It doesn't even seem high-minded. Not really.'

She gave a slight inward smile, not mocking. 'After all,' she said, 'you haven't done much good up to now.'

Stephen answered:

'Someone died last night.'

'I know.' It wasn't the fact she was acknowledging, but the expression on the faces round her: faces dark and closed. Then she said:

'Well. It was a quick death.'

It might have sounded affectless: but in her aseptic fashion she was trying to console them (the most habitual consolation, the nature of death, the only one which Stephen could offer Bernard's parents). She was exactly Stephen's age, but as they had talked she began to appear older – not maternal, for that wasn't in her nature, but more like a sharp-witted spinster, or even a male whose own life was behind him but who wished them well. Certainly, Tess was thinking, half-passionately resentful, half-longing that he was being moved, Stephen was taking more from the girl than he had ever done from her. He began to speak to her with an off-hand intimacy:

'You may as well know. We're not sure that it was altogether an accident.'

'I don't follow.'

'It's only a suspicion. But he may not have known what he was doing. He may have been drugged.'

She stared at him.

'He may have been drugged on purpose,' said Stephen. 'I mean, some madman may have thought it was a good idea. I suppose as a kind of practical joke or a nice parlour trick.' He said it without relenting.

'I wonder,' said Sylvia.

'We thought it was Lance Forrester who did it,' Stephen continued, 'but that may not be right.'

There was silence.

'It's a pity,' said Stephen, 'but it's possible we shall never know who it was.'

'I can't help you there,' Sylvia said. She was wearing her inward-looking smile or tic, neither mocking nor amused. 'I fancy though if you had to lose anyone the way Kelshall went – he was the one you could best spare.'

'How can you say that?' burst out Tess.

'Oh, I meant to tell you, but it wasn't as important as the rest. He was the one who gave you away.'

'I can't believe it.' Tess gave that loud angry cry.

'You'll have to. It's true.' Sylvia then spoke softly to Mark: 'I'd have told you yesterday, but I wasn't positive. I wasn't keeping anything back.' She turned back to the others. 'I found out for certain this morning. He was working for them from the beginning.'

While Tess was still protesting, and also breaking out 'Oh, why?' Stephen said, in a stern oppressed tone, to Sylvia:

'This isn't just an opinion, is it? You actually know?'

'I shouldn't have said anything unless I did. You ought to realize that.'

She asked Mark: 'You do, don't you?'

'How long was he working for them?' To Stephen, the detail seemed imperative, just as to someone jealous in love.

'Almost from the time you started.'

'God,' said Stephen, and added flatly: 'I must say, I'm surprised.'

'I'm not in the least surprised,' said Mark, his eyes flashing.

Yet, apart from that flash of excitement from Mark, Sylvia was astonished – at a loss as she hadn't been before – to find that their mood had become almost instantaneously more sombre, perhaps more corroded, than since she entered the room. She had expected the news to be of interest, but not to stir them like the good news she had brought. But the emotional air had turned passionate, in the oldest sense. That she couldn't help but feel. She couldn't perceive why the fact – a fact she had thought assimilated – of being betrayed should hurt them so much: or why the fact of knowing who had betrayed them was worse, seared deeper, than when it was left unknown. For herself, she would have declared, she would choose certainty rather than mystery, in any circumstances, any trouble, at any time. Pehaps she had still to learn.

21

THE mood wasn't broken, but jagged into, by a patch of house logistics. Mark had offered to 'organize' supper. That seemed matter-of-fact and easy: it would have been so at Thomas Freer's. But this wasn't Thomas Freer's. In his father's absence, Mark was supposed to be looked after by a housekeeper and a maid. He was at his most spontaneous and most tender with them, he talked to them, listened to their worries, ferried them into the town. They were fond of him, called him by his Christian name, and did as little for him as they could. Each vacation, he lived as though he were camping out in this big house. That evening, both housekeeper and maid came into the drawing room and argued as a matter of right that there was no food at all. Mark was patient and apologetic. There must be some food, it didn't matter what it was. At last, with the same air of righteousness, a tin of corned beef was produced, a loaf, a hunk of cheese, and a little butter. Mark gave grateful thanks. He went away himself, and managed to discover a couple of bottles of claret. That they drank along with their corned beef, apart from Sylvia, who pointed to the gin bottle and said she would stick to this. None of them realized that the wine was splendid. None of them – interruption aside – had found anything specially absurd in the domestic scene. Even Sylvia, not so egalitarian by principle as they were, used to a well-run house, though not one as wealthy as this, was a child of her time as much as they were, and wasn't comfortable about having servants, much less about disbelieving them.

In the midst of the housekeeper being explanatory and patronizing, the maid confiding to Mark that she had too much to do, the picnic being finally served on Wedgwood plates which Mark carried in, a new suspicion had been half-formed, without shape, one of the phantoms that was going through their minds. Bernard had been the traitor. That was stark, they took it now as though they had known it for a long time. Did that mean that someone else had known or guessed? And had doctored his drink as some sort of indication, warning or sign? Had it been more than a piece of party foolishness, drunk or drugged? Was there a meaning to it?

Not much of that was said, but the thoughts passed round, and were sometimes thrust back as useless, foreheads furrowed under the bright neo-Victorian chandeliers. Once, after a question left unanswered, Sylvia observed: 'Well, if I'd been one of you, I shouldn't have been too pleased with him myself.'

As they sat round the table, it was another question which they couldn't leave alone, which preyed on them. Bernard had done it. *Why?* It was the cry which Tess had uttered as soon as Sylvia's announcement had sunk in. Now it recurred to her, to Stephen, to Mark. Even Sylvia was at times engaged, for the winding in and out of strain, anxiety, bafflement, sheer misery – like a smell at the same time piercing and heavy, such as hyacinths in a sick room – also infected her.

Why had he done it?

In the lorry drivers' caff, talking to Stephen alone, Mark had been brisk and dismissive about motives for treachery. He wasn't now. There he had mentioned money, people betrayed their side for money – he mentioned that again, about Bernard, only to reject it with something like contempt. That wasn't through delicacy over the dead; he was speaking with respect, but without sentimentality. He might be more tender than the others, but also he was the least sentimental of them. He wasn't sparing Bernard or anyone else, this was his own insight. Money wasn't the reason: the others agreed.

There was some speculation, the talk was whirling round at random, purposes and relevance hadn't yet re-formed, about how much he had been paid. They knew nothing of how agents were employed or chosen.

'Perhaps,' said Stephen, 'in the next ten years everyone will have to learn.' They couldn't understand why Bernard had been picked: and yet it had been a good choice. (Tess was thinking, ashamed that her intuition had misled her, how Neil had, in the students' common room, brought out Bernard's name: in his abstract fashion, without any intuition or feeling he had got it right. He wasn't interested in human beings: it was humbling, it was maddening, that abstract thought had got it right, and feeling hadn't. Yes, Neil had come closest.)

Tess mentioned what he had said the morning before. That started other thoughts, but for the moment it was a distraction. Bernard had been picked out somehow, said Stephen, but it would have taken superhuman intelligence to arrive at him out of the blue. The first initiative must have come from him. At some time he must have offered himself. Again, why? Motives, even double motives? Why? About the whole mechanism, they were allowing nothing like enough to chance. None of them had so far experienced much betrayal in their inner lives. They hadn't met much motiveless malice. They knew about selfishness and cowardice, and, Stephen certainly, about cruelty. But all of them, except perhaps Mark, would have been at a loss with the quicksands of labile characters, the confidence men of this life. Yet that wasn't the cause of their being deceived: for they thought, and in this they were right, that with Bernard, however little they understood him, they were dealing with a personality no more motiveless, as strongly structured, as their own.

'Samson or Judas?' asked Mark.

'What does that mean?' Stephen couldn't match that flash of elation.

'Pulling down pillars. You know, I said something about nihilism the other night, didn't I? Tearing down the whole place just to see what happens. There are plenty of people we know who feel like that.'

'They're no good,' said Stephen.

'You couldn't feel like that if you tried,' said Mark, gazing at his friend.

'Nor could I,' said Sylvia.

'I might, you know.' Mark's face was candid, pure.

'Not for long.' That was Sylvia.

'Perhaps not for long.'

'You talked about building something.' Stephen said, also intimately. 'You can't build anything with people like that. I think – no, that's understating it, I know – I'd rather have most sort of conservatives than have anything to do with them.'

'I think you would,' said Mark. There was a pause.

'Anyway, that wasn't Bernard. It might be Lance, but it wasn't Bernard. He believed in order, in the long run, as much as anyone alive.' Mark smiled.

'Samson won't do. What about Judas? I mean, just playing both sides for the hell of it. Not really knowing which side he's on. Taking himself in more than anyone else. I bet you, a lot of double agents are just like that.'

'Do you believe that's like Bernard?' said Tess.

'Doing himself in, in the end. There must be a death-wish in most of them, mustn't there?' Mark glanced round for their response. Once or twice, since Bernard had been identified as the betrayer, the thought of suicide had recurred.

'Do I believe that was true of Bernard?' he answered Tess. He hesitated, and then went on: 'No, I rather wish I did. But no. Not for an instant.'

'No. He was clever, he was hard,' Mark was speaking with neutrality, keeping down his imagination. 'I believe that when anyone like that gives away his own side, it's because he's decided the other is going to win. I believe he was one of those who has to be on the winning side.'

Just then – they hadn't moved from the small table, though none of them, not even Sylvia, was drinking – Stephen, whose concentration was shot through and ragged that night, asked how they might have suspected him, what indications they ought to have picked up. He was a pretty good actor, said Tess. That's putting it mildly, said Mark. But really, she went on, he'd always been a bit apart from the rest of them, hadn't he? Always over-quiet? If one couldn't trust one's feelings, maybe one ought to watch for those who didn't behave like everyone else.

It didn't occur to any of them that others, watching their whole group, might have noticed that they didn't behave like everyone else. Their abstention from demos and protest, their discipline, their outward decorum (apart from Lance's breakaways) owed something to Stephen's own impact: that was his style, and Mark's too: they hadn't been much like their activist contemporaries. A very shrewd political observer, used to points of danger, might have

173

noticed that, and considered them worth watching. In historical fact, that had actually happened.

Stephen, forcing his attention back, was thinking about what Mark had said, not many minutes ago – about Bernard and 'the winning side'. As recently as Monday night, Stephen remembered, Bernard had said that the poor were always right in the long run. That was why he had to be an anti-Zionist. Stephen mentioned this, and said to Mark:

'He sounded as committed as anyone we know.'

'It must have been a cover,' said Tess.

Yes, his control (without that, those two years of sitting among them made no sense at all) had been absolute.

'But still,' said Stephen, 'I think he had a pretty clear vision of the future.'

'Perhaps too clear,' said Mark. 'I should say, he saw very clearly what we were up against. And liked it a good deal too much.' Mark added:

'You ought to have heard him talk to me in the botany garden. Yesterday morning. It sounded like an analysis. But it wasn't. He was admiring the power too much. He understood where the power existed, all right. He didn't believe it was going to topple for a long time to come. He wanted to get amongst it.'

'Did you feel that, at the time?' said Sylvia.

'I'm not sure. Sort of, perhaps.' Mark went on:

'He was brighter than most of us. He came from outside, more than we did. Perhaps he liked power more. Or the thought of it. It's a dangerous thing to like.'

To the others, it seemed that he might be getting near one motive, but they were left dissatisfied. Mark was more free from self than they were, often he saw deeper: yet here they felt he was over-simplifying, maybe he was too good or pure a soul to see all the turbulence and murk. Curiously enough, not one of them gave an instant's consideration to the most prosaic of thoughts. It wouldn't have occurred to them, not even as a possibility, that Bernard might have wanted to climb – not as his sole desire, but as part of it. He might have been tempted by the comfortable life into which they had been born. They could imagine him – this was Mark's version – aiming to be a backstairs eminence, among the secrets and the decisions. But they couldn't imagine that he might relish the kind of bourgeois life which that would bring.

They couldn't imagine it, because they liked that life so little, and valued it less. They knew it, moment by moment, since they were born: it had no hold on them. Even for Sylvia, who was drifting, apart from her love for Mark, it had no charm. Above all, it didn't bring them any moral calm. Stephen had enjoyed his father's house, the pictures were good to look at, he mightn't meet such comfort again: and yet he would have said, with simplicity, that he didn't care if he never set foot in such a house as long as he lived. He would have said that, not putting on any act, as a matter of plain truth. Of course, neither he nor the others could project themselves into their middle age. They couldn't predict the nostalgias, the regressions, even the pathos, that might be waiting for them. Nevertheless, the likelihood was that a change had occurred in people like themselves, that they were a sign of it, and that their statements expressed not only what they expected and wished to happen, but what actually would: or, as Thomas Freer used to ruminate, not only the future of desire, but the future of fate.

So it was natural that they couldn't conceive how Bernard would see in their lives, or their parents' lives, any kind of temptation. In that they were wrong: but still, in not crediting that that could drive him, they may have been right for the wrong reasons. For anyone as clever as he was, the way was open enough, he could have obtained a modest share of privilege, without doing anything more adventurous than taking his examinations and doing his research. If any of them had made that suggestion, though, it would have seemed over-simple too.

There was another temptation, different in kind, which they might have wondered about, Stephen most of all, for it was one he should have recognized. That was the temptation of superiority. It wasn't common, but it had happened before, for a man of gifts to feel himself elevated above those round him: and sometimes that sense gave a supreme freedom. I can act as I like because I am myself: it proves that I am myself. Some strange abnormal secret actions had been performed with that force behind them, perhaps mixed up with other forces which were shared with less arrogant men. No, arrogance wasn't the tone of those with this exalted certainty of their own powers, any more than humility was the tone of those who felt inferior. Not arrogance, but more like the condescension of a first-class player knocking about with club members on a local court.

If their temperaments had contained a trace of this themselves (but all except Stephen were devoid of it) they might have thought again about Bernard. Did he hug the secret joy of being more brilliant, freer, than anyone round him? Of getting away with moves that no one else could? Mark, in his compassion, would have said that that wasn't the whole of Bernard or anyone else. Perhaps it could be part. Certainly, until Bernard had come across Stephen, he hadn't met anyone remotely as intelligent as himself. It might have been easier for him to exist in a complex of superiority. Stephen himself had not been quite immune from it: but he had had to match himself, since he was twelve, against the competition of the English professional young, trained like racehorses. Some things, he had learned, he could do as well or better than anyone near him: at others he was only adequate. Even in his own field, people his own age had gifts denied to him. Others had kinds of insight different from, and maybe more valuable than, his own. Mark had. So Stephen as a very young man, despite a residue of pride that would live with him, had already learned some of his limits. It wasn't available for him, as it could have been for Bernard, to go on dreaming the megalomaniac dreams.

Only Mark had the psychological passion to persevere about Bernard's motives: the others were distracted by thoughts which, all through the evening, had been fragmenting everything they said. Practical thoughts. Selfish thoughts. Questions unanswered and perhaps unanswerable. At one point, the time was passing, after nine o'clock, Tess asked:

'Could he have committed suicide, after all?'

'It would be the nicest solution,' said Stephen.

'Except for his parents, I suppose,' she said.

'I don't see that it can ever be proved. Either way.'

'It would make sense,' said Sylvia. 'You know, it seems the obvious answer.' She was speaking, eyes lit up, with eagerness. Then she went on: 'But none of you believe it, do you?'

'I wish I did,' said Tess.

Stephen added:

'Yes. I keep thinking it might be true. Of course it might. But I'm afraid I don't believe it.'

'Nor did Neil,' Tess broke out: 'Do you remember, he didn't even stop to think. The moment we mentioned it, he just took it that the drug idea was right.'

They were remembering something else: Neil, at the first revelation that there was a traitor, crying out that he ought to be got rid of.

'Could he have meant that?' Tess asked.

'I think he did,' said Mark.

'I think he did,' Stephen repeated. Not even Lance had shrugged off what Neil had said. 'But – this would have been an imbecile way to try. It was much more likely just to keep him quiet, if he was freaked-out at all.'

They weren't irrational, even now. Yet the thought of Neil in action didn't leave them: Stephen didn't wish it to leave them, or himself. Tess, noticing his gaze down at the table, felt that under the stern expression there was relief. She wasn't sure what it meant, or aware that a new decision, or the chance of one, was playing with him.

22

It was about that time when Mark, bright-faced – the skin beneath his eyes showed none of the fatigue which was now visible in the others' – proposed that they should go and dance somewhere.

'Oh yes!' cried Sylvia.

Tess looked at Stephen, who nodded. He wouldn't sleep if he went home. Before they left the house, though, he returned deliberately to questions about Neil.

'I suppose he might have been trying just to put him (Bernard) out. He might have had some idea that, if he doped him, he wouldn't be able to leak anything more for a good few hours.'

'There wouldn't have been much point in that,' said Sylvia.

'Enough point for Neil.' Stephen was arguing like one wanting to believe. 'It would have given time for the word to go round.'

Glances were meeting his. Even Tess looked unconvinced. He went on arguing:

'There's no doubt that he'd identified Bernard. None of you denies that, do you?'

'I've told you what he told me.' Tess wanted to help Stephen, there was a desire emerging which she could begin to guess: but she was too honest to give way. 'I can't swear that he was certain.'

If Stephen's case were true, they asked him, would Neil have been so ready not to think of suicide? Would he have told them over the telephone that afternoon that he more or less accepted that Lance had nothing to do with it?

'All that could be a double bluff,' said Stephen.

He went on:

'Say that he did it. To keep Bernard quiet. That was criminally irresponsible. Death's too high a price for anything he did.'

'That was just a chance,' Sylvia said, high and clear.

'Still. If I was absolutely certain about this,' Stephen was speaking to Sylvia. 'I should feel inclined to follow your advice.'

By this time, both Tess and Mark had seen that he was hoping to abdicate from responsibility. This was an excuse, more than an excuse, a justification, for leaving Neil to stand alone. Stephen had been invaded by another surge of cowardly relief, of which he was ashamed, and yet to which he could try to reconcile himself.

No one said much more, either at the house, or as they were driving into the town. Stephen and Tess were sitting in the back seat of Mark's car, and Sylvia, in her own, was following behind. Stephen was in a state when he believed he was forming a decision. Yet underneath his intellect, he had (like Tess, sitting beside him, holding his hand) an honest mind. He wanted to convince himself, and couldn't yet. He was angry with everyone else's doubts, most of all hers, jaded and angry about his own. Once or twice in that journey – lighted houses serene and taunting in the streets – he had intervals of beautiful, wish-fulfilling lucidity.

The discotheque in — Street, which they all knew, was dark and noisy and crowded, but they found a table in the corner where, in the blare, they didn't need to whisper, though they kept their voices low. All round them were bodies, sitting and dancing, multinational, mostly their own age, class and occupation indeterminate; some foreign students, a group of Indians, probably employed in the town, young native business-men and girls, and a few Caribbeans.

As the four of them pushed towards their table, they met casual smiles, an acceptance of a different kind from that which Mark and Stephen had received from the Anglo-Saxon lorry drivers two nights before. They weren't looked at as though they belonged to an alien species. It was unexacting: and though in retrospect they found it strange to recall, and stranger that they had agreed to visit that place on that special night, they were at home.

Although in the spattered dark, getting up for their first dance, Tess and Stephen could scarcely see the other two, they took it for granted that they were enjoying it. For Tess and Stephen had seen before this how all Sylvia's self-consciousness evanesced as soon as she danced: she became as easy as Mark, and was taken over by grace and joy. As for themselves, facing each other, Tess once came near and spoke up to his ear:

'Don't decide anything tonight.'

'I wish I could.'

'No, don't decide anything tonight. Promise me.'

For a while he didn't reply, but she wouldn't let him stay silent. At last he said:

'All right. I promise.

She wasn't alone in trying to break into Stephen's mood. Soon after they had returned to their table, Mark leaned across and said:

'Someone's got to help Neil out. I mean, in public. Is that right?'

'I thought so when you (Stephen looked at Sylvia) told us

what was happening. But now I don't know –' the words dwindled away, he spoke without determination, half-angry, half-injured because others were not following him.

'I'll do it for you,' said Mark.

'I feel rather inclined to let you.'

'I'm more expendable than you are,' Mark went on. 'I shan't involve so many people.' Then he gave a smile, clear, candid, percipient. 'Also I shan't care anything like as much.'

Sylvia, listening with anxiety – caused not so much by danger to Mark as by the precipice-edge feeling she some-times had when he spoke naturally of himself – thought for long moments that Stephen was going to accept the offer. But, after a pause, in which his expression was sombre, he shook his head. 'No. If anyone is going to do it, it has to be me.'

Another pause. 'I confess I don't see why,' said Mark, but he didn't doubt that Stephen meant it.

'We don't want to waste effort.' Almost for the first time that night, Stephen's tone was business-like, authoritative. 'I'm a shade better known. They would probably listen to me more.'

The others had to agree. But Mark said:

'Is that really why you'll do it? Is that all?'

'It's enough.'

Tess broke out:

'I want to come in with you.'

'Of course you do.' To Sylvia, who had a curiosity about their relation, over-youthful for her age, his smile – since she arrived, he had scarcely smiled at all – came as a sur-prise. It was sharp with complicity and trust.

'Of course you do.' It was the kind of taunt, utterly loyal, that a married couple could have bandied about. 'I couldn't let you. It's unnecessary. It's romantic. One person can do anything that can be done. Which may be nothing at all. Two persons would add absolutely, not a thing – and increase the liabilities. It would bring in your father, it would be bound to. Quite foolishly. I couldn't have that.'

As he spoke, his tone had remained business-like and firm, as they had often heard it. He had used 'romantic' as a term of dismissal, and that was in his familiar style (perhaps the scorn a shade overdone because he had to keep down the same extravagance in himself). But, as they danced again, Tess saw his expression revert to what it had been earlier that evening, preoccupied, oddly soft or undefined, like a man procrastinating. She thought she could read all his expressions, but this was rare.

Sitting at their table, all four heads close together, he said:

'I don't know.'

They waited.

'I don't know how much I have to do.'

He was meaning, and the others understood, how far his obligation went. If Neil had been blameless, if this new suspicion had nothing in it (like others of the past three days), then he had been loyal throughout: if so, there wasn't any equivocation – or way out. He had to receive support. Yet the suspicion could be true, he might have brought all this upon them: he might have been irresponsible beyond the limits of irresponsibility. Then surely, despite the past, despite the time they had worked together, Stephen was released from obligation: there wasn't one left to discharge.

In snatches, inconsecutive, words hanging in the air – less articulate than usual, since they were talking of conscience – they showed that they understood. It was after another spell on the floor that Mark suddenly said:

'You oughtn't to try to think of everything.'

'What do you mean?' Stephen's reply was guarded.

'It's a mistake to try to work out all the combinations. It never helps. Whatever you do, you must do it in your freedom.'

That was a phrase which Sylvia hadn't heard but which was a reference back to Cambridge arguments. Stephen said:

'This doesn't seem much guide.'

'I'm telling you, it's simplier than you're making out. This man is innocent of what they're nailing him for. He's gone along with us. Whether that means he has a claim on you – that's for you to choose. It's a free choice. You can forget the rest.'

He said it with urgency, though whether he was being unambiguous, whether he was really pointing out the choice, no one could be certain. But Sylvia was quite unambiguous when she danced with Stephen, the only dance they had together that night. He was too self-intent to have perceived that she was in a state of intense excitement: in rapture because she had been so close to Mark, the kind of rapture which – since she was young in matters of love – seemed to her to belong not to the senses but to the soul. As well as rapture, she was showing other signs of excitement, a kind of active protective restlessness, an edge of strain and anxiety. Her lit-up eyes staring at Stephen, she said, as urgently as Mark: 'For God's sake get out of this.'

'I'm not sure that I can.'

'Of course you can. You've done enough.'

'I've done nothing.'

'You've done enough for honour, really you have. Now you'd better save what you can.'

Among the pressures and the contradictions – that is, if

Mark had been impelling him to act and Sylvia, believing that, had made the opposite plea – Stephen sat back in their tenebrous corner. At last he said:

'I think I'd better see the lawyer, Hotchkinson, tomorrow morning.'

He went on, as though talking to himself:

'I needn't commit myself, naturally. I needn't make up my mind. There's plenty of time to play with, there's at least twenty-four hours.' He added:

'No, there's no need to settle it yet awhile.'

It seemed to the others, and even more heavily to himself, that he was still procrastinating, snatching at each excuse, and was discontented and guilty as a result. More than at any time since the previous Saturday, he wasn't at one with himself, he didn't speak or look as though he were at one. Yet, although he didn't accept it, the decision was already made: like all decisions, it had been made faster than one likes to believe: like many decisions, it ran counter to much of his nature, and made him unhappy. He had none of the liberation of a decision made. There it was, resolved on but not ending the conflict, leaving him with a sense of emptiness, self-doubt and perhaps self-accusation.

23

THAT night Stephen's sleep was broken. Oblivion, and then full bleak lucid wakefulness. It was dead quiet in the precinct, not even the distant surge of traffic, the only sounds the chime of the clock, and once or twice the windows rattling in a stir of wind.

He lay on his back, staring into the black room. He couldn't deny his thoughts. He had to let them follow their course, as though he could still delay, as though he were unaware of his resolve, or could renege on one already made. At moments he had waves of relief, the same cowardly relief he had felt in Mark's drawing room. He had done nothing yet. Time, a few hours, perhaps a day or two, lay ahead. At moments there still seemed a choice. Hankerings, retreats, pretexts, feelings of free will, lasted long after decisions and alongside them. But he had none of the comforts of confusion. Whatever he did, would be wrong. The consequences were clear and lucid, stamped like lines of figures on the darkness. He went to sleep again, and then woke into the same unrelieved lucidity.

He had wakened for the last time, and was shaving when the telephone rang.

'It's me.' Tess's voice, quiet, concerned. 'How are you?'

'All right.' That was what they said when they weren't happy. He wasn't putting on a front, he was fending her off.

'Anything I can do?'

'If there is, I'll ask you. Of course.' He didn't hear, but she did, that his tone was warmer than for days past.

'What about you?'

'I'll see the lawyer this morning, if I can. I haven't settled anything.'

'No. You'll tell me?'

'As soon as I've made up my mind, I'll tell you. Of course.'

'Bless you.' A pause, then quickly: 'I know no one's any good to you just now. But –'

'That may not be quite true.'

He might not have been aware of it, but he had spoken without cover, and felt easier because of it. Just as he might not have been aware that shortly afterwards he spoke to his father not without cover, but with care and deliberate politeness. With the same politeness he was not avoiding his father that morning, but went down to breakfast at the sacramental time, a quarter to nine. Kidneys and bacon were sizzling on the hot plate. Thomas Freer entered on the stroke, and they said good morning as they helped themselves.

'I hope you slept well,' said Thomas Freer, but diffidently.

'Moderately, thank you,' said Stephen.

'Good. Very good,' said Thomas Freer, with exaggerated enthusiasm.

As they were eating, which concealed an interval of silence, Thomas Freer said 'I suppose it's too early for you to know what you'll be doing today, isn't it?'

The question could have been evaded, was so tentative that evasion was provided for. But Stephen answered:

'As a matter of fact, I'm thinking of calling on Hotchkinson.'

'That sounds very sensible, I must say.' A side-glance, up from the breakfast plate. 'I wonder, have you made an appointment?'

'No, not yet, I haven't.'

'I suppose,' said Thomas Freer, 'it wouldn't be any help if I arranged it for you? It wouldn't be the slightest trouble, you understand –'

Stephen was on the point of replying that he could do that easily enough for himself. But he realized that his father was pleading to do him a service. In the new control which was composing Stephen that morning, he felt it wrong to say no.

'That would be very nice of you,' said Stephen. 'Thank you very much.'

'I'll do it the moment I get to the office. And let you know at once. That shall be done.' Then, encouraged, Thomas Freer asked, as though vaguely: 'I take it, though, you haven't any very precise idea of your present plans? That is, I suppose you're waiting until you've seen Hotchkinson –'

'No, you're right, I've no idea.' Stephen said it politely, but so that one step shouldn't be followed by another. Thomas Freer did not attempt to do so. As he was spreading honey on his toast, he went off on a side line:

'I imagine you must have seen Matthew Hotchkinson once or twice, haven't you? I wonder, you might have met him in this house –' Actually, it was unlikely to have been anywhere else.

'Only once, I think.'

'Did you have any conversation with him?'

'It was years ago. No, not much.'

'Perhaps, I'm not sure, but perhaps I might tell you that he's never been specially disposed to go in for – what shall I call them? – social emollients, shall we say. I fancy it's probably fair to say that. Between ourselves, I used to think that was – Uppingham. The result of Uppingham. But I don't know. I *don't* know. Anyway, we shall see what your impression is, shan't we?'

A few minutes before eleven o'clock, Stephen was walking in front of the City Hall, twentieth-century civic Stalinesque, looming heavy in the misty morning. Hotchkinson's office was close by, in Bishop Street, a couple of blocks away from Thomas Freer's. Apart from geographical proximity, Stephen, who as a child had enjoyed visiting his father's office, thoughtfully unmodernized, leather-bound books on shelves, black boxes with clients' names in white letters, found that this one struck strange. Five floors up, new building, waiting-room smelling of flowers, not books. He wasn't kept waiting long, and Hotchkinson's own room was just as beflowered, also with windows instead of walls, airy, agoraphobic.

'You're on time,' said Hotchkinson, as though that were an obscure grievance or a failure in courtesy.

'Yes,' said Stephen. To add another incongruity in that tycoon-like room, Hotchkinson, was wearing a suit of heavy ginger tweeds. He was a very big man, heavy-shouldered, thick through the chest. In a doughy small-featured face the eyes were shallowly set with full flesh or underlids beneath them, which gave him an expression assertive and surreptitiously salacious. His voice was strangulated, husky, and high, such as one sometimes hears in star games players or other massively muscular men.

'We might as well sit down,' said Hotchkinson, leaving his desk and walking soft-footed to a sofa which faced the longest window. In front of them, as they sat, was a low

189

glass-topped table on which stood a cigarette box and an ash tray.

'Any good to you?'

Stephen thanked him and shook his head.

Hotchkinson said:

'I don't understand why you're here.'

'I thought my father had told you –'

'I know all about that. I don't understand why you're here.'

'Didn't he arrange for you to act for me, if necessary?'

'It isn't necessary.'

Stephen said: 'I'm afraid I'm not so certain. I want some advice.'

Hotchkinson answered:

'All the advice you want is four words. Keep your mouth shut. K.Y.M.S.'

'It isn't quite so simple –'

'You clear out and keep quiet. And thank your lucky stars.'

'No, I haven't made up my mind. I want your advice. On what's going to happen, so far as you know.'

'It's a waste of time.'

'Not for me, perhaps.'

Stephen hadn't been prepared for this kind of attack, but he had equipped himself by now. In another mood, before the crisis, he would have been amused by his father's euphemisms about Hotchkinson not being specially disposed to go in for social emollients, meaning that he was remarkably rude. Stephen would have been amused too by his father's explanation, referring to a respectable school as though it were some kind of Borstal: to an outsider, prosperous lawyers in a provincial town might have seemed much of a muchness, but Stephen had grown up knowledgeable about the Byzantine social hierarchy in which his father's imagination at happy moments moved. But Stephen couldn't afford such detachment now. Hotchkinson was as a matter of routine remarkably rude. He seemed to be so whoever he was with, and by itself that would not have mattered much. Stephen was indifferent to rudeness and not got down. But there was something more. Hotchkinson was not only rude, but also hostile. He was ready to act for Stephen and the others because Thomas Freer asked him to. For Stephen he might feel – and this wasn't a consoling thought that morning – something like a class solidarity. Nevertheless, he detested everything that Stephen believed, everything that they had done and stood for. He would gladly have seen them transported: and, looking at those fierce sly eyes, Stephen felt he might, if he had the power, show them less mercy than that.

Even that, though, wasn't the end of it. Stephen had listened to his trustees and his father's professional musings, but had never had a legal interview in his life. This was a bizarre one. The lawyer was hostile, he wasn't on their side: and yet he couldn't avoid, as they went on talking, no sympathy between them, behaving like a real professional. And, Stephen soon realized, having a respect for professionals and experience in judging them, like a very good one. He loved his job. He didn't look intelligent, but his mind was as hard and undecorated as Stephen's own. Further, he appeared to possess a singular amount of inside knowledge – far more than he should have done, to those who innocently believed in the sacrosanct propriety of legal processes. To Stephen, however, used to the toing and froing of his father's friends and their local connections, that didn't come as a surprise.

The first sitting of the inquest on Kelshall next morning

(Friday) would be formal, said Hotchkinson. Nothing but the immediate cause of death. The inquest would be adjourned. Next time, there would be the post-mortem findings. They were searching for a trace of drugs in the bile duct. Drugs would be mentioned. Coroner's verdict: anyone's guess, almost certainly inconclusive, quite certainly irrelevant. By that time St John and Forrester would have been arrested. Warrants would be issued within hours or days. Hotchkinson had already told St John so.

Charges?

Forrester: possession of cannabis, L.S.D., heroin: trafficking in cannabis and L.S.D.

St John: possession of cannabis: trafficking in cannabis. When Stephen heard that last rough, confident statement, he said:

'Nonsense. He's never possessed a gram.'

'That's your story.'

'I know it.'

'You can't know it.'

'I'm absolutely certain. What's the evidence?'

'Stuff found in his room. Not much. Enough.'

'Planted there,' said Stephen.

'That'll get you nowhere,' said Hotchkinson, with contempt.

'Just possibly left there by – someone else.' For once, Stephen's sense of fact, of possible accidents and chance, had weakened him.

'You can believe that if you like.'

Stephen did not attempt to persuade the other man. There was a wall of ice, or something rougher than ice, between them. Kelshall's death couldn't be mentioned at the trials, said Hotchkinson, but it would be remembered. Some people who knew the whole story would consider that in breaking secrecy he had performed a public service: Hotchkinson made it obvious that he thought so too. Stephen did not respond. Not even Mark, who had the freest psychological imagination of them all, had reflected that what was treachery to one side was loyalty to the other, or that Bernard, whatever his other motives were, might at the same time have felt dutiful, or a partisan in reverse. Stephen wasn't capable of disinterest then; he was trying to cut through his own hostility and this other man's, occupied with one thought alone, how this man could compartmentalize his mind, and apply himself to do his best about their tactics. To that extent, Stephen – though his temper was impelling him to telephone from that office for another lawyer – found himself trusting him.

The two would go for trial?

For certain.

Findings?

For possession, guilty for certain. For trafficking, guilty, but could be made to appear minor and amateur transactions. Youth would be invoked, also pattern of student behaviour. Finlayson's evidence would be knocked about. Enough left to convict, but they would not look like serious pushers.

Sentences?

Forrester. Heavy fine. Suspended sentence, probably nine months.

St John. Also fine, but less. Also suspended sentence, six months.

Both kicked out of the university.

(These forecasts proved to be very nearly accurate. From this stage onwards, the legal fates of Neil and Lance were predictable, and nothing unlooked-for happened. There was to be no reversal of fortune and no drama, except the normal ritual of the courts. Hotchkinson did not foresee that there would be student protests when they were expelled from the university. These happened, but weren't prolonged, probably, so it was thought, because Neil had, by a political calculation, cut himself off from other local activists. With that – apart from one exception – the external consequences of the core's actions dwindled away though to the members themselves there had, simultaneously, been others.)

'What difference should I make,' said Stephen, 'if I gave evidence for Neil St John?'

'What can you say?'

'I've known him well for two years. I've never seen him take a single reefer. He's always been dead against it.'

'They won't believe you.'

'That's their privilege. I can go on saying it.'

Hotchkinson gave him a sharp, ferial glance, and said:

'You wouldn't be a bad witness.'

'What difference should I make?'

'Not a sausage.' Hotchkinson wore an angry scowl. 'No, that's nearly right, but it might be going too far. These things aren't so cut-and-dried. They wouldn't believe you, they wouldn't let him off. But it might save him a few pounds off his fine.'

'That makes total nonsense of it.'

'Total. It's as likely as not.'

Stephen, expression hard and set, asked about the other charge.

'What can you say about that? Have you ever seen him with Finlayson?'

'No.'

'Then what in hell can you say?'

'Nothing. Except he's no more likely to peddle drugs than I am. Or than you are, as far as that goes.'

'Character reference. Useless. Coming from you.' Then Hotchkinson asked: 'What about the other man? Do you want to say that you've never seen him take a single reefer?'

'No,' said Stephen. 'I shan't say that.'

After a pause, he added:

'I could say that I don't think it's likely for an instant that he's ever sold any of the stuff. Why should he?'

'That's a very moderate statement,' Hotchkinson gave a hoarse laugh. 'What do you think a jury's going to make of that?'

'I've not decided whether I shall go in front of a jury. That's why I'm here.' Stephen went on: 'If I do I might only feel obliged to give evidence for St John. It's not all that simple –'

Hotchkinson waited for him to finish, discovered that Stephen had fallen into an abstracted silence. Hotchkinson said:

'I've told you already. Keep out of it.' Then, in a tone a shade less peremptory: 'I'm assuming you realize that it would do you some personal harm. You'd have a black mark against you. I don't know what your plans are about jobs, but I guess that Cambridge wouldn't want to give you one.'

'That's been thought of.'

'It's your affair. You're old enough to look after yourself. But you're also involving other people. You'd better be clear about that.'

'That's also been thought of.'

'Has it? It would involve your family. You can't do it. For no benefit to anyone at all.'

'You said there conceivably might be slight benefit.'

'A fleabite. Against involving your family.'

'I shall have,' said Stephen, 'to be the judge of this.'

They confronted each other. Perversely, the hostility was not so hard. Stephen had mastered his temper, he was talking as he might have done to his doctor.

'I have to tell you something else,' said Hotchkinson. 'If you take part, you may be asked how you got mixed up with these fellows. That could fling your whole political game wide open. Nothing grand, just a silly scandal. There wouldn't be any names mentioned except your own, but all you seem to have a fancy for would get into disrepute. I take it, you wouldn't find that specially agreeable?'

Which, as Hotchkinson made apparent, he as a private citizen most emphatically would. Yet he had brought the eventuality into the open. Perhaps – Stephen was neither then nor in retrospect able to be certain, for Hotchkinson under the surface was not an unsubtle man – he was using it as the argument most likely to deter Stephen. Perhaps it was merely produced by professional conscience.

'How likely is this?' Stephen asked.

'Can't be sure.'

'I should have thought it could be stopped.'

'Possibly. I can't guarantee it.'

Stephen had regressed into silence, into a state – though the lawyer could not have understood it – similar to that of the night before, bringing back moments of uncertainty, confusion, relief. At last he said:

'Is there anything else?'

'Not until you tell me what you want to do.'

After a pause, Stephen said:

'I've still not quite decided. I'll let you know when I have.'

At that Hotchkinson stood up. He didn't offer to shake hands, and gave only a nominal reply to Stephen's good morning. As Stephen left the room, however, he was followed by a shout: 'Give my regards to your father.'

24

FOR half-an-hour Stephen walked, without any purpose, round the middle of the town. Shops, bright and busy, chainstores now, not the old proprietorial shops, but busier than they ever were, he glanced at but didn't see. Or rather he saw them as though it were through dark glasses. It was the same when he had lunch at home with his mother. They had some civil conversation, utterly remote from what they were both thinking, remoter still to Stephen because her voice seemed to come from outside the envelope from which he hadn't yet escaped.

He would have said – and later he did say – that he spent all those hours, from the evening before to this Thursday afternoon, making up his mind. When he told Hotchkinson that he had not 'quite decided', he wasn't pretending; he believed that to be the truth. And yet the decision had been made hours before, probably in Mark's drawing room (there isn't a precise time for the first crystallization of a decision), certainly by the time he had spoken to Tess on the telephone.

Sometimes, but very rarely, in a state like Stephen's, a fluke happened from outside, and one could back out; then one felt judicious, for not having made the decision in a hurry: in everything but the act, one had. Usually – and this was just about to happen to Stephen – there was no chance of backing out and one moved, or was passively transported, to a second crystallization. At this point – it could be very sharp – the decision, already made but shied from and submerged, became conscious. Then one had it.

Analysts of the emotions had made that discovery about love a long time ago; but it was just as true, and sometimes more significant, about unerotic states. Until the decision was conscious, then one felt free and also conflict-ridden, as Stephen had done, with intermissions, up to this Thursday afternoon. Even when it was conscious, there remained consequences, new choices where (perhaps one deceived oneself) one still felt free. One decision was forming itself clear in the open, in front of Stephen. When he couldn't resist it, there were others which he hadn't let himself bring to mind: but they were waiting there.

In the middle of the afternoon, Stephen made his way, strolling, even dawdling, as though absent-mindedly, towards Neil's room. He had not rung up to say that he was coming: all through that week (and also in times without crisis) their appointments among themselves were punctilious: this was the first one to be left to chance. By this time, Stephen realized what he was doing. It was a piece of superstition or self-defence. He would be glad if Neil were out.

Actually, as Stephen could see from the windows, lighted in the cloudy afternoon, Neil was in. He was not alone. When Stephen tapped and entered, Emma was sitting on the divan, looking flushed and sullen. Lance Forrester sat, not lounging but half-forward, in the armchair. From Emma's side, Neil said:

'It's you, is it?'

Lance gave a sharp smile. 'Welcome,' he called out.

In the bare room, they had, as though by instinct, packed themselves close together. Their voices were unhabitually quiet. They gave the impression that they were having to think about ordinary physical reflexes, such as how to control their breathing: rather like exiles, who, in their new country, think twice about the most routine of activities, as it might be finding their way to a lavatory door. That was true of Lance as much as of Neil. If they had been prisoners of war, their C.O. would have trusted them to behave well – but out of training, not first nature. Lance, without a drink or smoke that day, hadn't lost his nonchalance but was having to force it. Just as he said now:

'The other night, I told you, we shouldn't come back to this pad. It brings bad dice. Here we are again!'

'Never mind that,' said Neil.

'Never mind what?' Lance wouldn't stop. 'You can see how right I was.'

Ignoring him (as a companion, it was better to have a coward than someone who insisted on forcing hangman's jokes), Neil spoke to Stephen, who had taken a canvas chair, some way apart.

'I suppose you know.'

'I think I know everything you do.'

Voice hard with suspicion, Neil said:

'Not to say a damn sight more.'

'You've seen Hotchkinson, have you?'

'Yes.'

'What did you think of him?'

'He's all right. He's a decent chap.'

Even at that moment, this seemed to Stephen a curious encomium. It passed by. There was a quick exchange, suspicious on Neil's side, but factual and competent. Hotchkinson had given Neil precisely the same opinion as he had to Stephen, though apparently without bullying. He had discussed the defence in more detail. Everything would be challenged, they had nothing to lose. But Hotchkinson hadn't pretended that there was a chance of getting them off. As to the outcome, his prognosis had been as unqualified as to Stephen. The sooner they got used to it, the better.

'So we're ready for them to pick us up,' said Lance. 'Well, you can't say it isn't interesting.'

'They've organized it bleeding thoroughly, you have to give them that.' Neil's anger broke out, but the force, the sense of outrage, were not as powerful as on the previous afternoon; they still assuaged him, but did not totally heal him. 'Blasted drugs in this place. Organized. Planted. I keep asking you' – this was to Lance, in a ringing whisper, and Stephen heard the echo of recriminations recurring, uselessly circling, for hours before he arrived – 'whether you ever left any of your fucking stuff here –'

'I keep telling you, not likely. Too precious.' Lance didn't resist adding, and this again he must have done before: 'That is, unless I was too high, one of those sessions.'

'By Christ!' Neil's suspicions flashed simultaneously at Lance and at the police. 'All organized. When you take on the whole machine, they make the rules and don't stop at smashing every single one of them.'

He stared at Stephen with an expression fixed, unyielding.

'Well. You're sitting nice and pretty, so it seems. You're safely out of it, aren't you?'

'They're not charging me.'

'It shows you what influence can do.'

The blood was rising in Stephen's face.

'That may be too simple,' he said in a level tone. 'I've no information.'

'We can guess,' said Neil. 'The bourgeoisie looks after its own.'

'This isn't very useful,' Stephen made an effort to keep his tone unchanged.

'It's just as well to understand how the machine works.'

'Have it your own way.'

Neil let out a soft, jeering laugh, edged with contempt, not so much for Stephen, though that existed, but much more impersonal contempt.

'So you can sit by and watch, can't you?'

Stephen was angrier than he had been at any time that week. He might have been presented with a last excuse. It was one he couldn't take.

'No,' he said, 'I shan't do that.'

'What the hell do you mean?'

Even now, decision not only made, but crystallized, committed, the false reliefs, the attempts at a moral solvent (convincing no one, not even himself) did not quite subside. He said:

'I suppose you weren't the fool who doped Bernard Kelshall, were you, by any chance?'

'In God's name, what's that got to do with it?'

'It might have had a lot.'

'If it gives you any satisfaction – no, I wasn't.'

Stephen asked: 'Have I got to believe you?'

'You can believe what you bleeding well like.'

There was a longish pause, in which Lance, half-aside, said that they weren't going to find the answer to that one. For his money, it could just as well have been suicide. Neither Stephen nor Neil paid any attention.

At last Stephen said:

'I shall give evidence for you. It won't be much help.'

'What evidence?'

'You've never had anything to do with drugs in your life. I can say that. It happens to be true.'

'Not a scrap of use.'

'Very little use. More or less negligible.'

'Nice plushy young bourgeois giving me a certificate of character, that's what it amounts to, isn't it?'

'If you like.'

Neil said:

'It won't do you any good.'

'Perhaps not.'

'Getting into the scene by the back door, aren't you?'

Stephen did not reply.

'I don't see why you should,' Neil said.

'The reasons don't concern you.'

'Bloody Quixotism. Is that it? I've got no use for that.'

Neil was jeering again, unmoved, though there might have been a shade less contempt. 'You're going in for the luxury of honourable behaviour. So that you can feel good. Individual salvation, that's what you're after. There's no doctrine of individual salvation that doesn't get in the way in the long run. We have to eliminate all that stuff. Just fancy our positions were reversed. Which, by the nature of the system, is impossible. But do you imagine that I'd do as much for you? Not on your sweet fanny. Unless I thought two things. First, that I could have some effect. On the blasted trial. Second, that I was certain you were objectively useful. To the movement. If I wasn't certain of that, you'd have to take your chance.'

He went on:

'Of course I shouldn't be certain of it, either. I don't believe you'll ever be objectively useful to the movement. If you live a hundred years.'

'Perhaps it's as well for you,' said Stephen, 'that I don't make the same conditions.'

'It doesn't signify one way or the other,' said Neil. 'Whatever you do.'

He showed no more interest in Stephen's evidence, or even whether he had aborted it. It was possible that he knew Stephen well enough, and assumed – not with gratitude, but with indifferent respect – that that wouldn't happen. Instead, he began to talk about his future, or rather to revert to earlier talk about it, which had left Emma mutinously silent ever since Stephen entered the room. For herself, she would have behaved as Stephen was behaving: she had no feeling for Stephen, except maybe envy that he could make a gesture denied to her. While Neil was making the opposite of a gesture, something her imagination revolted at, and saw as too dingy to be borne.

Neil had been talking prosaically about his future – and, with Stephen now present, he did again. The trial; suspended sentence. He couldn't take risks while that lasted. Or for long after. They would have tabs on him. Anyway, student politics were no good. Foreign politics were no good. Instant revolution was a blink in a middle-class eye. Fatuous talk about alternative societies. All middle-class nonsense. He wasn't going to waste his time.

Defeatist, said Emma.

The only real politics left in a country like this was on the shop floor. That was where he was going. Marxist politics on the shop floor. He would go back to Liverpool. He could pick up with people he knew. Not in the docks, more straightforward in a big firm. They would have it against him that he'd been to college, but he'd get round that in time. The union would look after him. It didn't matter that there were tabs on him there. Marxist shop stewards had tabs on them too. He would be one himself some day. Then he could do some real work. 'How long?' Emma had said it before, in rage, in anticlimax.

'A few years,' said Neil. He would have to win their

confidence, he said. If he knew the people he had come from, it wouldn't be all that easy.

'Then little strikes in the shop!' cried Emma.

'Of course. That's what it's all about. To begin with.'

'It's running away,' she said.

'Don't be childish. It's the opposite.'

'It's letting everyone down.'

She meant, letting her down, or her dreams about him. She wasn't heartbroken, her kind of passion was too wilful for that. But she was deserted. Not many people had seen Neil as romantic, but she had. He had been her new-style hero. She had imagined conspiring for him when he went to prison, keeping him when he came out. She had pictures of standing beside him in the streets, when the rising broke through. She wasn't over-rating herself. She had as much physical courage as anyone not insane. She would have been splendid among the Paris students a couple of years before. Yet she wouldn't have been so splendid after the revolution had succeeded, or any revolution that had happened or could ever happen. It was like dreaming of a lover, and then settling down in marriage to find out what he was like in the boredom of ordinary days. It was like that with Neil now. The flat routine he was setting himself, the boredom of slow talk on the factory floor, the keeping sight of ten years ahead, the calculations, the analysis, the union climb – that took away the aura he had once had. That wasn't the hero she wanted. That wasn't for her.

She had all the unsentimentality of the romantic, perhaps unsentimentality doubled because it was mixed with sex. She could snatch at men to replace him. It wouldn't take her long. There were activists less rational than these had been, projects and visions more inflamed, danger, a new existence, round the corner. That was where the excitement lay.

During the morning, Stephen had foreseen most of the external consequences for them all. But those which were already in train within them – they were still hidden. This was the first to break surface. Stephen had nothing to say to her. He had no claim, and not much influence, upon her. Although, at least in terms of intellect, he understood Neil's choice in a way to which she was blind. For, although he and Neil had little in common – they had been allies without a personal relation between them, except perhaps subliminal resentment or dislike, sharpened that afternoon – they were searching for a purpose, and by this time (as another consequence) it had to be a disciplined purpose. That was what Neil was looking for in shop floor politics: possibly, more likely than not, he was already home. Which Stephen wasn't. He was going on the same search, but the answer might take him a long time to find.

Soon afterwards Lance, with an air of casualness, asked: 'What about me?'

Since he first saw Lance in that room, Stephen had been preparing himself for this. Now, uncomfortable, suddenly ashamed, he pretended not to understand.

'I mean, do you feel inclined to give a bit of evidence for me?'

Lance had put on a brash, impudent smile.

'I've thought about that.' Stephen's reply was slow in coming.

'I wonder, do you feel inclined to say you've never seen me smoke anything but a nice Virginia cigarette?'

'No. I can't do that.'

'I suppose you can't. Perhaps that wouldn't be too convincing.' Lance's expression was changing. 'But you could tell them, couldn't you, that I've never gone in for pushing. It doesn't make sense. I've looked after myself, that's all. I've never sold anything in my life. You could tell them that.'

An empty pause.

'It wouldn't do any good,' said Stephen.

'You said you can't do Neil any good. But you're appearing for him all the same.'

'No,' said Stephen. 'I didn't say quite that. I can give concrete evidence about him. I can say, I shall say, that I've been here with him often enough and I've never seen him touch a spot of grass. Either here or anywhere. That might make five per cent difference for him.'

'You could say you've never seen me sell a spot of grass.'

'That wouldn't make the slightest difference at all.'

'So you don't feel like playing?'

When he had been brazen, overdoing it, it had been easier for Stephen. Not instantaneously, he said:

'No. It would be useless.'

'Oh, come on. In for a penny, in for a pound. It won't get you in much deeper.'

'There's no point in it.'

'I've been one of you, haven't I?' The front had dropped right away, Lance was pleading. 'I've done my whack.'

Stephen didn't answer.

'You're not still thinking I'm responsible for poor old Bernie, are you? I swear that I had nothing to do with it.'

'I haven't a view on that. It doesn't enter.'

'Well then. You might as well say a word for me.'

'It would be valueless.'

'I dare say it would. Just for the look of it, though.'

Stephen's voice sounded harder than he intended.

'No. Not for the look of it, I can't.'

'Of course you can. Why not?'

'Have I got to tell you?'

'You'd better.'

'It's your fault that we're in this situation. With hindsight I think they'd probably have stopped us anyway, but they wouldn't have made us look ridiculous into the bargain. You've done that. With your drugs. No one minds what you do – providing it's no danger to the job or anyone else. This has been. I'd come to the rescue if I could really help you. But as for tokens, I don't think they're called for. I've tried to think it out. It seems to me the obligation is cancelled.'

Lance had listened without a twitch. He said:

'You knew all about me before you took me in.'

'As a matter of fact, I didn't.'

'You should have done.'

'That's fair.'

'Anyway, you soon did know. You should have told me to stop.'

'That's fair too.'

'We were too democratic, we never interfered with anyone. Someone ought to have been in charge,' Neil broke in. Lance said to Stephen:

'I'd either have played or got out. I wouldn't have blown any secrets. You could have trusted me.'

'Yes,' said Stephen.

'Well then. Won't you think again?'

'No. It wouldn't make any difference. I've thought enough. I'm sorry.'

Lance gave an imitation of his impertinent smile. He gazed steadily at Stephen, and said:

'Right ho. There's never any harm in trying, is there, though?'

It was that flick of jauntiness which, as Stephen left them, on his way to meet Tess, recurred to him, made him unreconciled to the decisions he had made, and once, like a shame jabbing back into memory, forced him to shut his eyes and stand stock-still.

25

OVER the telephone to Tess, in a hurry, possible meeting-places for tea leaving him blank as though he were a stranger in the town, Stephen had finally come out with the name, Simpkin and James'. It was an unlikely rendezvous for them. This was the local Fortnum and Mason's, a grocery for the genteel, not long after this to be, like other small genteel emporia, closed down. Stephen had sometimes been taken there for tea when he was a child, but had not been inside since. There, in the café upstairs, overheated, over-scented, full of provincial ladies, at a side table Tess was waiting for him. As he went towards her, he seemed to be the only man in the room.

'How's it gone?' she said.

She already knew something about the interview with Hotchkinson, and that Stephen was seeing Neil that after-noon. During that lunch-time telephone conversation, Stephen hadn't told her what he had decided, or if he had decided anything: but that she had guessed, or more than guessed. So, when he repeated what he had said to Neil, she nodded.

'It's no use trying to get you to change your mind, is it?'

He shook his head, thinking that, if there had been such a hope, he would have gone to her before this.

'I don't think I want to,' she said. 'It's difficult. But I don't think I want to. Most people wouldn't have done what you're doing, though.'

'Lance was there. That was a nuisance.' Stephen was pressing on a sore. 'He wanted me to do the same for him.'

He went over the scene for her, as he had done within himself – not getting free – since he left Neil's room.

'He accepted that it would be absolutely useless. He knows that as well as I do,' said Stephen, as though she were arguing with him.

'I think he just wanted not to be left out,' she said. She hesitated, and then went on: 'Perhaps we got him wrong. We thought he was only after sensation. And adventure. And didn't care a rap for anyone else. Perhaps that's wrong. Or perhaps people like that want a bit of affection, like everyone else.'

'That's the blackmail of pity,' said Stephen.

'You wouldn't say that,' she replied, 'unless you thought so too.'

They were picking at the neat little sandwich triangles.

She understood that he was distracted and guilty. In their own shorthand, fragmentary, sentences not finished, he was saying that they had tolerated everything, they hadn't interfered with, or criticized, anyone's 'private life' (that was the phrase they used, prim when it was referring to activities anything but prim). It was part of their creed. Still, no one should let his private life mess up others or the job in hand. They had excluded people from the core, close friends, whose private lives might have been a danger: such as a clever man, a very good man, whose homosexual pickups went too wide. It was easy to see that they ought to have excluded Lance. That was their mistake. Had they the right to blame him for it now?

'I think so,' said Tess.

'Have we?'

'He's never thought about anyone but himself.' She added: 'Is he worth while?'

'Who is? I mean, can we say that against anyone?'

Suddenly Tess was finding herself more positive than he was. This was a kind of discrimination which they didn't like making, which didn't fit the climate they had been brought up in, or their hopes. But to Tess, left to herself, it came naturally enough, gave a sign of how her character would later show itself, like bone so far almost hidden under the flesh.

She didn't choose to argue with him that afternoon. She wanted to ease him, she tried another way.

'Darling. Would you feel better if you spoke up for him, after all?'

'Possibly.'

'I'm sure you would.'

He held out his cup for her to fill again, but didn't answer.

'It wouldn't make much more unpleasantness for you, would it?'

'A certain amount.'

'Never mind. You could take it. We could take it, couldn't we?'

'That goes without saying. It wouldn't really count, one way or the other.'

'Well then. Do it.'

He was sitting back, she watched the clear profile. Then he turned to her with an affectionate, intimate smile, and she was sure that she had resolved him. He said:

'No. That's not for me.'

He went on, still intimately, almost lightly: 'I'd better get it cut-and-dried. I'll ring up the man Hotchkinson before we go. I'll tell him that I shall give evidence for Neil, and then I shall call it a day. That's as much as I shall do.'

It came to Tess as an unmitigated, unprepared surprise. She was certain that he meant it, and that this was how he would act. She was as certain that he had spoken honestly a moment before, and wasn't being moved by a last residue of prudence, or loss of nerve. It was a mystery, perhaps as much to him as to her. It seemed to cut clean across his nature. He spoke and behaved as though doubts, or even scruples, had at last been wiped away. She wondered if he were feeling the release of exerting his will. Exerting his will in a vacuum or without cause, after being at others' mercy all those days. She wondered how often he could be so hard.

In a matter of minutes, she was due for another surprise. He had said he was thirsty, and ordered another pot of tea.

Tea cups clinked on the next table, there was the sound of women's voices, the smell of scent.

'There's another thing,' said Stephen.

He was looking down at the table. What hadn't he covered, what was coming, one more threat to take care of, she thought.

'I think we ought to get married pretty soon. If you agree. Will you?'

She had imagined so often hearing him ask her. She had doubted whether it would ever happen. Her hopes had been strong, but she had tried to sink them down. Often her imagination had been too much for her. But it hadn't produced a scene like this, not the two of them in the midst of a crisis, sitting in the feminine well-to-do café, crowded, public, so that he hadn't even taken her hand. Astonished, taken aback, the shock wave not yet followed by delight, she found herself, in reply, asking the singular question:

'Why?'

'I need you.'

'Is that enough?'

'It is for me.'

The shock wave was receding now. Tess said:

'Darling. Of course I want to marry you. More than anything on earth. I'm not coy. But for you – Is this the right time for you to know what you want?'

'What is the right time?'

'No. I'm serious. I've got to tell you the truth. God knows, I wish I hadn't to. But you've been under great strain. You still are. So have we all, but you've felt it worst. I don't think you're in a state to make up your mind – about anything like this.'

She went on, determined, almost fierce, cheeks flushed dusky.

'I've got to tell you something else. You won't like it. You're strong, but you're vulnerable too. A lot of supports have let you down. Your parents have let you down. You were prepared for it, in one way, and in another way you weren't. You want to get rid of everything that's let you down. I believe that's right for you. But I don't believe it's a good reason for marrying me.'

Stephen didn't respond at once. Then he said, as though thinking to himself: 'All that is absolutely true.'

Tess felt a seep of desolation, empty inside. She had been honest with him, she had thought of him. She had harmed herself, he wouldn't make the same choice again.

'All that is absolutely true. Most of it had occurred to me, you know.'

Suddenly he gazed full at her. 'But it doesn't count. I want you to marry me.'

'Leave it for two or three months. Then see.' That was her last lame honest effort.

'Will you marry me?'

She remembered afterwards that immediately she had said something like 'of course', but that was a false memory. In fact, she had, by way of delight, as an emblem of acceptance, asked how he had been thinking of her.

He said:

'These last few days, I've realized that I didn't know you before. Not properly.'

'Now?'

'Now I know a bit more.'

'Do you?'

'I'm not a romantic, am I?'

'Aren't you?'

'But I love what I know.'

It was actually then that she said both 'yes' and 'of course', as though answering to a single question. She reached across the table, took his hand, and kissed it. Whether anyone at neighbouring tables noticed, she couldn't have told.

When Stephen said that he was not a romantic, he was half-deluding himself. If he had been born a little earlier, he probably would have been. Nevertheless, there was a certain truth in his statement about not really knowing her. They had been to bed within a few days of meeting. Even with her, sex had come first, and knowledge afterwards. With him, a long time afterwards. With him, though not with her, sex had for a while got in the way of knowing. It was a curious converse to their parents' courting. Though their own children might in due course think that they had found their way to the same end.

Across the table, Stephen was being practical, liberated,

after the bitterer practicalities, to cope with this one. They had better get married in the spring. He wanted her to finish her degree course, he was enough of a professional for that, he didn't like unfinished business, he said. As for their plans together, she knew already that there was his trust to live on, and he would get an academic job in the autumn. His subject made him more independent than most men: he could do it anywhere. His decision about Neil, his involvement in this case ahead, might shut some doors, not all.

'That won't be too difficult,' he said. He added:

'It'll be more difficult to be some use outside. For both of us.'

He had told her of Neil's intention. That wasn't open to them: they couldn't have accepted that kind of politics; yet they were committed. Committed to what? They didn't make it vocal to each other, even now: perhaps any answer would have seemed too inflated for their taste. They might have admitted, but then their mouths would have been wry, that they couldn't just look on: they were living in this world, they didn't like it, they had to work for a better. That seemed flat enough. Yet they were committed. Time might play tricks on them, but they wouldn't alter as much as sceptical onlookers would expect, or hope. These last days had affected them, but hadn't altered them. Stephen's thoughts had darkened, so had his pessimism, but, when it came to the future, he still believed, as much as Tess, in the possibilities men had, almost in what Tess's father would have called grace, and had as much irreducible hope.

'It'll be more difficult,' he said. 'There I haven't much to offer you.'

'Never mind,' she said. 'We'll carve something out.'

'I don't see it clear.'

'Maybe we can't do much. But we'll do something.'

She was good – it wasn't art, it was nature – at giving him no more encouragement than he could take. They didn't say any more about the future, but he was more comfortable, and she also, because something had been said.

Before they left the café, Stephen went to a telephone (women's voices in the background) and rang up Hotchkinson. Mr Hotchkinson was at home. With pressure, Stephen extracted the home number. He heard the high strangulated voice. 'What do you want?'

Stephen said that he had decided to give evidence for Neil St John.

'Think again.'

'No. This is definite.'

'So much the worse for you.'

'Will you note it? I don't want any misunderstanding.'

'Noted.' Hotchkinson didn't indulge in useless argument. 'It's on your own head.'

Hotchkinson inquired about Forrester, evidence for him? No, said Stephen, in a sharp emphatic tone, he wouldn't do that. A grunt at the other end of the line. Hotchkinson then said, issuing a brusque communiqué, that the warrants had now been duly issued and that the two would presumably be arrested that evening. About getting them bailed out – For Stephen, who hadn't been near a criminal case, that hadn't entered his mind. Money? Forrester was no problem. 'If money's needed for St John –' Stephen began, and Hotchkinson said: 'Point taken.' He added: 'That's about all,' gave Stephen time and place of the inquest ('Nothing will happen') the next morning, and there was a clink of the receiver ramming down.

The café closed at half-past five, and Stephen, as they walked through the market place, stalls bare, waiting for

Saturday, vestigial smells of fruit in the frigid night, told Tess what had just been said.

'All fixed,' she said with acquiescence.

'All fixed. Except going through with it.'

It was a strange mood for her, after the proposal, this mixture of joy and dread. The joy was deeper, reached nearer the springs of life, than the dread, and yet, at some moments, it wasn't written on her face, and a passer-by would have thought her anxious. Her nerves were firm, when she was herself concerned, but now they were attuned to his.

They had threaded through the market place, and came out, without any aim (there was nowhere to go yet) into a side street, oddly old-fashioned, like the market place itself, in the glossy town. They passed a shop giving out the smell of cheese. Stephen said:

'I shall have to tell my parents about us.'

'They won't like it much, will they?' But a passer-by would have seen the anxious expression vanish and joy take over.

'I have other things to tell them.' He meant, as Tess took for granted, his resolve about Neil and the trial. 'They'll like those less.' In a moment, he said:

'I'd better go and see them: I may as well finish it off.'

Looking up as they walked, quite slowly, together, fingers interlaced, Tess said:

'No, darling. Not tonight.'

'Why not?'

'No, don't do any more tonight. You've made enough efforts for one day. Haven't you?'

'It's nice to get things done.'

'It can wait till tomorrow. Nothing more tonight.' She smiled at him and hugged him. 'Now be said.'

She was mimicking her mother, using a homely old idiom that Stephen hadn't heard until he met her. He smiled back, not arguing any further. He was willing to be guided by Tess that night.

Nevertheless, though it was a respite, the two of them together, there was nowhere for them to go. As soon as six o'clock struck, they turned into a pub small, obscure, unknown to them: there they sat in the quiet chintz-curtained saloon. Without breaking the news they couldn't return to either of their homes. Quite unexpectedly, time was going slow. Glasses in front of them, they were talking, but thoughts, marriage blended with the events not far away, trial and shame, would not leave them free for long.

If they had had a place of their own, they would have gone to bed. But Tess, reposefully happy under all the rest, might have admitted that she wasn't sorry they were prevented. Examining herself, she would have felt a sense, perhaps a primitive survival, perhaps more profound, that it was somehow fitting that evening to stay chaste. Solemn, superstitious even, but she didn't mind that. Not even when it meant hours stretching ahead, nowhere to go, nothing to do.

At one stage, she told Stephen that she might speak to her father later on. 'He'll be very glad,' she said. Stephen replied 'Of course. Do that.' But she hadn't asked whether she should, she had simply told him. There was no more tentativeness or touching wood. They were each of them learning what trust was like.

They had a snack at a sandwich bar, but neither was hungry. Then, not only time going slow, but words also, they went – it was the opposite of a climax to a decisive day, the most decisive they had known – to a cinema. The film had no suspense. They sat with arms round each other, and Tess felt so sleepy that her eyelids drooped. Shaking herself awake, she noticed that he was sleepy too. They left before the film was over. It was not yet ten o'clock.

In the street, she said:

'Now you'll have an early night.'

'I'll take you home.'

'You won't. I love you very much. It's much too far.'

'This doesn't happen every day, does it?' She saw the trace of his sarcastic smile.

'That's why,' she said. 'Not a time to drag yourself about.'

When she hadn't been certain of him, she had been uneasy because he was dutiful and polite. He understood, and kissed her, standing still while the crowd on the pavement pushed by.

'You can see me to the bus,' she said.

After she had left him, Stephen walked home. Near the cathedral, the streets were as quiet as they had been on Saturday night. In Thomas Freer's house, the drawing room lights were shining over the lane. Stephen took care to make no noise as he unlocked the door and as he went upstairs. He passed the drawing room door, the sound of Bach came from within, no one had heard him.

He reached his room. As Tess had said, it would be an early night for him.

26

HE woke, as he used to wake in placid times, to the clang of the cathedral bell. The prospects of the next hours swam into mind: he felt, or began to act as though he felt, that he had them mastered now. He telephoned Tess. That early morning call was going to become ritual until they married. Yes, she would see him at the inquest. Remember to put on a black tie.

As on the previous day, he arrived down at breakfast with his father. Outside, the morning was slate-grey, but the wall-lights shut it out, islanded the room. As on the previous day, there were good mornings, inquiries about sleep. On the hot plate this morning stood poached eggs on haddock.

After a while Thomas Freer said:

'I've been thinking, I suppose it's just possible that you might consider attending this inquest today –?'

He already knew, Stephen was certain.

'Yes. I think I have to go.'

Thomas Freer glanced at him, surreptitiously, with his eyes half-veiled. His expression was melancholy but inquisitive. He brought out one of his random questions:

'Have you ever met the coroner?'

'I don't believe so.'

'He's a *nice* little man.'

Stephen's attention was elsewhere, but on other occasions he had observed that his father's use of the diminutive often referred less to physical size than to social standing.

'It is rather convenient, don't you agree, that his office is just across the way. It is rather convenient, you'll only have to slip along, won't you?'

Thomas Freer spoke with obscure satisfaction, as though he had had some part in contriving it himself. As it happened, the coroner's office was in the street opposite the cathedral, along which Stephen and the others had walked up and down so many times, probing the first news, the Saturday night before.

'Of course, in my opinion, for what it's worth, nothing will happen this morning. *Nothing* will happen. It will be adjourned after five minutes.'

For an instant, his lids were raised.

'Or perhaps you are better informed?'

'No. That's what I am told.'

It was also what his father had been told, Stephen was more certain still. He also suspected, more than suspected, that his father had been told more than that. He had been warned – had the other lawyer done it 'in terms' as Thomas Freer would say, or wrapped it up? – that Stephen would give evidence at the trial. Thomas Freer already knew that a decision had been made, that there was a conflict coming inside that house as well as publicity ahead. Which he hated more, it would have been impossible for Stephen, hard for himself, even in his introspective moods (more naked than Stephen imagined) to disentangle. That morning at breakfast he was half-inviting Stephen to declare it all, half-making defences against hearing what he didn't want to hear.

In fact, Stephen had no intention of speaking yet awhile. The invitations, if that was what they were, he was – quite gently – opaque about. With ambiguous relief, Thomas Freer went into a disquisition about *Humanae Vitae* and world-conservation in Stephen's life-time. Before they got up from the table, Stephen announced that he would be at home that evening. It was understood by both to be a promise to speak: but Thomas Freer scarcely seemed to listen, in a hurry talked of something else, as though not wishing to regard it so or for Stephen to be bound.

The inquest was down for eleven o'clock. Before he left the house, Stephen – as though casually, though it was part of his programme for the day – called in at the drawing room. As he expected, his mother was sitting there, spectacles on nose, holding the newspaper right down on her lap, doing the crossword puzzle.

'Hallo,' she said. There was no lift in her voice.

Seating himself in a chair close by, Stephen said that in five minutes he was going over to the inquest. Really, she answered. Then Stephen, still trying to sound matter-of-fact, gave her the same message as he had given his father. He would be at home that evening. Like Thomas Freer, she must have understood. She didn't attempt any sidetrack of conversation, to pretend that they were both at ease or postpone disquiet. All she said was: 'Oh, we shall expect you in for dinner, shall we?'

For an instant, as the door shut behind him, the strain slackened, despite where he was going. He went out without a coat, not noticing the bitter air. The matins bell followed him all along the three or four hundred yards: it hadn't finished as he reached the office, just audible, no longer palpable, as he went upstairs.

The coroner's office, one floor up, was smaller than the drawing room Stephen had come from. It had probably itself once been the drawing room of an eighteenth-century house, though one slightly less spacious than Thomas Freer's. Even now, in spite of the desk, books, paperasserie, jury's chairs, if one looked at the wainscot and the shape of the fireplace there was a ghostly domesticity: which wasn't reduced because of the couple of dozen people present, some standing apart as though at a party where they hadn't been introduced. The Kelshalls, she all in black, he with an armband, were sitting in two chairs by themselves. A secretary, already in place behind the table, faced them: jurors took their seats already knowing that nothing was required of them that morning. Someone from Hotchkinson's office was standing up, so were a solitary press man, Constable Shipman, and a superintendent in plain clothes. There was, although Stephen didn't identify him, a doctor from the infirmary. The Bishop, having escorted Tess, was talking quietly to the coroner; he lifted up a hand as he saw Stephen, who brought a chair by Tess's side. Although they had expected him, Mark had not come.

Two minutes past eleven. The coroner, a doctor called Evans, rapped on the desk. He was shining-faced, heavily muscled, in no language except Freerese a little man. He had the kind of presence which simmered with high spirits, impatience not far from the surface, and rapid shifting moods.

Thomas Freer's physical designation might have been inaccurate, but his prophecy about time wasn't far out. Shipman gave formal evidence about being called to the body on the pavement. The doctor, reading from a script with the curious air of insincerity that reading aloud produced, as though these weren't the facts but had been composed by a committee, reported the arrival at the infirmary.

'Yes. He was dead on arrival,' said the coroner, hurrying the young doctor up. 'You examined him –'

More reading aloud. 'Extensive laceration of the skull. Extensive fracture of the vault of the skull. Depression of the bone into the brain matter. Laceration of the brain forcing the brain down into the skull casing. Cone compression of the brain stem, pressing on the respiratory cortex: thus causing death.'

To Stephen, the mechanical words were more ominous than the sight had been.

'This is exactly what you might expect from a fall from a fifth storey window,' said Dr Evans, quick and uninflected.

'Yes, if he fell in a certain position.'

'If he fell in the position which he obviously did.' Dr Evans glanced towards the superintendent. 'We haven't established, though, how he came to fall. I understand that there are inquiries still proceeding in this matter.'

'Yes, sir. I am instructed to ask for an adjournment.'

'You're conducting a post-mortem?' That question to the infirmary doctor puzzled those who had heard nothing about drugs: there had been no mention that morning.

'To be exact, a post-mortem is being conducted.'

'Yes, yes, yes. Adjourned for seven days. This day week.' Then the coroner, tone suddenly deepened, leaned forwards towards the Kelshalls. 'Before you go I want to say a few words to you. Strictly speaking, I ought to wait until we're finished, but I'm not going to. This young man has died, and it's terrible for you. It's terrible for any parents when a young man dies before his time, however it happens. It's specially sad when we hear that your son possessed most brilliant promise. My whole heart goes out to you in sympathy.'

He added:

'I wanted to tell you that.'

He stood up, and immediately began conferring with his secretary. Emotion, or emotional words, had compelled emotion, and Mrs Kelshall, who had listened to the doctor's evidence with her features like a blank sheet, covered her eyes. The others had risen, and Stephen and Tess, the Bishop close to them, moved hesitatingly towards her. Stephen hankered to pass out unnoticed behind her, could have done so, stood with Tess's hand on his arm, at last was impelled to speak. He took a couple of steps in front of the Kelshalls' chairs, looked down, neck inclined, and said, quiet but staccato:

'Mrs Kelshall. I'm sorry again.'

Her hands dropping into her lap, she gazed ahead. Her face had gone stiff.

'I do not understand.'

'I'm sorry. I can't say any more than I did that night.'

'I do not understand. They do not tell us what happened to Bernard.'

Just for an instant her eyes fixed on his, then gazed ahead again.

'You have said nothing, Mr Freer.'

She went on:

'I hoped you were a friend.'

She spoke with pride, and that Stephen had confronted in her before, but also with hate. He had no reply, and as he returned the yard or two to Tess, not only his cheeks were pale, but his lips too. He was flinching too much to imagine any of the pictures she had constructed since the Tuesday evening, the people utterly mysterious to her, the wild parties in houses such as she had never been inside, the lies, even the conspiracies against her son. Stephen was the only one she had known by sight. When she saw him now, she could imagine anything of him, the sight was hateful. But really, since she was so mystified, felt so ignorant about these people round her son, her only recourse was her pride.

It would be her only recourse for months, and perhaps

years, to come. She was to derive no comfort from one phenomenon about memories of Bernard which no one had foreseen. As a matter of fact, she remained once more in total ignorance. The inquest, in a week's time, proceeded according to the lawyer's prediction. The medical evidence about the traces of drugs wasn't firm and was given with scientific dubiety: Dr Evans wouldn't take it as proved, and blarneyed the jury into giving a neutral verdict. The presence of Bernard in Lance's flat, and his death, were mentioned at the trial, as explaining the first police search. That wasn't allowed to go further, and soon afterwards it seemed likely that Bernard's name was forgotten. But it didn't happen quite like that.

The core had organized their network of contacts with professional thoroughness – so much so that the information couldn't be damped down now. True, the politicians, the public relations men and the journalists could, because of legal dangers, say nothing. That however didn't prevent gossip seeping round the way-out left in half-a-dozen universities. There was so much secrecy, so many mutters of drugs and double agents, that the gossip became distorted and for a time – not to a mass extent, largely to persons who liked the air of conspiracy and of being in the know – Bernard became a cult hero of some fringe groups. He had killed himself to keep a secret, was one rumour. Another was that the C.I.A. were teaching 'our people' how to make away with the real leaders who were going to bring 'the system' down. Bernard was one of the real leaders. In one university, photographs of him were on sale. It helped that some of his remarks, pro-Arab, anti-Zionist, were on record; they had been made at a meeting of pro-Arab Jewish students, and were the only ones of his to be preserved.

The curious thing was, Emma came to believe in this apotheosis of Bernard. In order not to compromise Sylvia, Stephen, Tess and Mark hadn't revealed to the others who had betrayed them, or that they had a source of precise information. Stephen had, on the afternoon before the inquest, given an indication to Neil, but not of how certain he was nor of how he knew.

Although they soon died away, there were one or two mentions of Bernard in newspapers during the months after the inquest. In a demo in the summer term, a small file of students, parading outside the Israeli Embassy, chanted 'What about Bernie Kelshall? What about Bernie Kelshall?'

Mrs Kelshall did not read any newspaper except the local evening one, and was not to know.

That Friday morning, the Bishop had watched what had taken place between her and Stephen. He patted Stephen's arm.

'Never mind,' he said. 'It's only natural. Poor folk, poor folk.'

He went himself and talked to them. His face was open with empathetic sorrow. Stephen heard Mrs Kelshall say 'Thank you, sir. Thank you.' She and her husband began to cry, and the Bishop talked on, sustaining a background of brotherly murmuring.

Soon he shook hands with them, taking in turn each of their right hands in both of his. 'God bless you.' It was all part-brotherly, part-paternal, just a shade episcopal, as Stephen and Tess observed him: he had given at least a moment of consolation, altogether beyond their power. And yet, as he walked with them down the office stairs, into the narrow street, it was Stephen who was thinking of the Kelshalls, not the Bishop. The Bishop had seen too much bereavement to carry it away with him: you shared it when you were in its presence, and then you left it behind; it might have seemed like professional callousness, but the Bishop, if he had thought about it, wouldn't have felt guilty: he, like a doctor, had to live like a war-correspondent of mortality, it was the only way to live.

As they came into the harsh, throat-biting air, he gripped Stephen's arm.

'I must say, Stephen,' he said, with a joyous countenance, 'this is splendid news!'

He went on:

'When my girl told me, you could have knocked me down with a feather.'

He glanced lovingly at Tess, who herself was looking up at Stephen, knowing his concentrated moods better than her father did. He gave her a flicker of a smile. He said:

'I've been very lucky.'

'I hope you've both been very lucky,' said the Bishop. 'If I say so myself, she is a good girl.'

'Don't I know it,' said Stephen.

'And I believe that you are a good young man.'

Suddenly, after all the cosiness, he had spoken with surprising sharpness and authority. Stephen replied in an identical tone.

'I can't let you think that.'

'Others have to judge it for you, you know.'

'I'm not sure what it means,' said Stephen, 'or whether it means anything at all.' (Tess was thinking, indulgent, irritated, that this wasn't the time for semantic quibbling.) 'But, in any sense that you could use it, it doesn't begin to be true.'

'You're very honest, aren't you?'

'You always have been,' put in Tess.

'Not even always that,' said Stephen.

'Do you think any of us are always that?' the Bishop asked. He was beginning to understand something of what his daughter had told him about Stephen. He was arrogant often, but didn't like himself much. The Bishop thought that too much self-dislike could splinter a character: and yet, though this young man was accepting no assurance that morning, there was something enduring about him. 'We shall see! We shall see!' the Bishop was enunciating cheerfully to himself. They had arrived opposite the cathedral gate, and he said: 'Come to the office, just for a mo'.' Then, as they walked across the yard, he ruminated, again cheerfully: 'Marriage is tactically disastrous. But strategically vital.' That was not the kind of comment he made at marriage services, and until they were sitting down, opposite the crucifix, he was telling them what sounded more like the conventional wisdom.

Then he said:

'No announcement until it's all cut-and-dried! We don't want any leaks.'

He put a finger to the side of his nose, with an air of preposterous cunning. Tess must have told him, Stephen realized, that the news was not yet broken to the Freers.

'Announcement as soon as possible,' said Stephen. 'Monday or Tuesday.'

'Very good, very good.' The Bishop regarded them. 'There's one thing you might remember. The minute this is public property, it'll give people round here (he waved a short arm) something else to think about. People aren't very much use at thinking of two things at once. Perhaps it's a bit of a bonus to you now.'

To Stephen, that seemed a piece of superficiality, not relevant to the situation, less worth listening to than anything the Bishop had said, either this morning or two days before in that office. But it wasn't entirely so. The Bishop didn't approve of the worldliness of the world, but wasn't unaware of it. Neither Stephen nor Tess had given it a thought, but a respectable marriage might save them both some slander.

'Well then. Well,' said the Bishop to his daughter. 'I think it's time I took you away.'

That came on Stephen unprepared. Seeing that Tess made no resistance (he had relied on having her to himself) he misunderstood, and thought it was a piece of misplaced tact, leaving him alone before the evening confrontation. But it was nothing like that. The Bishop's wife cherished strong and dutiful family feelings, and she had a sick sister coming to stay. Before the Bishop and Tess left home that morning – and before Tess had told him of the engagement – Mrs Boltwood had said that she expected them to join her at the station. It hadn't escaped the Bishop that Tess had chosen to speak to him in her mother's absence: strong and dutiful family feelings weren't so harmonious as outsiders took for granted, including Stephen, who still believed they were simpler, warmer, more homely (in the English sense) than his own. The Bishop wasn't prepared for Tess to let him give the news to her mother at second-hand. So he was making her do her duty at the railway station. Tess, because she was happy, was agreeing to be obedient that day.

Thus, before midday, Stephen was left alone. He had a sandwich at a pub, and then went to the reference library, near to Hotchkinson's office, to get out of the cold, sitting there with boys from the local grammar schools. He tried to read some of Einstein's letters, on the unity of all things, on the God (which was an atheist God) expressed in the order of the natural world. What majesty, what repose:

but the words wouldn't stay in his mind, even the grandest of men made existence easier, more conformable with their desire, than it truly was. For a time, he day-dreamed. It was not until half-past three, when he could expect the house to be empty, that he returned home.

On the telephone pad was a request to ring a number, Mark's. They hadn't met since Wednesday night, a day and a half ago.

'Hallo.'

'Hallo.' This was Stephen. 'I was going to call you anyway.'

'Any news?'

'I've been settling various things. Tess and I are going to get married.'

'Oh, I'm delighted.' Mark's voice was spontaneous, fresh, generous. 'It's the best thing for both of you. Much the best thing.' Then he went on, still eager: 'I must see you. Right away.'

'No, not now.'

'Yes, I must.'

Stephen explained that he had to speak to his parents: about his decisions, including this one. 'It won't be nice.'

'When are you doing that?'

'This evening. The sooner I get it over, the better for everyone.'

'I must see you before that.'

'Let's meet tomorrow.'

'I'm sorry.' Mark was gentle, inflexible. 'I'll be round in half-an-hour.'

27

AFTER that telephone conversation, Stephen lay back on the window-seat in the drawing room, gazing out, seeing nothing, neither the cathedral spire against the clouds nor the reflections of the room's lights in the murk outside. He was thinking, not at all of Mark, but of how to get the evening over and to finish with what he had to do.

It came almost as a surprise, something he had forgotten, an interruption that was irrelevant and irksome, when Mark came into the room. His face was radiant.

'It's wonderful about you and Tess,' he said, and, crossing over to the window, shook his friend's hand.

'I wasn't sure you'd have the sense,' he added, giving out pleasure that was absolute and free from envy, infused with knowledge of Stephen's earlier passions.

'Perhaps I've learned a little,' said Stephen.

'Perhaps.'

Stephen, still awkward because of this interruption, said that it was too late for tea, was it too early for a drink?

'No, no. Nothing for me,' said Mark. 'You're getting like your father, you know.'

'Not much, I think.'

Mark had spoken lightly, and hadn't expected the hard reply. For once, his antennae had failed him.

Stephen had left the window-seat, and they sat opposite Thomas Freer's favourite picture, glowing under the hidden light above.

'You've settled some other things, did you say?' Mark asked.

'I shall do what you wanted me to do.'

'What's that?'

Stephen said that he would give evidence for Neil. There was no going back on that.

'Good. Very good.' Mark went on, in an eager, intimate tone:

'And you decided that without knowing everything. Maybe that was better.'

'I don't understand.'

'Oh, you will soon. I mean, on Wednesday night – you know, we were at my house – you thought you might have a way out, didn't you? That is, if you could persuade yourself that Neil had done the doping, you only had to persuade yourself, that would let you out–'

'You're right.'

'And you couldn't persuade yourself.'

'I knew I was making an excuse.'

Mark, expression washed clean, gave a brilliant smile, eyes shining.

'I wasn't honest with you that night. I don't know why not, as a rule it's easy to be honest. It is now.'

'What about?' But that was a formal question.

'It wasn't Neil who did it. It was me.'

Blankly, with extraordinary loneliness, Stephen asked: 'What ever for?'

'The honest answer is, I just don't know.' Mark went on: 'I don't believe that I had a reason that you could call a reason. Of course, I knew he (Bernard) was the one who'd given us away. But I could take that easier than you could. Perhaps I wanted to mark the fact that I knew, all right. But I didn't put a few drops in his drink on the off-chance that he'd begin to talk and tell us all about it. Or to immobilize him for a few hours, while we got on with the job. That was someone's bright idea, wasn't it? Oh no, it was nothing like so rational as that.'

Then he said, with a baffled, open air:

'No, it seems to have been just something that I did.'

'Good God, is that all you can say?'

'I don't know what else there is to say.'

'And now you're going to have this to live with –'

'I'm not even sure about that,' said Mark. 'It's easy to be honest, but it doesn't give the answers you expect. The truth is, it seems such a little thing.'

Stephen said, brutally, harsh with pain:

'It might have seemed a little thing if you'd stuck him with a knife.'

Mark replied:

'I dare say it might.' He had spoken absently, as though struck by wonder. He had not imagined the innocence of an act which neither they, nor anyone else, were faced by, until the act had consequences which seemed to exist in another dimension from the three dimensions of the flesh. A sexual act: writing words on a piece of paper: a stroke of one's arm: they were all so simple, so concrete, disconnected from, not in the same world as, the results which flowed from them.

'But still,' said Mark. 'Putting a few drops into someone's glass. Without any reason. God knows, I might have done that in yours. Any time in the last few years, if we'd had the stuff to hand.'

'That's softening everything for yourself.'

'It doesn't feel like that.'

'Are you also going to say that he committed suicide?'

'No.' Mark's gaze was steady. 'If I'm being detached, I should say that we shall never know.'

'You're being too detached to be human.'

'Am I?' Mark said. 'I was going to tell you, I don't believe he did.'

'You're sorry that he's dead?'

'Of course I'm sorry. I'm sorry for anyone who dies young. But I won't pretend. Even that may be sentimental. I'm really sorry for those who loved him.'

'You'll have that on your conscience for the rest of your life.'

Mark said:

'You have a lot of conscience, you know. I don't think I have that much.'

At that, Stephen, whose tone had become even more bitter, because he seemed to be suffering the more and couldn't shake the other, was more angry and bewildered. When the Bishop had said that he, Stephen, was a good man, he hadn't tolerated it: he knew, as well as he knew anything, that it was false. But in secret, all through their friendship, he had thought Mark was good. Different from the rest of them, in some way set apart. He had sometimes wished, for Mark's sake, that he was nearer ordinary human earth. He could be a bit of a saint. It made him seem more fragile. Even now, that evening in the drawing room, after Mark's confession, Stephen couldn't help still thinking of him like that. The aura hung about him. And yet he said he had no conscience, and behaved like it. It was a contradiction that men like Stephen had met before, and never understood. Did conscience, as Stephen had to face it, and the constraints he felt upon himself, belong alone to ordinary sinful men? With their share, like his own, of sensual treachery, venality, cowardice, cruelty?

'There's something I should be sorry for,' said Mark. His tone was friendly, but Stephen's cry in return was harsh.

'What's that?'

'If you let anything I've done, or anything I've said to-night, get in your way. Remember what I told you in that caff the other night. I meant every word of it. Don't let anything I've done upset it. You need that kind of hope, don't you?'

'Don't you?'

'Nothing like so much.' Mark went on:

'I should be sorry, you know that, if I'd made life darker for you.'

'This is rather late in the day.'

'Never mind that. Listen to me. That's the only thing I ask you.' He added:

'You see, I shan't be with you much longer.'

'What do you mean now?'

'Oh, I've been making some decisions too. What you're doing is right for you and Tess, I'm sure it is. I don't mean just getting married. You want a different world here and now, or anyway before you're too old, don't you?'

Stephen couldn't have said that without embarrassment, but it was true. 'And you'll try and plug away somewhere,' said Mark. 'I used to think I wanted that too. Perhaps I do. But I haven't the patience to stick at it. So I'm getting out.'

'Where to?'

'I shan't go back to Cambridge. This time last week I expected to be there, by now. It seems strange. I shan't go back. I'll take myself somewhere among the really poor. Somewhere like Calcutta. Where things can't be worse. I'll find a job in a hospital. I can't do much, of course, but I expect I can do something. Anyway, I think it will suit me.'

He said it, just as casually, as though it were automatically obvious, as when, a year before at Cambridge, he announced that he was taking a week-end off.

Stephen, now distressed as well as angry, began to argue – began with a flat platitudinous argument. Just as he wanted Tess to finish her course, so he urged Mark. Only two terms to go. Bad to leave loose ends. Mark would get a certain First. For the first time that night, Mark showed a trace of malice, when he laughed at him. 'You're as hidebound as they come, aren't you? You like people keeping on the rails, in the long run, don't you? What the hell does a First matter?'

'You never know.'

'I do know.'

If he had been tranquil, Stephen realized, he wouldn't have made that mistake: this made him more furious still. He uttered a curt remark about individual salvation. That was the phrase Neil had used the afternoon before. In the past, they had all agreed, no decent men went in search of that. It couldn't be justified, either in morals or intellect. Now Mark was falling into that trap, that tinselly romantic trap.

'Not a bit of it,' said Mark.

'What else is it?'

'No, I'm not saving myself. I'm not interested in that.'

'Then whatever are you doing?'

'Just getting on the move.'

'I suppose you might be trying to be happy –'

'Wrong again. I think I should be about as happy wherever I was.'

Stephen gave a bitter shout. 'This is as irresponsible as it comes. You're more irresponsible than anyone I've ever met.'

Later, there were times when Stephen and Tess speculated to each other about Mark's self-exile. It could have been, they wanted to think, the sign of remorse breaking through: the kind of remorse that he wouldn't admit, but showed itself in action. They wanted to believe it, but yet they couldn't quite. It was too tidy, too schematic, too much of a solution. They had had to learn that anyone's motives, their own, Mark's least of all, weren't as linear as that, and were left more mystified, less positive, than when they first met him and loved him.

Listening to Stephen's reproaches, Mark simply said:

'I don't think this is the right time to quarrel, do you?' He went on:

'You know, I don't think this is the right time for you to quarrel with anyone. I should like you to have a drink with Neil tonight. Us two and Tess. It would be a good thing to do.'

'Are you suggesting we ought to have a celebration?'

Mark disregarded him.

'He's done you no wrong,' said Mark. 'You know it all now. He's been absolutely loyal. You ought to count the good things. I'd like you to be reconciled wherever you can.'

Stephen didn't speak, and Mark pressed on.

'Tess would like it. I'm sure of that. She's got to live with you, you know.'

Just then, Mark had the stronger will.

'I'll organize it,' he said, in his freshest, most eager tone. 'We'll pick you up after dinner.'

Within a few minutes, Kate Freer, not having taken off her fur coat, entered the drawing room. Mark sprang up and kissed her.

'What have you been doing?' he cried.

'Bridge,' she said. 'Nothing interesting. Just bridge.'

'You must be tired. I'll get you a drink.'

He knew his way about the house, he was as familiar there as Stephen was. He didn't need to ask what was her evening drink. He brought her a tumbler of whisky, tinkling with ice, and settled her in her habitual chair. 'There,' he cried. 'Now I must go. I'll see you later,' he called to Stephen, as with light steps he walked out of the room.

'He's so kind,' she said. 'He has such style.' She was looking, not at Stephen, but at the door through which Mark had departed, as though this were the son whom she would have liked.

28

BEFORE Mark's visit, Stephen had wanted to come out with his decisions, and get the evening over. He had felt controlled and able to do it cleanly. Now he sat with his mother in the drawing room, not willing (or more unable than that) to stir from his chair, on his face an absent expression which she misread. If he had been in a state to notice, he would have realized that she and his father had been preparing themselves all day: they had foreseen, or discovered, some of what he had to tell them: she took it for granted that this mood of his was because of that.

'Come on,' she said, awkwardly, as though trying to sound like a companion. 'I suggest you have a drink.'

'No,' said Stephen, from among his thoughts, and had to make an effort to thank her.

It wasn't that Mark's confession, by distracting him from what he had to say, made that easier. In some fashion, the stresses added to each other. He felt drained of energy. He didn't even want to stand up. He scarcely spoke. When Thomas Freer came down from his study, a few minutes before dinner, he glanced curiously at his son.

Still nothing was said. The dinner table was quiet, the other two making a little conversation, Stephen silent. They had their soup and their chicken pancakes, a dish which Thomas Freer requested once a week. Then, all of a sudden, pushing aside his pudding, Stephen began to talk. He said it in rough harsh bursts, without any of the civility, or the touches of affection, which he had resolved to use.

There was anti-climax. He was going on, when he had to accept that they knew: certainly they knew that he was in no legal danger: they seemed to know most of the detail of the proceedings, and that he had undertaken to appear for Neil. What added to the anti-climax, they had made themselves ready to deal with him. Resignation, no anger, recrimination all brushed aside without hard words, everything civilized.

'I take it,' said Thomas Freer, fingers together, even now revealing the gratified smile of inside knowledge, 'that one is right in assuming that once this unfortunate accident had given – what should one call them? – given your opponents a handle, they didn't want to proceed to extremities. In fact, they would have been very foolish to do so, from their own point of view.'

'I suppose so,' said Stephen.

'Minimum force,' Thomas Freer murmured. 'It's usually a good maxim. They have those two young men, that's quite enough. I take it one wasn't too far out in judging that you yourself would probably be left alone. If you didn't insist on getting into the public eye.'

'Yes.'

'I think I remember telling you. I *think* I remember.' Thomas Freer spoke with subfusc satisfaction. 'However. Things might be worse. Yes, they might be worse.'

'You are getting into the public eye, though, aren't you?' Kate Freer's glance turned to Stephen, then passed him. Her voice wasn't full: she could keep out excitement or hysteria, but it sounded thin.

'To an extent. To an extent,' her husband intervened. Stephen said:

'I've told you just how much.'

'It may develop.'

'That's a possibility.' Stephen's tone was as restrained as hers.

'I wish you'd explain why you're doing this.'

'It's not easy.'

'You look as though you know it's wrong yourself.' Once more she had misread him. Now he had made the announcement, his thoughts had left the three of them, were casting back, not giving him peace, to what he had heard from Mark. Again he had to make an effort to answer her.

'I don't know it's wrong. If I did, I shouldn't do it.'

'You're only making a gesture. Gestures are stupid.'

'Sometimes,' said Thomas Freer, 'we all have to make them, don't we?'

Neither his wife nor son had attention to spare, or they would have been startled to see him trying to be so unapprehensive, or even to forget himself. At another time, his wife might have wondered when she had ever seen him make a gesture.

'I don't like them,' she said. 'They always do harm to other people.'

'Perhaps some good.'

'Perhaps some harm to people nearest to you.'

Stephen did not reply. Thomas Freer said:

'Don't you see, my love, he believes that it's his duty?'

'Duty's usually an excuse.'

'What for?' said Stephen.

'For doing what you want to do. Especially if it does harm.'

All their voices had remained quiet. An onlooker might have imagined that no voice had ever been raised in that house, and no emotion uttered in the open.

There was a long silence, in which it seemed there was

more to be said, but as though everyone was holding back. But once they had held back, no one chose to speak again.

With an appearance of relief, Thomas Freer concentrated on his cheese. They hadn't drunk wine at dinner, but with elaborate, emollient indifference, he mused aloud: 'I don't know about you two, but I'm rather inclined to fancy a glass of port.'

'I might as well join you,' said his wife.

Stephen said 'Not for me, thank you.'

'Oh, I do wish you would,' said Thomas Freer. Just in time, Stephen recognized that this once more was a kind of plea. 'Yes,' he said. 'I'll change my mind, may I?'

The decanter went round. There was another silence, except for Thomas Freer murmuring, as he tasted: 'Reasonably good. *Reasonably* good.'

Stephen sipped, and said:

'I may as well tell you the rest. I've proposed to Tess Boltwood. And she's said yes.'

There were two kinds of astonishment. For both the Freers, this news was an absolute surprise. The other they had been expecting, and had rehearsed how to meet it – though his self-discipline had (and it would have seemed strange to anyone who knew them) proved stronger than hers. But about this they had no warning at all: Stephen had had other girls: they had often imagined him making what they still called 'a good marriage', and had considered Sylvia, and had speculated as to whether that was good enough.

The other astonishment was Stephen's. For whatever response he had expected from his mother, it was different in kind from this. She gave a loud, hearty, almost raucous laugh, and broke out:

'Well, I must say, you haven't been exactly idle recently, have you?'

She asked, practical, participating as she used to when he first went away to school, about the date of the wedding, where they intended to live.

'Wherever I get a job,' said Stephen.

'Not Cambridge?'

He shook his head.

'You'll have children?'

'I dare say.'

'I wonder how you'll like that.' There was a flash of remote sardonic amusement (absent from her since Tuesday night), half-sarcastic, half-detached. 'Anyway,' she remarked, 'we shan't be seeing so much of you, shall we?'

'No, not so much.'

'We shall all have to get used to that, shan't we?' she said. 'It was bound to come, of course.'

She was looking happy, much younger, more than that, liberated, free from care. Maybe – long before the danger – this was a relation which (to herself, in privacy) she couldn't sustain. She was one of those who weren't independent in action but in privacy answered only to themselves. But also, there was something healthier, or at least more commonplace, than that. Marriage was something to cling on to. Marriage would make him safer. Marriage had both confined her, and made her safer. Perhaps it would do the same for him.

She enjoyed meeting him when there was no open feeling between them. She had often asked herself what her true feeling for him was. There might be an animal tie. She had been vain, because he was clever: she respected him, because he was on his own: otherwise, in the past years, she had often been afraid of him. In time, as he became more like the rest of them (this was what his marriage promised her), all that would be easier. She couldn't resist the thought – malicious, cheerful, like a young woman's teasing – that his children, her grandchildren, might cost him the embarrassment that he had cost her.

Meanwhile, Thomas Freer, expression not anxious but melancholy, was reflecting. Underneath all his façades, despite the ingenuity of his defences, he didn't often, or not continuously, deceive himself. He wasn't going to lose only his son's company, which unlike his wife he had basked in and enjoyed. He was – not dramatically, not with words but nevertheless in a sense which both of them recognized – going to lose his son. That was what this meant: marriage didn't matter, but the timing of this departure did. Some of it was his own fault. Some of it was circumstance. That didn't matter either. The parting did. Thomas Freer loved his son: mixed up in his deviousness, it was nevertheless the simplest thing about him.

Still, his defences were getting to work, and getting to work in their labyrinthine fashion, concealing much, concealing what he felt and didn't wish to face. Lucidity could be masked over: and Thomas Freer was letting himself mask his with some social lucubrations. The girl wasn't a brilliant prospect. She had her points, she wasn't unattractive, she was bright enough. But not a brilliant prospect. Bishops weren't what they used to be. The Bench had descended several steps down the social scale. Bert Boltwood was a nice little man but – He might go a little further. Probably not, he was a bit too wild. Still, even now, even at that, a Bishop's daughter *would do*. She would *just about do*.

Thomas Freer found this conclusion vaguely consolatory. It was only he – and then intermittently – who knew the holes in such defences.

Suddenly, in a resonant tone, he announced:

'We shall have to ask them in. We shall have to.'

This was another form of defence. Social arrangements were the plinths of an ordered life. Neither of the others recognized what he was doing, confronting each other as they had been for instants without any defence, unguarded.

Kate Freer, brought back to daily things, asked:

'When? Tomorrow?' (That was Saturday, precisely a week after the dinner party.)

'No, I should have thought that was a shade too early. One doesn't want to rush things.'

'When then?'

Thomas Freer considered.

'I'm inclined to think that Sunday would be reasonable. Does that suit you?' he asked Stephen. 'Yes, Sunday evening would be reasonable.'

'Won't he be preaching?'

'We'll ask them for nine o'clock. He ought to have finished by then. He *ought* to have.'

Not long after, while they were still sitting round the table, Thomas Freer engrossed in protocol, nine o'clock on this Friday night struck from the cathedral. Stephen was listening for the downstairs bell. Mark wasn't late. Stephen said: 'That does seem to be about all, doesn't it? If you'll excuse me –' He contrived to keep his tone as level as though they had been discussing nothing but a cousin's anniversary, and left them there.

29

MARK was waiting in the hall. As they went out into the lane, the air was still. The last time they had walked along there together, the bells were going through their combinations, but it would be twenty-four hours before there was another practice, and no sound came from the cathedral tonight. The building stood in the dark, unlit and empty as a ruin.

For an instant, Stephen felt a superstitious tightening or shudder ('someone walking over my grave', the old housekeeper would have said): it was a relic from the past, a sense that people had prayed inside there that week, prayed for him. Certainly the Bishop had prayed. It was possible that so had Thomas Freer.

Mark was saying that he had brought Tess in his car.

'By the way,' he went on, 'I've told her all I told you this afternoon.'

'Have you?'

Mark smiled: 'I didn't want to be with you both tonight on false pretences.'

'How did she take it?'

'She can accept anything. Much more than you can, you know. You'll find that out.'

As they came to the bottom of the lane, Mark suddenly stopped, resting one hand on a bollard. He said:

'I don't think anyone else need know. Or ought to.'

'She's discreet.'

'So are you.' Mark added: 'If it helped, I shouldn't mind

all that much. But it wouldn't do any good. It might give some unnecessary pain.'

He moved out on the street, and then back, one foot restless.

'I had to let Sylvia know that I was going away. I think she'll be waiting in the pub. She wants to look after me.'

'Yes.'

'I haven't told her about Bernard. You can see why, can't you?'

'I think so.'

'She wants to look after me. It would mean that I was asking her to.'

'I wish you could.'

'Sometimes I do too,' said Mark. 'Then Bernard – that would be the first thing I told her. But –'

He hesitated. His spontaneity had left him.

'She's a good person. Of course she is. She's so proud. Only a good person can throw away her pride as she does.'

Quickly Mark began to walk across the street, towards the parking space. Stephen, beside him, had already crossed that street, in this identical place, on his way to the coroner's office not many hours before.

Tess was sitting in the warm car. As she got out, she caught her breath in the sharp air. She looked expectantly at Stephen: yes, it was all done, he said, she and her parents would be invited to the Freers' house on Sunday night. 'With a certain amount of formality.' Stephen smiled at her.

'Oh, I shan't mind that! I shan't mind that.' She laughed, kissed him, was delighted, almost as though she hadn't till now emerged from incredulity.

Taking his arm, pressing it, she walked between them, as they turned to their right, along the street. Stephen noticed that, after a short time, but as though by a conscious decision or effort, she took Mark's arm also, and pulled him closer to her.

He was leading them to the pub in which they had conferred, after the first alarm, trying to predict the future, the previous Saturday night. It wasn't an habitual meeting-place of theirs, but Mark seemed to be choosing to remind them: some of the future they had tried to predict was past by now: he might have been doing it out of irony, but, so the others took it, more likely to give them what he could of reassurance and peace.

The sign of the turbaned head shone floodlit opposite the darkened shops. They quickened their steps, getting inside out of the cold. The lounge, on a Friday night, was half-empty: as Mark had expected, Sylvia was already there, sitting at a table by herself, a glass of gin in front of her. Her great eyes lit up when she saw them. She had paid more than usual attention to her face, blotting out the etched precocious lines.

'Well!' she said, as Tess sat beside her and Mark brought tankards of beer.

He remarked without emphasis:

'Sylvia doesn't know about you two. I thought you'd like to tell her yourselves –'

'Yes,' said Stephen. 'We're getting married.'

'Oh, what luck,' cried Sylvia. Immediately, without any of her self-consciousness, she leaned round and kissed Tess on the cheek. The two were nothing but acquaintances: so far as they had a relation, it was one, not quite of dislike, but of suspiciousness or something near to mutual jealousy. Yet, though Sylvia was herself careworn, at least for a moment all that was discarded. Everyone there had made a discovery, or would do so when they could look back, which comes to those undergoing a crisis: that personal

250

relations were a luxury, except the rooted ones. The likings of the nerves, the hostilities of the nerves, they all got washed or swept away. A common danger or purpose, and you were living alongside those whom fate had given you. It was only outsiders, elaborating on their own feelings, who attributed the same to people in action: thus misunderstanding the quality of action such as these had gone through, or action on a bigger scale. Mark might have known this by instinct, but Stephen had learned by now: some feelings were simpler, compulsorily simpler, than until inside them one would ever think.

Then Neil arrived, was bought beer by Mark, and also told of Stephen and Tess.

'Good for you,' he said. 'If that's what you want.'

He was gazing hard-eyed at Sylvia, whom he had neither met nor seen before.

'Are you in on this?' he said.

Against that kind of attack, she was composed. She said: 'I know there's been some trouble.'

'You'll know some more before you're much older.'

It now appeared, what Stephen and Tess hadn't realized, that Mark had attempted to collect the other members too, perhaps as a sign of good-bye, of all suspicions having been taken from them now, or a silent acknowledgement of what he couldn't say.

'Where is Emma?' he asked.

'Gone off.'

'Where to?'

'How the hell should I know?'

That was all. He added that she'd probably get into Trotskyist hands, or some such foolery.

'What about Lance?'

'I called him.'

'What did he say?'

'He said he'd rather take a trip on his own.'

Stephen did not suppress a grim smile. Mark said:

'I wonder. I wonder if we oughtn't to do something about him.'

'What can we do?' said Tess.

'You could say in court what a splendid guy he is,' said Neil to Stephen. 'That would be bleeding nonsense. It's bleeding nonsense what you're doing for me.'

'Not completely.'

'Stuff it. You'll have to stop this sort of nonsense. If you're going to be any good to us.'

Neil was repeating what he said the day before, without alteration or concession, any concession, though he interrupted himself to buy a round of drinks. He said that the only test of an action was objective, did it help the cause or not, nothing else entered. He broke off:

'You needn't worry your guts about Lance.'

'Why not?'

'He'll survive.' He went on: 'And if he didn't, it's his own funeral. He wouldn't be any loss.'

'I can't take that,' said Tess.

'Take it or don't take it. He'll survive. Or else he'll dig his own grave.' He stared round. 'We've been in a war. In a war somebody is going to get hurt. We lost this one, but we haven't done so badly. Lance might be a casualty, that's the only one.'

Others were thinking that, since Stephen had in effect told him that Bernard had been the penetrator, Neil didn't so much as mention him, as though even his name didn't exist.

'I'm all right,' said Neil. 'I suppose you two are all right.' He was speaking to Tess and Stephen, and then turned to Mark. 'I suppose you are. We shall keep at it somehow.'

'I'm going away,' said Mark. Sylvia, eyes not leaving him, once more heard him, with an expression open and relaxed, announce his plan.

'You're giving up hope, are you?' said Neil. 'I can't say I'm surprised.'

'No, I'm not giving up hope. But it's not the same as yours.'

'There's only one kind of hope in this world.'

But there were different kinds of hope, strong and passionate, round that table. Tess's, flesh and spirit at one, able to assimilate her knowledge of Mark, still certain that human beings were capable of good – that she would sometime, not too far ahead, in her own time, find a better life: Stephen's, more shadowed, remorseful and less able to assimilate, his mind not trustful and becoming less so, and yet his emotions in tune with hers, more simply so than his mind told him: Mark's, which, since he hadn't a religious faith, he didn't explain, but seemed to rest in existence itself: and Sylvia's.

When Mark got up to fetch their final round, she couldn't stop herself speaking to Stephen. He was sitting next to her, but her question, abandoned, out of control, could have been heard by others.

'Have I any chance?'

Stephen said: 'I hope so.' He didn't know what to predict. He repeated: 'I hope so,' and meant it.

She said:

'Shall I go after him? Wherever he goes?'

'Could you?' He was thinking, despite her spirit, she was a conventional girl at heart, she wasn't made for the reckless choice.

'I ought to.'

Before Mark returned, she just had time to say:

'Steve (she hadn't called him that since they were children). I envy you, you know. You've found your way, haven't you? I haven't. And God knows he hasn't either.'

When at closing time they left the pub, and the five of them walked back – without the argument, the agitations or the false optimism of the Saturday night before – through the empty museum-like streets, Stephen couldn't get those last words out of his thoughts. Yes, he and Tess had found a way. So had Neil. Give and take the chances of life, part of what was to come one could already see. It gave confidence, it gave one's own kind of hope. Not so with the others. Indeterminacy. The word from his own trade chased through his mind. One couldn't foretell their fate – except the fate that must happen to everybody. Did that give them, even Sylvia, a glimpse of limitless expectations? Was there something lost, when one had found one's way?

Of course there was. But not to lose it, was like not cutting the ties of youth. Stephen was thinking of those two as though they were younger than he was. Sylvia would renounce limitless expectations that moment, if only she could change her fate for Tess's. Would Mark change with him? Mark had never known limits, he behaved as though complete free will was his. Sometimes such expectations gave others a flicker of envy, the mirror-image of Sylvia's: but, Stephen thought, his concern wouldn't be over, no, they wouldn't be safe until they had found a way.

They were all standing together, in sight of the cathedral (no shudder for Stephen now, no footstep of someone walking over his grave). They were all, except Sylvia, talking with a kind of comfort, like passengers having got over mountains in an aircraft, the air still turbulent, but with the assurance passing round that the worst of it was over.

MORE ABOUT PENGUINS
AND PELICANS

Penguinews, which appears every month, contains details of all the new books issued by Penguins as they are published. From time to time it is supplemented by *Penguins in Print,* which is a complete list of all titles available. (There are some five thousand of these.)

A specimen copy of *Penguinews* will be sent to you free on request. For a year's issues (including the complete lists) please send 50p if you live in the British Isles, or 75p if you live elsewhere. Just write to Dept EP, Penguin Books Ltd, Harmondsworth, Middlesex, enclosing a cheque or postal order, and your name will be added to the mailing list.

In the U.S.A.: For a complete list of books available from Penguin in the United States write to Dept CS, Penguin Books Inc., 7110 Ambassador Road, Baltimore, Maryland 21207.

In Canada: For a complete list of books available from Penguin in Canada write to Penguin Books Canada Ltd, 41 Steelcase Road West, Markham, Ontario.